LORI WICK

Jessie

HARVEST HOUSE PUBLISHERS

EUGENE, OREGON

Unless otherwise indicated, all Scripture quotations are taken from the King James Version of the Bible.

Cover by Dugan Design Group, Bloomington, Minnesota

JESSIE
Copyright © 2008 by Lori Wick
Published by Harvest House Publishers
Eugene, Oregon 97402

ISBN-13: 978-1-60751-272-1

Printed in the United States of America

For Rachel —

precious daughter of my heart
and gift to my Matt.

Thank you for being you.

⇥ ACKNOWLEDGMENTS ⇤

Some books are harder to write than others. Some flow, some pour, and some trickle. As excited as I am about this story and the people in it, this book trickled. At the same time, precious people played a part, all of whom helped me to finish. Indeed, I would not have finished without them. I wish to thank…

> Tim and Andrea—You literally came in at the eleventh hour. Your words were few but just what I needed. Thanks for listening as I poured my heart out and then saying just what I needed to hear. You are utterly dear to me, and I am so glad God put you in my life.

> Ab—What can I say? You are so much more than a daughter. Thank you for finishing strong. The goals you set so many years ago have remained, and I'm indescribably proud of your accomplishments. Thanks for battling strong alongside me and reminding me so often of how much the cross is worth.

> Matt—Your heart and work ethic are amazing. Thanks for listening with such humility. Having you home for this time is a huge blessing. You are very loved.

> Merry—What an amazing friend you are. You don't know how much you encourage me. Thanks for this season of time we've had together. Thanks for your laughter and precious friendship. You are so very loved and needed.

> Pearl—The walks and your listening ear have been amazing. Thank you for your constant hospitality and welcoming heart. You are a treasure to my life.

> Bob—Wow. It's been a time. At one point in the story, Seth says he does not want to go back in time and learn things all over again. And so it is with you and me. Thanks for coming the distance with me. Thanks for learning and growing ahead of me and with me. God can do amazing things in a humble heart. Thanks for keeping yours so soft. I love you.

1873

Jessie Wheeler—owns and operates Wheeler's Mercantile
Seth Redding—stranded in Token Creek
Jeb Dorn—Jessie's cousin
Patience Dorn—Jeb's wife
Pastor Larry English—Jeb and Patience's pastor
Brad and Trace Holden—ranch owners who live outside of town
Jeanette Fulbright—Brad and Trace's aunt
Theta Holden—Jeanette's sister and Brad and Trace's ill mother
Becky—lives with and cooks for Jeanette

1884

Nate Kaderly—Token Creek's sheriff
Rylan Jarvik—pastor of the church
Bri and Danny Jarvik—Rylan's wife and son
Cassidy and Joey Holden—Trace's wife and son
Meg, Savanna, and Cathryn Holden—Brad's wife and daughters
Heather Wales—lives with and works for Jeanette Fulbright
Hannah and Clancy Wheeler—Jessie's daughters

From Texas

Eliot McDermott—Seth's brother
Cassy—Eliot's wife
Nate and Lindy—Eliot and Cassy's children

Part One

June 1873

Chapter One

Token Creek, Montana Territory

JESSIE WHEELER CAME SLOWLY downstairs from her apartment into the mercantile below, the familiar sights and aromas a comfort and a distraction all at the same time. She shifted a stack of heavy cotton pants on a shelf and then fronted a few cans in one aisle before heading to the front counter, behind which sat rows of mailboxes.

Jessie was alone these days. Her father had been gone for more than a year, and her mother had been dead for three. She had grown up in this store so taking over had come naturally, but running it alone, ordering supplies, and keeping the books was sometimes a burden. She could find help for the backbreaking tasks of unloading and loading in the storeroom, and she had a cousin whom she trusted to run the register and help in any way needed, but the decisions were all hers. Some days the responsibility was a weighty one.

A customer was waiting when Jessie opened the store, and that suited her fine. It did no good to think about things that weren't going to change, and she knew getting busy was the best cure.

"What can I help you with today, Mrs. Carlisle?"

"I've got quite a list, Jessie. I think we'll start with lard and beans."

"Will do," Jessie said congenially, doing what she did best, knowing her own store and seeing to customers' needs.

Marty Carlisle's husband, Bart, was a rancher outside of Token Creek. Marty didn't get into town very often, and when she did, the list could be significant. Today was no exception. The two worked together for the better part of an hour, putting the order together and then transferring it to Marty's wagon.

Marty paid in cash and also settled the bill for the ranch, always nice for when Jessie needed to order items that had to be paid for in advance. After seeing Marty off, Jessie took a moment to right the register and grab the broom. Someone had come past the front of her store in muddy boots, and the boardwalk out front needed attention.

She swept for a time in peace, heading back inside only when Kaleb Heydorn, the train stationmaster, delivered a small sack of mail. He explained that it had been on the late train the day before. Jessie set to sorting it. She was still in the midst of this when a stranger walked in.

"Hello," Jessie greeted.

"Good morning," a man said, his voice deep.

Jessie set the mail aside.

"Can I help you?"

"Actually, I was hoping I could help you."

Jessie looked at this tall, self-assured man and waited.

"I was hoping the owner might want to hire me," the man continued.

Jessie knew she would do no such thing but asked, "Are you new in town?"

"Just passing through," the man said.

Jessie's brows rose. It wasn't normal for someone looking for a job to admit such a thing.

"I woke up when the train stopped here," the stranger went on, "and found my money gone from my pocket. I have to find work because I'm broke."

Jessie wasn't sure she believed this but asked, "Where are you headed?"

"Texas."

"It's early on your journey to be stranded."

"My thoughts exactly."

The words were spoken so dryly Jessie smiled. The stranger smiled too, and Jessie had to admit that he was very good-looking.

"I'm Seth Redding, by the way," he said as he put his hand out.

"Jessie Wheeler," she offered, shaking the hand.

"Your family owns this store?"

Jessie nodded, not willing to admit to this stranger that she was the only Wheeler left.

"Do you think your family can use me?" Seth tried again.

"Do you have any experience in mercantile work?"

"As a matter of fact, I've done a little bit of everything. I worked at a general store in Kingdon for about two months."

Jessie nodded and decided to lay her cards on the table.

"What guarantee do I have that you won't come in here and steal everything you can lay your hands on?"

Seth looked thoughtful for a moment and then lifted the large satchel he was holding and put it on the counter.

"This is everything I own in the world. You're welcome to look inside and then put it anywhere you like. I won't leave town without it."

There was no missing the earnestness in his face and voice, but that didn't mean he wasn't acting. Jessie took the liberty of looking inside the satchel and thought that if he was lying, he was very good. She noticed the clothing certainly, but also two family daguerreotypes and some legal documents.

"And you're really going to let me tuck this bag away until the end of the day?"

"Yes, ma'am," Seth said. "I'm broke, and I'll be visiting Token Creek until that changes."

Jessie couldn't help herself. She was drawn to the man and the way he said things. He was also easy to look at, very tall with broad shoulders and wavy, dark hair. His chin looked a bit stubborn, but his gray eyes were warm and friendly.

"I don't know if I can use you more than today," the mercantile owner tried next.

Seth shrugged. "I'll take any work you can give me."

Jessie nodded and said, "That door back there leads to the storeroom. You'll find some crates of canned goods in front of the shelves they go on."

"I'll get to it," Seth said and started that way.

Jessie stared after him and knew the exact moment he stopped and looked back at her.

"Thank you," he said quietly. He then turned and went through the store, disappearing into the storeroom.

Jessie stood for a moment and thought about the exchange. She dearly hoped she would not regret hiring him and in truth didn't think she would. Just to be sure, however, she did tuck the satchel away in a spot where he wasn't likely to find it.

"I made you some dinner," Jessie said several hours later, finding Seth in the storeroom, working on the fifth task she'd given him.

"Thank you," the man said in genuine appreciation, stopping his work on the large crocks that Jessie wanted cleaned and rearranged and taking the plate she offered him.

"You can use the table there, and don't feel like you have to rush."

Seth thanked his employer again and did indeed turn for the work-table that sat near the rear of the storeroom. Fresh air and light came from the two windows behind him. He sat down in the only chair available and looked at the plate of food she'd prepared, impressed with the amount. He tucked into beef and biscuits covered in gravy and thought about his employer.

So far he'd not seen anyone else working. He didn't think she owned the store on her own but knew if she did, he would be the last to hear about it. And she was clearly no stranger to the business. There was no hesitation in her as he finished each job. She knew exactly what she wanted him to do next and took no time in telling him. She didn't check on him constantly, but he was fairly certain it would take hours of searching to find his bag.

Seth heard her just then, clearly helping a customer, and realized he liked the sound of her voice. It was deep and little bit husky and suited her. He'd not met a woman so attractive in a long time, and never one so unaware of it. She moved with grace and unconscious ease as she walked or spoke, and she didn't seem the least aware of herself. Seth did a lot of looking when she was in the room, but if Jessie noticed, she hid it very nicely.

While he was still thinking of her, she appeared.

"I don't want to rush you, but I've a big order I'm working on out here. When you're finished, you could load it for me."

"Certainly. I'll be right there."

Jessie thanked him without ceremony and slipped from the room. Seth, watching all the while, smiled after her. He hadn't planned to spend more time in Token Creek than he had to, but if he could spend it in the company of Jessie Wheeler, it might be worth sticking around.

"Well, Pastor English," Jessie greeted the older man who had come in a few hours before closing, "how are you today?"

"Doing well, Jessie. How about you?"

"I'm fine."

"Busy today?"

"About normal for a Wednesday," Jessie said with a smile. "What can I get you?"

"Just my mail today, thank you."

Jessie thought he looked a little tired but didn't comment. She was reaching for his mail when Seth came to the front with a question.

He was gone again before Jessie could introduce the two men, but the pastor asked about him.

"New worker?"

"Today, anyway," Jessie said before going on to explain the situation.

"Stranded, did you say?"

"Yes. He says someone took his money while he slept on the train."

"Does he need a place to stay?"

"He probably does. He's working in the storeroom. Feel free to talk to him."

The older man nodded and went that way. Jessie had no idea how long he was in the store because she ended up with an indecisive customer who required all her attention in the clothing aisle. The woman could not decide if the blue serge was going to hide stains better than the black, and each time Jessie tried to leave the woman to look at the fabrics on her own, she had another question. At last she decided on the blue serge, but she took so long that by the time Jessie had seen her off, Seth was standing by, waiting for more work.

"All done in the back," Seth said.

"Good. Did Pastor English find you?"

"He did. He invited me to stay with him."

"Will you?"

Before Seth could answer, a man showed up, carrying a large piece of luggage that told Jessie he was selling something. Jessie didn't know him personally, but she did know what to expect.

"Hello." Jessie greeted him cordially, but if the man had known her, he would have noted that her smile didn't quite reach her eyes.

"Hello, young lady. Is the owner around or perhaps the manager?"

"I'm the manager."

"Well now, you're a young one, but that doesn't bother me if it doesn't bother you! Cal Worth at your service," the man added, putting his hand out.

"I'm Jessie. What did you need?"

"I've got some very fine pocket watches to show you today, and I know you're going to want to carry these in your store."

The man proceeded to open his case and pull out the timepieces. Jessie took time to look, but when the man started quoting prices, she put her hand up.

"I can't make a profit with those types of prices. I'm sorry. I'm not interested."

"Oh, but if you buy ten or more, I can give you a rate."

"I can't sell ten," Jessie said, this time on the move. "Thank you, Mr. Worth," she said as she walked away from the man.

"If I could see the owner," Cal Worth said, continuing to try to speak to her, but Jessie disappeared into the storeroom and found something to do. Thankfully the man took the hint and left without following her. Seth found her in the back, dusting a shelf.

"How often does that happen?"

"It varies. Sometimes off and on all month, and sometimes not at all."

Seth nodded, his eyes still watching her. Jessie looked back for a few moments, their eyes catching briefly.

"Do you want me to do anything else today?"

"No, but thanks for the offer. I'll get your pay."

"Is that what you usually do, pay by the day?"

"No, but I didn't assume you'd be back."

"Can you use me tomorrow?"

"Sure," Jessie said, but at the moment she wasn't certain what he would do. The thought of never seeing him again bothered her, and if he was telling the truth, he genuinely needed the work.

"What time?" Seth asked.

"I open the doors at eight o'clock."

"I'll be here."

Seth started away but came swiftly back. Jessie looked at him, not sure what he was about until he said, "It would be nice to have my bag."

Jessie had to smile, and Seth knew he liked that smile more than a little. He took his bag and left with few words, planning to find the pastor's house, but in his heart he thought he could easily spend the evening in the company of Jessie Wheeler.

"Hello, Jeb," Jessie greeted her cousin midmorning on Thursday. "How are you?"

"Fine. Yourself?"

"Can't complain," Jessie said, smiling at the man who was old enough to be her father. Jeb had been her father's first cousin, and he and Jessie had always been close and especially fond of each other.

"What is Patience doing today?" Jessie asked of Jeb's wife.

"She's making pie fillings that have to be done for a church social this weekend, and she's run out of cinnamon."

Before Jessie could grab the item from the shelf, Seth came from the back. He did not interrupt, but Jessie naturally introduced him to Jeb Dorn.

"It's good to meet you," Jeb said, thinking about the different folks Jessie and her parents had hired over the years. The list was long. "Are you in town long?"

"I think just passing through, but right now my plans are unsettled."

Jessie's brows rose on that bit of information. Just the day before he had planned to go to Texas.

"Well, maybe we'll see you around," Jeb said. He waited until Seth had asked Jessie a question and returned to his work before speaking again to his cousin. "Do you need me Saturday?"

"I do, Jeb. Is that going to work?"

"I'll plan on it. All day, do you think?"

"If I have to pick, I'll take you earlier over later."

"I'll be here, Jess. Can you put the cinnamon on my bill?" Jeb asked as he left.

Jessie smiled and said yes, but they both knew she wouldn't. She paid her cousin when he worked, but unless he or Patience came in with a large order, single items were never accounted for.

Jessie suddenly remembered she'd not made any plans for dinner. For a moment she stood and wondered at herself. Normally she woke up with the day's events and needs on her mind, but this morning her first thoughts had been for Seth Redding.

Well, it's too late now, Jessie thought. She knew she would probably end up asking Seth to head to the hotel and bring them something. She preferred her own cooking, but the choice had been taken from her hands. Going back to work on an order she needed to place for more tinware and some iron pots and pans, Jessie told herself it was time to get her mind back on the job.

Thursday and Friday went by with plenty to do and plenty of customers and orders to see to. Seth worked with the stock, making two trips to the train station for orders and unloading them and carrying customers' purchases to their wagons, his demeanor calm and pleasant. He was good-looking and confident, but it was more than that. Something about Seth Redding was comforting and trustworthy. In fact Jessie had watched more than one woman take a second look, and Seth, very much a man, was not above flirting or complimenting the pretty women he helped.

On Saturday, however, Jessie had no time to notice such things. This was always the store's busiest day, and from the moment she opened her door, she and Jeb were on the run. Seth helped out and filled in wherever he could. He had not yet worked out front at all, but being on hand to find things in the storeroom or wrap, box, and carry orders left Jeb and Jessie free to see to the next customer.

Jeb stayed until midafternoon, and then Jessie was on her own. There was a lull about four o'clock. With only an hour to closing, Jessie slipped into the back to find some tin funnels they were out of in the front. She was tired—there had been no time for dinner—and she misjudged her steps and backed into a shelf. Without warning a can resting on the edge fell on the top of her head. The corner cut into her scalp.

Jessie stood still, her hand gripping a nearby shelf, her eyes closing as she willed herself to breathe. The pain was intense for a few minutes and then settled into a persistent throb. Jessie wished Jeb were still out there seeing to folks, but with only Seth in the store to help, she knew she had to stay on the job.

A very subdued Jessie made her way back to the store aisles, carrying the extra funnels. She placed them on the shelf with the rest of the tinware and went to the front counter. It was in pretty good order, so for the moment Jessie just stood.

She was still just standing when Seth came in from sweeping the front walk and found her doing nothing. Not that he would have criticized. He'd never seen a woman put in the day of work she had today. He assumed her store was closed on Sunday and also that she looked forward all week to that day off.

"Anything specific you need right now?" Seth asked, having just noticed she was frowning a little.

"I don't think so. What time is it?"

"Four-twenty."

Jessie did not need to answer or even nod because Ingrid Stillwell came in. Her husband, Pete, owned the livery. She had a sizeable list, but all pretty basic, and Jessie had her out the door with a minimum of effort. The moment she left, however, Seth faced her across the counter. He leaned his arms on the wood surface until their faces were on the same level.

"There is blood in your hair," he said quietly.

"I figured there might be. A can fell from a shelf and hit me."

"And you didn't feel a need to say anything?"

Jessie shrugged, looking very tired. "I have a store to run, Seth. I didn't see I had a choice."

Seth didn't comment, but neither did he agree. He certainly hadn't had much of a look at her head, but he felt it needed attention over the store.

"We close soon," Jessie said, ignoring his look. "I'll see to it then."

"And if you need a doctor?"

"I'll go find him," Jessie said pragmatically, wishing she could lie down and sleep for a while.

Disapproval radiated from Seth's entire being, but he said nothing. No other customers joined them, and right on time Jessie paid Seth, thanked him as he left, and locked up for the night.

She was tired and hungry and desperate to lie down, but realized what she must do. Slipping out the rear door of the storeroom and locking it behind her, she went to the Dorns'. Patience cleaned the wound, put something on it, and forced Jessie to eat a little supper.

Less than an hour later, the mercantile proprietress made her way home, enough food in her to let her sleep. Doing little more than slip from her clothing and wash her face, she climbed into bed and slept all night. Not even the noise from the Saturday night crowd in the bars on Main Street disturbed her.

Jessie did not sleep in. Though she was naturally an early riser, she did lie around on this Sunday, her head paining her a bit. It was not miserable, but the missed dinner and small supper from the day before had worn on her. Headache or not, she knew she needed food.

Sunday was her day to cook and enjoy. She cooked most other days as well, but this was the day she could relax and savor what she'd made. This meal was no different. She had planned to keep it simple—a few eggs and some toasted bread—but once she got going, she made herself a feast. She added bacon and potatoes to the menu, and brewed extra coffee to enjoy.

She wasn't two bites into the meal when she knew it had been worth it. Putting her feet up and opening the weekly newspaper she didn't have time or energy to read during the week, Jessie began to enjoy her day off.

Pastor English had made the offer in total sincerity, but he was not surprised when Seth did not show any interest in joining him in church. The young man was polite and kind, but his interest in spiritual things was not just greatly lacking, it was nonexistent.

The pastor even invited him to the pie social they were planning for that afternoon, but knew with a fair amount of certainty that he would not see Seth Redding. Seth helped him with the dishes, but even before the pastor left for the church building, the younger man was on his way out the door. He didn't take his bag so Pastor English knew he would still be spending another night, but he strongly doubted he would see him the rest of the day.

Jessie's head felt fine by late morning, but the apartment was growing a little warm. Not moving very fast, she cleaned the kitchen and put her shoes on. After putting the apartment in order, she headed downstairs and through the storeroom. She was outside and had locked the door before she turned and spotted Seth Redding sitting under a tree watching her. Jessie stared at him a moment and then started that way.

"I wondered if you were ever going to come out that door," he said, pushing to his feet as she neared.

"Is that what you're doing here, waiting for me?"

"You're surprised?"

"I didn't know if I would see you again so, yes, I'm surprised."

"Meaning you don't need me to work, or you thought I would be leaving town?"

"The latter, but I just remembered you told Jeb you might be sticking around."

"At the moment I don't know what I'm doing," Seth admitted, and then added, "How's your head?"

"It's doing all right. Patience checked it for me."

"Patience?"

"Jeb's wife."

"Are they family?"

"Jeb and my father were cousins."

Seth nodded, his eyes watching her. Jessie looked right back.

"Would you care to walk along Token Creek, Miss Wheeler?"

Jessie, simply liking him and the way he said things, smiled. Seth took that smile for a yes.

Chapter Two

"PASTOR, MAY I ASK you a question?" Jeb began, having caught the man after the service.

"Certainly, Jeb."

"You mentioned during the sermon that a young man is staying with you right now. Is it Seth Redding?"

"It is. Did you meet him at the store?"

"Yes. What do you think of him?"

"He's very polite and grateful for the meals and the bed." The pastor stopped and looked at the other man a moment. "Are you worried about Jessie?"

"Not worried exactly—she takes care of herself very well—but I know if you had a concern I could talk to her about it. She listens to me."

"I don't have a concern about Jessie's safety, Jeb. I'm not sure Seth is planning to stay in town very long. And as far as I can tell, he's been honest with me. We've talked a little in the evenings. He has very little family alive and no real roots. He also has no interest in biblical matters—that does concern me no small amount—but then I know Jessie doesn't either."

"That's true. I'm hoping someday that will change, but she's her father's girl. Hiram Wheeler didn't feel he needed God for anything.

He had his store and his strong back and hands and believed that was all he needed."

"That was my impression too. How would you say Jessie has done with his being gone?"

"I think she does fine. I'm thankful to say she comes to us when she has a need."

"That's good to hear. Maybe if Seth stays in town for a while, you'll have an opportunity to have him and Jessie over. That way you can see firsthand what he's like."

"That's a good idea, Pastor," Jeb said. The men had worked together on Saturday, but there had been no time for socializing in the store on that day. Jeb realized his attention had drifted a bit and added, "I don't think I would have thought of that, so thank you."

The men said their goodbyes and Jeb found Patience. On their walk home, he told her what their pastor had said and what he had in mind.

"You actually run the store by yourself, don't you?" Seth asked when they'd walked for a time.

"Yes. My father has been dead for more than a year."

"And your mother?"

"She died two years ahead of him."

"No siblings?"

"I'm afraid not."

"You sound like you have regrets."

"It wasn't my choice, but some days it would be nice to have someone else who cared."

She was doing odd things to Seth's heart, and he knew she wasn't even trying. It didn't hurt that she was beautiful, but it was far more than that. He liked her toughness and her confidence.

"What's in Texas?" Jessie suddenly asked.

"My brother."

"What's he doing there?"

"He's from there. We didn't have the same fathers and haven't lived together that much."

"Where are you from?"

"Kingdon way."

"When did you decide to move to Texas?"

"What makes you think I'm moving?"

"Well, you told me all you own is in your bag. That doesn't sound like a man who's planning to return."

"Eliot, that's my brother, likes it down there," Seth said by way of an answer. "He thinks I will too."

"Will he wonder what happened when you're delayed?"

"We're pretty independent, and he knew I would have to work my way along."

Jessie nodded before asking, "Who do you think took your money?"

"I don't know, but it's my own fault." Seth's voice held a level of disgust. "For some reason I moved the bills to my shirt pocket and then nodded off. If I'd left them in my pants pocket, no one could have gotten to them."

"Well," Jessie said, working not to like him too much. "You could be stranded in worse places. Token Creek is a very nice town with many fine folks."

"Including Jessie Wheeler?"

"I don't know about that. I'm just a store owner with usually more work than time."

"You must look forward to Sundays all week."

"I do look forward to the day off, but I also close at five, so I have my evenings too."

"Was that a hint?"

Jessie blinked at him. "A hint for what?"

Seth almost accused her of hinting that he ask her to dinner, but he could see by her face that she was doing no such thing. Instead he changed the subject.

"Pastor English invited me to a pie social the church is having this afternoon."

"Are you going?"

"If you are," Seth felt bold enough to say.

"I wasn't planning on it."

"Fair enough, but it might beat walking the creek line in the June heat."

Jessie nodded thoughtfully and made sure she was looking at him when she said, "You could always come to supper at my place."

The interest in the eyes watching her was unmistakable, and Jessie decided to be very clear. "*Just* supper," she added.

"Just supper is fine," Seth said smoothly, smiling at the way she read his mind.

"You're sure about that? Because I wouldn't want there to be any misunderstandings."

"I'm sure. What are you having?"

"Chicken and dumplings."

Seth nodded, looking pleased but not saying what was on his mind. He didn't know when he would have enough money to get himself to Texas, but that might not be as great a factor as it once was. This woman was simply too good to be true, and Seth thought he might need to stick around long enough to find out if he was wrong.

Trace Holden sat down at the pie social with his aunt, Jeanette Fulbright, and was swiftly followed by his brother, Brad. The pie social was being held on the grassy area between the church building and the parsonage.

"How is Mama today?" Brad asked. He was Trace's senior by 21 months, but the men looked enough like twins to be mistaken for such on a regular basis.

"She's doing well. Becky stayed with her," Jeanette added, referring to her cook. "Do you have time to come see her after we're done?"

"We're planning on it."

Jeanette looked at their handsome faces and tried to think about how much her sister, Theta, was missing. Two years earlier her husband, Wes Holden, had come home drunk and beaten her almost to death. She had never been the same. Wes had taken off and not been heard from since, but the boys continued to run the ranch on their own. Jeanette had taken her sister into her home in town and cared for her every need.

"What pie did you get?" Jeanette asked her nephews, working not to think about Theta just then.

"I started with berry," Trace said. "Now I'm working on apple."

"Lest you feel faint before supper," Jeanette teased gently, bringing a smile to the youngest Holden's mouth.

"How about you, Brad?" Jeanette asked.

"I'm still on my first piece—it's apple—but I think I'll have the berry next."

His aunt couldn't stop another smile, and Brad caught it, his own eyes twinkling.

"What kind did you bring, Jeanette?" Trace asked.

"Peach crumble."

"Oh," he said softly, almost reverently. "I'll have to have some of that too."

This made Jeanette laugh outright but also reminded her that she hadn't had pie. As it was, the three of them made for the pie table at the same time.

"This is nice," Seth said, standing in Jessie's living room several hours later and having a look around. It was one large room with three doors leading off of it. The door he'd just come through led to the stairs. He assumed the other two were bedrooms or a bedroom and a closet, but the doors were shut.

Large windows looked over the street, and to the left of these was the kitchen area. A small dining table with just four chairs sat in front of the windows. Between that area and the stairway door was what Seth saw as the living room. There was a long sofa and two comfortable-looking chairs. Dark wood tables sat next to the chairs, and two ottomans rested before the sofa. A brightly patterned rug brought all the furniture together. Against one wall sat an oak bookshelf that held knickknacks and a dozen books or so.

Jessie thanked Seth from her place by the stove but didn't turn to face him. She had let him in the storeroom door and led the way upstairs but, suddenly nervous, had gone back to cooking as soon as she could. She had never had a man in her rooms. She didn't know where the boldness had come from to invite him, and now that he was there, she was at loose ends.

"Be careful," Seth said, suddenly near enough to see that she had just about burned herself.

Jessie pulled her hand back and looked as uncomfortable as she felt.

"Are you sorry you invited me?"

Jessie turned to him, ready to deny it, but was honest instead.

"I don't usually do this."

"Do what?"

"Invite men for dinner."

"Well," Seth said slowly. He certainly hoped this evening would lead to much more, but he didn't like seeing her upset. "You have to eat supper, and I took you at your word that it was a supper invitation, and that's all I'm here for."

Jessie stared at him.

"You did make enough, didn't you?" Seth asked, doing well at looking stern without meaning it.

"Yes," Jessie said, a grudging smile coming to her lips.

"Is it ready?"

"Just about."

"Well, hurry it along. I'm half-starved."

His teasing relaxed her. Jessie finished the meal, and they were sitting down to eat just ten minutes later. Jessie waited for Seth to taste it, trying not to be obvious, but looking very pleased when he filled his fork, tasted it, and then chewed very slowly.

"This is good," he said at last.

"Thank you."

"Are there things you can't do?" Seth suddenly asked.

"Many, I can assure you."

"Such as?"

Jessie only shook her head at him and didn't try to answer. Seth ate for a time but found that his questions would not remain inside.

"So what happens now?"

"About what?"

"About you? Do you keep running the store forever on your own?"

"I hadn't thought about it," Jessie admitted with a small shrug. "It's all I've ever known."

"Do you wish for change?"

"For some things, but not in leaving the store."

"What type of changes do you want?"

"It would be nice to have a house. Living and working in the same place gets old."

"Where would you build?"

"Someplace close, so when the weather changes I don't have far to go." Jessie stopped and smiled. "I guess that's the one advantage to working and living in the same place. I don't have to go out into the cold to get to work."

Seth smiled at her smile and went back to eating.

"So who did you leave in Kingdon?" Jessie asked.

"No one. My mother lived there for a long time, but she met someone and moved on."

"Why didn't you go with them?"

"I wasn't invited."

"Where is your father?"

"I don't know. I've never known him. My mother's last name is

Handley; Eliot's is McDermott; and mine is Redding. We're not what anyone would call settled."

"When was the last time you saw your brother?"

"It's been awhile. He visited two houses ago."

Jessie digested this a moment before commenting, "It sounds like you've moved around quite a bit."

"Not too far from Kingdon. Most of our places were in that area."

"Where all have you worked?"

"I've done some mining, something I *don't* plan to do again. I worked on a ranch for about five years, but other than a beef dinner every night, it wasn't a life I enjoyed. I've worked in plenty of saloons and a mercantile too."

"What was your favorite?"

"You won't believe me if I tell you."

"Try me."

"The general store."

Jessie's mouth opened for a moment, but then doubts flooded in. Was he just saying that to be charming?

"I knew you wouldn't believe me."

"I didn't say that."

"You didn't have to."

Jessie went back to her meal, but she couldn't quite stop the small smile that turned up the corners of her mouth. She made herself not look at him, but suddenly every part of her being was glad she had invited him.

When the meal ended and they talked for a little while and he took his leave without once hinting for more, Jessie was glad again. Indeed, she had to do everything in her power to hold her heart in check.

"Is that you, Seth?" Pastor English asked when he heard the front door.

"Yes, sir."

"How was your day?" the older man asked, coming from the kitchen with a dishtowel in his hand. "I've got some stew here if you're hungry."

"I've eaten, but thank you. How did your pie social go?" Seth remembered to ask.

"It was fine. Most everyone sent an extra piece home with me, so if you've a hankering for pie, just name the type."

Seth laughed, but in truth pie sounded good. He chose a piece of peach crumble, and Pastor English took mince.

"How is Jessie today?" the pastor asked, assuming that's where Seth had been.

"Very well. She just fed me chicken and dumplings."

"I've heard she's a very good cook."

"She seems to be good at everything," Seth said.

"She certainly knows her way around that store, but then I guess that's to be expected."

"Have you lived here long, Pastor English?" Seth asked.

"I have. I've known Jessie since she was a girl."

There was no threat in the words, but Seth was reminded that even though Jessie lived alone, she was not alone in this town. Seth had no plans to dabble with her heart or do anything that they both didn't agree on, but this gave him pause.

The conversation ranged to a few other topics before they turned in. Pastor English mentioned what he was studying for his sermon, but Seth only half-attended. As with the rest of his waking moments since arriving in Token Creek, his mind was on Jessie.

Tuesday rolled to an end, and Jessie knew what she had to do. It was hard, but she reminded herself that she had a business to run and that was the bottom line. She watched Seth lock the front door, and the moment he turned to her, she spoke.

"I've had you do everything in the back, Seth. Unless you want to learn the workings of the store or do some painting, I don't have more work for you."

"You would teach me how to run the store?" Seth asked.

"If you're interested."

"As a matter of fact, I am, but just last night Pastor English mentioned some work he hoped to get done around the church and the parsonage. He won't let me give him anything for staying there, so I want to lend him a hand. He also said he'd heard that workers are needed and they're paying well at the foundry. I thought I might check into that."

"Fair enough," Jessie forced herself to say, not wanting him to know that she wished he would just stay at the mercantile. "I'll settle with you tonight, and you can come back if you want."

"You don't need to settle with me now," Seth said, but Jessie was already headed to the cash register. She returned with the currency in her hands, but Seth did not reach for it.

"I'll be back," he said.

"But if you don't make it..." Jessie began, but stopped when Seth shook his head.

"I'll be back."

"Seth." Jessie began to look impatient. "You probably won't be back this week, and that way we'll be settled."

"I'll be back this week," he said, watching her.

Jessie's look told him she was not happy, but Seth still did not reach for the money.

"You like to have your own way, Jessie Wheeler. You know that, don't you?"

Jessie's mouth opened in surprise. She had never seen herself that way, but it was the very thing her mother used to say about her father. The memory was not a happy one, and soon the surprise gave way to anger.

"It's just the way I do things, Seth. Take the money!"

Seth's brows rose in amusement, but there was also a good measure of stubbornness thrown in.

"I'll be back," he said quietly as he turned away. Unlocking the door he'd just latched, he slipped outside and walked from the store without a backward glance.

Jessie didn't know when she'd been so surprised and frustrated. Just barely remembering to relock the door, Jessie returned the money to the till, nearly throwing it in. She wasted no time milling about the store but made for the stairs. Half of her hoped she would never see Seth again, and the other half hoped he would come back just so she could deny him entrance. It was not a good start to the evening.

"Well, Seth," Jeb spoke to the hot, sweating man who had just come from the foundry midmorning on Friday. Jeb had been cutting past the building and on his way home and caught Seth as he came outside. "You done at Jessie's already?"

Seth took a long drink from the bucket and ladle outside, even as he shook his head no. When he'd slaked some of his thirst, he explained.

"I'll be back there, but this was good money and just for a few weeks. But hot," Seth said, looking at Jeb from a face that was thinner than the last time he'd seen him.

"Definitely hot."

"Why did I think you would have moved on by now," Jeb said, no censure in his voice.

Seth smiled a little before saying, "My plans may have changed."

"Does that have anything to do with a certain mercantile owner?"

"Well, it certainly doesn't have anything to do with this foundry work," Seth said dryly, using his sleeve to wipe the sweat from his brow.

Jeb smiled at his tone but wasn't done.

"Does Jessie know?"

"That I'm staying around town for her? Probably not. That last time I saw her she was mad at me, so we'll have to see how it goes."

"What happened?" Jeb asked, but then put his hand up before Seth could answer. "Let me guess, you wanted her to do something different concerning the store."

Seth studied the older man before asking, "What is that about?"

"I don't know. Her father was the same way. In most ways she's easygoing, but when it comes to working the store, there is only one way. And no one can really argue with her since she and her family have always made such a success of it."

Seth looked as though he were pondering something, and Jeb wondered what he was thinking. Seth seemed decent and hardworking, and Jessie was no one's fool, but Jeb was determined to have his say.

"Jessie doesn't need me to cosset her, but I want you to know that I care about her, as do many others."

"I can see that," Seth said, but didn't comment on his intentions toward Jessie. They were not altogether selfish, but some certainly were.

"I'm glad it's clear to you," Jeb said, his eyes watching the younger man.

Until that moment, Seth had not taken Jeb's full measure. Seth had gauged him to be very kind, like an older uncle who visits the family once every few years, but there was more to him than that, and the serious eyes watching him made that clear.

"I'd better get back to work," Seth said.

"I have to get along too," Jeb replied. "I'll see you around, Seth."

The younger man waved and headed back inside the foundry. He still looked hot, but a small amount of his confidence had evaporated, and that gave Jeb Dorn no small amount of peace.

"Did you miss me?" Seth asked, leaning on the counter five minutes after Jessie opened the store on Saturday morning.

Jessie looked up to find his face very close, his warm gray eyes telling her he was much too pleased with himself.

"Why would I miss you?" she asked, working hard not to smile.

"Isn't it obvious? I'm a wonderful, charming person."

Jessie couldn't stop the smile that peeked through, and Seth's own satisfied smile told her he'd seen it.

"Are you here to work or to lean on my counter?"

"I need a work shirt. I ruined one of mine at the foundry," he said. "I'm also here to work if you can give me a quick lesson on how things run."

A lot of things Jessie wanted to say from their last encounter slipped from her mind. She was amazed at how glad she was to see him again. When he hadn't come in all week, she'd assumed he was gone, and that had been hard.

"Jessie?" Seth said when she didn't speak. She caught herself, and only just in time. Two customers came in together, and Jessie recognized one of them as someone who always meant business.

"You do know how to make change, don't you?" Jessie asked, keeping her voice low.

"Yes, ma'am," Seth said with yet another pleased smile.

"Well, try to keep up, and for goodness' sake, don't offend anyone."

Seth didn't comment. He was amused by the look she gave him and also the way she made a beeline for a woman in a garish hat.

"Good morning, Mrs. Theel. What can I help you find?"

Seth watched Jessie in action until he noticed a pile of mail waiting to be sorted. Stepping behind the counter, he knew he was headed into the deep end but figured there was no better way to learn.

Chapter Three

July 1873

"WHAT'S ON THE AGENDA for tonight?" Seth asked when the clock showed minutes to closing. It was the sixth Saturday Seth had worked at the mercantile. He spent his weekdays at the foundry, building up a nice bankroll, and had even found a room at the boardinghouse. He hadn't pressed Jessie in any way, but their awareness of each other was hard to ignore. At the moment they were both behind the main counter, but Seth was the only one working, straightening a jewelry display that no one had taken time with during the day.

"The normal," Jessie answered.

Seth stopped long enough to face her and ask, "Which is?"

"I find something to eat and then fall into bed."

Seth nodded in full understanding. He could have mustered some energy if he tried, but he knew just what she meant. The activity in the store on Saturdays was nonstop. It wasn't a great weight when all you did was stock shelves, but dealing with people was exhausting.

"How about tomorrow?"

"I don't have any plans. Do you?"

"Only to see you."

"You sound as though that's a foregone conclusion."

Without warning, Seth cupped her cheeks in his hands and kissed her. He took his time about it, and when he was done Jessie felt flushed all over.

"It is a foregone conclusion," he said quietly, gently kissing her one more time. "I'll see you tomorrow, Jessie."

By the time Jessie had found her voice, he was long gone.

Jessie walked downstairs and through the storeroom early the next day. She didn't really have anyplace to go, but she was sure if she lay around as she usually did, Seth would be waiting. He was far too confident about himself in her opinion; the kiss had certainly proved that. She assumed that when he came, he would sit out back and wait for her. Well, by that time she would have already enjoyed her walk along the creek line and be back home. She would enjoy knowing that he would sit in the heat for nothing.

Jessie mulled all of this over as she let herself out the back door. Not until she had the door locked and the key in her pocket did she find Seth leaning against the back of the building, quietly watching her.

"Good morning," he said, his eyes a bit knowing.

"What are you doing here already?"

"Catching you before you can get away."

Jessie's chin came up. She'd been caught in the act but wasn't about to admit it.

"You're much too sure of yourself, Mr. Redding."

"And you're not very honest, Miss Wheeler. You are as attracted to me as I am to you. When are you going to admit that to yourself?"

Jessie didn't look at him for a moment, and when she did, her face registered pain. Seth, who had been keeping his distance, came closer.

"What's wrong, Jessie?"

"I am attracted to you, Seth," Jessie said, her voice sad. "There's no getting around that, but there's also no getting around the fact that you're passing through. If we get involved, I'm going to someday find myself alone, possibly with a child, while you finally make that move to Texas."

Seth knew he'd asked for it. He told her she wasn't honest, and she'd surprised him by giving him as honest as it gets.

"I wouldn't do that," Seth said, but Jessie was already shaking her head.

"I don't think you would mean to, but it could still happen."

Without permission Seth took her in his arms. He held her close, his heart clenching with feelings that were new for him. Jessie hugged him in return and admitted to herself for the first time that she wanted him to stay forever.

"Walk with me," Seth invited, taking her hand and stepping away from the door.

Jessie told herself to refuse, but she couldn't do it. Even knowing that spending more time with him would only lead to heartache, Jessie let her fingers link with his and went along.

"Is that Jessie and Seth?" Patience asked Jeb as they walked home from church. The couple was at a distance, and Jeb squinted that way.

"It looks like them."

"Have you talked to Jessie lately?"

"Not since I helped her out last Saturday."

"How did it seem between them?"

"There was lots of teasing and fun, but I didn't get the impression that they had much of a relationship beyond the store."

The Dorns watched Seth slip an arm around Jessie and pull her close. Both wondered if this was something new or if Jeb had completely missed the signs.

"I'm going to catch the morning train," Seth told Jessie at the end of the day. They were in Jessie's living room late Sunday night, standing close. They had spent every hour together that day, their eyes saying things that their mouths refused to voice. "But I'll be back."

The smile that slanted across Jessie's mouth was sad, as were her eyes.

"I mean that," Seth said, his hands caressing her shoulders.

"At the moment I'm sure you do, but Texas is a long way from here, and you know firsthand the way plans change."

Seth took her in his arms. Never had he dealt with a woman the way he'd dealt with Jessie. All his life if he had found a woman desirable, and certainly one as alone as Jessie, he would have found a way to make their relationship intimate. But not Jessie. The idea of leaving her alone with his child was too much for him. No one before Jessie had ever talked so plainly about it, and it was not something he could ignore.

"I'll be back," Seth repeated, kissing her this time with greater insistency, but making himself pull away.

Jessie didn't see him downstairs. She watched him leave the apartment, her eyes swimming with tears, but hadn't the strength to go after him. At the moment she didn't feel she had the strength to do anything ever again.

Through swollen eyes, Jessie opened the store on Monday morning, hoping beyond hope that it would be a slow day. On warm days she propped the door open wide, but on the chance that she would notice the whistle when the train left the station, she kept the door shut this morning.

She'd not taken any extra time on Saturday evening to clean up, so she was in an aisle putting things to rights when she heard the door. She knew she should at least call a greeting or head to the front but had no energy to act on the thought. It took a moment for her to realize she wasn't alone. Seth was standing ten feet away, watching her. Jessie pushed to her feet and stared at him.

"I bought my ticket," he said quietly, his voice rough from lack of sleep. "I was in my seat and my bag was stowed, but I couldn't go."

Jessie licked her lips and told herself not to cry.

"Marry me," he said quietly.

Jessie was in his arms as fast as she could move across the floor. She threw her arms around his neck and kissed him for all she was worth. When they broke apart, Seth laughed.

"Should I take that as a yes?"

"Yes!" Jessie said and pulled his head down to kiss him again.

"You're getting married?" Jeb asked, his face showing his surprise as he looked at the young couple on his sofa.

"Yes," Jessie said, her face aglow. The day in the store had been the longest of her life. Long before suppertime she had wanted to run to the Dorns and tell them the good news, but she made herself wait until closing.

"Congratulations," Jeb finally said, realizing he was genuinely pleased. "When is the day?"

"That depends a little on you, Jeb," Jessie said, her eyes searching his. "We want to go away for a few days. I thought we could close the store at noon on a Saturday and get married that afternoon, but then we want to stay away until Wednesday."

"And I would work on that Monday and Tuesday?"

"Right."

"Which ones?"

"You tell us," Seth said, wishing it could be this Saturday.

"Patience will be home in about half an hour," Jeb said, consulting his watch and knowing how pleased she was going to be with this news. "Can you wait so I can check her calendar?"

The couple willingly agreed, Jessie settling a little closer to Seth's side. The three of them talked until Patience made an appearance, and much to Seth and Jessie's delight, Jeb agreed to mind the store in just two weeks.

"Who is going to marry you?" Patience asked, having already hugged her husband's young cousin.

Seth and Jessie looked at each other, having completely forgotten this necessary portion of the agenda. Their surprised looks made the older couple laugh, which got all of them to laughing.

Patience was ready to put coffee on and serve an impromptu dessert, but Seth knew that Pastor English did not stay up very late, and they wanted to talk to him that night. With excitement filling them and a little bit of fear that he would say no, they didn't linger with the Dorns but headed for the parsonage.

"Are you coming up?" Jessie asked when Seth walked her home a few hours later.

"Do you want me to?" Seth asked, studying her face in the swiftly fading light.

Jessie nodded, and Seth stared at her. He knew that many people would say he couldn't love this woman in less than a month's time, but they were wrong. He loved her completely, and for that reason he found himself shaking his head no.

"We'll be married in less than two weeks," he said, more for himself than for her.

Jessie sighed, not sure if she appreciated the gesture or not. She had never been in love before, and in her mind this was perfect.

"I love you," Jessie said, wanting to say it over and over.

"I love you too," Seth said, having second thoughts about waiting but then hearing a door slam and a man's voice somewhere behind them. Jessie had a reputation in this town, and he would not damage that.

"I'll see you in the morning," Seth said, giving her a swift kiss and moving on his way.

Jessie sighed as she unlocked the back door and then shut it behind her, but this time it was one of contentment. She would see him in the morning and every morning for the rest of their lives.

December 1873

Seth and Jessie Redding took to married life and running the store with the ease of breathing. Neither one minded rising early, and they genuinely enjoyed their customers, but come Sunday, they did little but enjoy each other's company.

They had taken a short trip after the wedding and had to come back way before they were ready, but neither one minded overly much. They had their evenings to themselves and all day Sunday. And the in-between times as well. Seth was always ready for a hug and kiss, and more than one morning the store opened late because he was still teasing his wife by chasing her around the living room furniture.

"Look at the time!" Jessie said to him when they had been married for more than four months and Christmas was just a few weeks away. "I have to get downstairs."

"Jessica," Seth said in a coaxing voice as she darted around the sofa, stalking her very slowly. "Come and kiss your husband one more time."

"No, Seth. You dislodge the pins from my hair."

Seth pulled to a stop and put his hands in the air. Very deliberately, Jessie watching him all the while, he put them behind his back, causing his wife to smile.

"No hands," he promised.

"Just one kiss?"

"Yes."

"No hands?"

"Yes."

Seth grinned wickedly as Jessie came near, but he was good at his word. They were about five minutes late getting the store opened, but no one was waiting.

"I'm going to have to take the time to check the front walk from an upstairs window," Seth commented as he began to straighten the counter.

"Why is that?"

"Well, if we can see that no one is waiting, we can steal a little more time alone."

Jessie smiled and went up on tiptoes to kiss his cheek. Seth looked down at her, asking himself why it had taken so long to find her. She was 21 and he was 23. They weren't old by anyone's estimation, but it felt as though too much time had been wasted not knowing and having each other.

"Good morning," Pastor English greeted the couple as he came into the store. "How are Mr. and Mrs. Redding today?"

"Doing well," Seth answered. "You certainly picked a cold day to be out."

"Yes, I did, but I have a list of things I need, and it won't wait."

"What can I help you with?" Jessie offered.

"I need to order some paper," the pastor said, all the while praying that the couple would show some hunger for more than each other. His mind went back to the night they'd come to him. Yes, he'd agreed to marry them, but not before telling them that whether or not they wanted to hear it, a life lived without God was no life at all. They had listened patiently, with every sign of politeness, but he could tell he'd not gotten through.

Looking at Seth now, as he stayed close and watched Jessie find the item in the catalog and start the order process, he realized he'd not been surprised when they had fallen for each other. He had seen in Seth that Jessie was special to him. He also saw signs of selfishness, but he was not without conscience. He could see that Jessie's settledness in the apartment and the mercantile was appealing to him. The wise pastor also knew that it didn't hurt Seth's feelings that Jessie was a beauty. She was also kind. He knew she was not perfect, but there was much to like about Jessie. Seth had made a good match.

"Now, don't forget," the pastor said when he'd thanked them for their help, determining also to say what was on his mind, "I continue to pray for the both of you, and you know where I live."

"Thank you, Pastor," Jessie said, much as her father had over the years.

Neither Redding spoke further of it after the man pulled his coat collar high and went on his way. Indeed they would have said there was nothing to talk about. Pastor English was peddling God, and Token Creek's newest married couple was simply not interested.

March 1874

"What do you mean you moved the tobacco?" Jessie asked, her face showing how completely she disapproved.

"I think if it's near the pipes, we'll sell more pipes. That's how men think."

"I want it on the front counter," Jessie said, a note of finality to her voice. Seth ignored it.

"Let's try it here and see what happens."

"No," Jessie said, and this time Seth grew angry.

"Why can't I try anything? Why must nothing be changed in this store?"

"Because it works," Jessie said, turning to walk away.

Seth looked after her, frustration filling him, and decided he'd had enough. He had started by asking her if he could make changes, but she always said no. Then he'd gone to changing what he wanted but always switching it back when she noticed and grew upset. This time he dug his heels in. The change was a good one. If she wanted it changed back she could do it herself.

"I thought I told you to put the tobacco back," Jessie said an hour later, finding Seth working the storeroom.

He faced her, speaking quietly. "I'm not your employee anymore, Jessie."

"I didn't say you were," Jessie replied, not catching on at all.

"But that's the way I'm treated. You order me around as though I work for you."

"I wouldn't have to do that if you would leave things as they are."

Seth stared at her and saw that she meant what she said with all her heart. No matter what he said, she was not going to change. When he spoke, his voice sounded sad, but inside there was more resentment than sadness.

"I can see that you don't really need me out front. I'll just go back to keeping the storeroom in order and getting the orders from the train station."

Jessie looked as stunned as she felt, but Seth didn't comment. He collected his hat and coat and walked through the store, heading out the front door. Jessie didn't see him until minutes before it was time to close for the day. He came in without a word to her and headed to the storeroom to hang up his coat. Jessie followed, hurt by his actions but much calmer than she had been earlier.

"Where have you been?"

"Just out," he said, not mentioning the saloon he'd sat in all afternoon. "There was nothing at the train station, and I knew the storeroom was in order."

Jessie asked herself how this could happen. They had been doing so well. What was wrong with the way she had the store?

"What's happening to us, Seth?"

Seth had been ready to head up the stairs, cold and hungry, but he made himself stop.

"I want to be more than your servant, Jessie. I'm a man with a brain, not some mindless idiot. If I have an idea, I want to try it."

"But my father," Jessie began, but Seth had heard this before and put his hand up.

"I don't want to hear about your father. He's dead."

This would normally have made Jessie mad, but this time she was only surprised and hurt.

"I just don't want him to be disappointed in me," she admitted for the first time.

"Jessie," Seth said, calming some but not about to agree with her. "You don't even believe in heaven. Where is it you think your father is sitting and being disappointed in you? You have a flesh-and-blood husband in front of you, but you care more about your dead father!"

Jessie's hand came to her mouth in horror. It was true. Her father was gone, but she was more worried about his feelings than Seth's.

"I'm sorry," she whispered. "I didn't mean it that way."

Seth looked at her face and saw that he had her attention on this matter for the first time. He didn't want to fight with his wife. He loved her and loved the life they had started together. Moving slowly, even giving her time to pull away, Seth walked toward her. He put his arms around her and was surprised when she clung to him. Seth held back no more. He crushed her in his arms and hushed her when she continued to apologize.

"We'll work this out," he said quietly, fully believing they would do just that. What he hadn't planned on was Jessie getting pregnant that spring, and that driving the workings of the store completely from his mind.

August 1874

"None of my clothes fit," Jessie said in late summer. It was Sunday, and she was sitting on the side of their bed in her shift.

Seth lay against the pillows watching her and trying not to smile. He was delighted about this baby. Jessie was losing her waist, but it was not unattractive. Indeed she was growing fuller all over, and Seth was not put off in the least.

"Are you smiling about this?" Jessie turned to see his face.

"No," he lied shamelessly. "It's very serious."

Jessie rolled her eyes at him, giving Seth permission to chuckle.

"Why is this funny?"

"I don't know, but it is. You're only four months along, which makes me wonder how it's going to be in a few more months."

"I'll be even more tired and grumpy."

Seth didn't laugh then. She was very irritable at times, and that was not his idea of a good time.

"Well," he said before his silence got him into trouble, "Patience is feeding us when they get home from church, and that's always nice."

"Oh, that's right. How much time do we have?"

"More than an hour."

Jessie looked as though she wanted to lie down again. They had slept late, but Seth thought it might be good for her to sleep a little longer. He also knew, however, that she would want the time to get ready. He offered to heat water for her bath, and her pleasure over the offer was good for his heart.

"How are you, dear?" Patience asked after the women had hugged.

"I feel fat and clumsy."

"You don't look the least fat," Patience argued with her. "Does Seth say you're fat?"

"No, but he thinks my not fitting into my clothing is funny."

"You never know what's going to amuse a man. Oh, that bread smells done. Check that, will you, Jessie?"

While the women put the meal together, the men talked in the living room.

"How is she feeling?" Jeb asked Seth, having experienced a cross Jessie more than once in the past few months.

"Most days, fine. Some days she's not so easy."

"How are you holding up?"

"My favorite time of year is the fall, but this year I could skip right to Christmas and New Year's."

"When is Jessie due?"

"The doctor thinks the sixth of January."

"Maybe the baby will come early."

"A Christmas baby would be fun."

The temptation for Jeb to mention a certain baby at Christmas was very strong, but Seth was like Jessie, showing no interest in anything spiritual.

"Well, Seth," Jeb said kindly, still praying for the younger man, "if it's like most things in life, the time will fly by and that baby will be here before you know it."

Seth had to agree. He had been stranded in Token Creek 14 months ago and had been married for 12 of those. In hindsight it seemed like yesterday. In all honesty, he couldn't say where the time had gone.

Chapter Four

January 1875

"WHAT ARE YOU DOING?" Seth asked, coming in to find Jessie with a feather duster in her hand.

"Just a little cleaning."

"You cleaned yesterday and again all morning. You were going to take it easy this afternoon."

"But I feel good."

Seth leaned on the counter and watched her. The baby was two days late, and Jessie looked as though she'd never had more energy. Seth didn't think her middle could expand any further. And Jeb had been right, overall the time had flown by, but since the due date, time had seemed to crawl.

"Oh," Jessie said, bending a little as though in discomfort.

"What's the matter?"

"Nothing. I just thought I felt a little something."

Seth came toward her and took the duster.

"Be done," he said firmly.

"But I'm almost finished," she argued.

"It will wait," he said.

"What am I supposed to do?"

"Go upstairs and lie down. Read a book or take a nap."

"I'm not tired."

Seth looked at the frown she was giving him and decided it was no use. He handed the duster back to her, got the broom, and went out front to sweep. Jessie watched him, knowing what he was thinking without his having to say the words. Seth had told her many months ago that she argued with everything he said, and she'd argued even about that. For the first time, she saw that it was true and was again reminded how much she was like her father. Her mother used to accuse him of the same thing.

Jessie did finish the dusting, but she also went upstairs as Seth suggested. She wasn't at all tired and had no desire to read. She made a very nice meal for the two of them.

The conversation from downstairs did not come up again, and that was fine with Seth. He would rather they didn't fight as often as they did. He would take peace wherever he could get it. He was weary of the conflicts and his wife's moods since becoming pregnant and just wanted the baby to come.

It took another three days, but he got his wish. Mrs. Seth Redding presented her husband with a small baby girl. They named her Hannah.

September 1875

"What are you doing awake?" Seth asked the baby in the crib. Hannah, now eight months old, smiled up at him in delight. Seth lifted her into his arms and held her close, his heart burgeoning with emotion. Jessie was still asleep in the other bedroom, so he walked with Hannah to the living room and got comfortable on the sofa. He didn't have all morning—the store needed to be opened in about an hour—but for right now he just wanted this time with his daughter.

"Did you sleep well?" he whispered to her, smiling when she grinned at him in delight. "I can see that you did. You're such a good girl to sleep all night."

Having said this Seth realized it might not be true. Jessie could have been up while he slept through it. However, more smiles and some laughter told Seth he'd said the right thing, and this was the way Jessie found them.

"Good morning," Jessie said from the doorway, her voice still holding that early morning rumble.

"Good morning," Seth replied, smiling at her disheveled hair and sleepy eyes. "Look who's here, Hannah. Mama's awake."

Jessie snuggled closed to Seth's side, and he leaned to kiss her.

"Has she been awake long?"

"I found her awake when I got up."

"When was that?"

Seth looked at the clock on the wall and realized 30 minutes had passed. He had to get shaved and dressed for work.

"Do you have time to make me some eggs?" he asked as he handed off the baby.

"Sure," Jessie agreed, and with her normal, quiet efficiency she cooked Seth's breakfast, holding Hannah on her hip through most of the process.

Seth was downstairs on time, greeting the first customer just moments after he opened the door. Jessie and Hannah eventually joined him, but only for about an hour. Hannah was crawling, so Jessie ended up in the storeroom working at the table over the account books. Seth had barricaded a corner that Hannah could call her own, and that little girl was content to play as long as she could see her mother.

"What's this?" Jessie asked Seth some time later. He had come to the storeroom looking for a larger sack of brown sugar.

"Let's see."

Seth bent over the book and looked where Jessie pointed.

"That's the order from the Brown Company."

"It doesn't go there."

Seth had a customer, or he would have argued with her. He was certain he was keeping the books the way she liked, and now she was complaining. He turned from the table, found the sugar, and left.

Jessie assumed that his silence meant he agreed with her and started back to work, but that lasted only until Hannah made a noise. Jessie looked at her, realizing that Seth hadn't so much as glanced at their daughter. That was not normal. She was ready to search him out and confront him, but Jeb had stepped in the door and called her name.

"Back here," Jessie called right back. "What's up?" she asked when her cousin came into view.

"Patience wants to see this baby," Jeb said, going to the play area and leaning down to talk to the child.

"Come evening we're pretty weary, Jeb."

"Come for supper," Jeb invited. "We'll feed you, and you can put your feet up."

Jessie heard the entreaty in his voice and gave in.

"I've got a pot of stew on, but we'll come as soon as we're done."

Jeb had Hannah in his arms now, holding her close and kissing her. He didn't answer, but she could see in his eyes that he was pleased.

"I should have sent a warning with Jeb," Jessie said when the three Reddings visited at the Dorns' that evening. "She cries a lot in the evening."

"She does?" Patience asked, bouncing and walking Hannah to no avail. "I wonder what that could be."

"We wonder too," Seth said dryly, but if the truth be told, it made the evenings very long.

Jessie heard his tone and shot him a look, but Seth only stared at her. This was yet another issue they fought about. Jessie felt she could settle Hannah better than Seth could, but she got mad at him if he wanted to get out of the apartment and away from the noise. Not that he blamed her for not wanting to be left on her own. Hannah started to be unhappy each afternoon, and little could settle her outside of sleep. Thankfully she usually slept through the night, but not until her parents were exhausted and snapping at each other.

When they had first arrived, Jeb and Seth had been talking about Pastor English leaving Token Creek—his health was failing him—and the new, younger man, Rylan Jarvik, who had come to pastor the church. Seth had seemed genuinely interested, and Jeb had wanted to stay on this topic, but the older man could not ignore the exchange he'd just witnessed.

"So how is this affecting the two of you?" Jeb asked as Patience wandered off, bouncing Hannah all the while.

"We're fine," Jessie said, ignoring the stare she felt Seth giving her.

"Is that what you would call it, Seth?" Jeb asked the younger man, even risking Jessie's ire.

"I think we're ready to move past this part of Hannah's life. It's hard not knowing how long it will go on."

Jessie heard his weary answer and realized she could have admitted the same thing. Jeb was asking only out of concern, and she knew she had been too ready to defend her job as a mother.

"I'm tired," Jessie felt free to say. "I love my daughter, but she wears me out."

"I told you I can take care of the store," Seth put in, his voice compassionate. "You need to nap when Hannah does."

"What do you do when Hannah naps?" Jeb asked.

"Get as much done as I can or help in the store."

Jeb's eyes swung to Seth, and that man said, "I don't do things quite how she likes."

"Has business fallen off since Seth has been handling more?" Jeb asked.

Jessie shook her head no, not looking at either man. Things were great in the store. They had plenty of business and profit to show for it, but it was not just the way she wanted, and that irked her.

Before anyone else could comment, Patience arrived back, Hannah asleep in her arms. She smiled at the other three adults, and they laughed softly at her pleasure.

"Now," she whispered, taking the rocking chair, "the four of us can have a nice visit."

All four of them had to get hands over their mouths to keep from laughing loudly. The thought of having a whispered conversation was hysterical to each of them, but in truth that was just what they did.

May 1876

Seth reached for Jessie once they'd climbed into bed, but her stiff back made him swiftly draw his hand away. They had done little but fight for months now, and even though the last few days had gone smoother—Jessie had even welcomed his embrace a few nights before—his wife was evidently upset with him about something. Hannah had been fussy all evening, something they had actually seen less of, but much as Seth tried to help, nothing he did was right.

Seth rolled to his back and stared at the dark ceiling, wondering what happened to the woman he married. He had felt a stability with Jessie that he'd never known—love, trust, and caring too—but not anymore. Most days when she looked at him, she was frowning.

The bright spot was Hannah. If anything she was more work than ever before, now that she was walking and able to take things from the store shelves. But he loved his daughter in a way he didn't think was possible.

Jessie lay on her side and stared at the dark wall of the bedroom, wondering why the life she dreamed about was so hard. She had a beautiful 16-month-old daughter, her business was booming, and she'd married the man she loved, but all was not well. They were still tired much of the time and short with each other. Seth seemed quieter and more withdrawn with each passing week, and when they actually did have time alone, neither one said much.

Jessie fell asleep with no answers to her questions, no balm for the hurt inside of her.

Seth, in just as much pain and confusion, listened as her breathing evened out, asking himself what he was going to do about his life and marriage.

"What is this?" Jessie snapped at Seth for the fourth time since they'd opened two hours earlier.

"What does it look like?" Seth gritted out, not sure he could stand much more.

"It looks like a huge mess!"

"In case you haven't noticed," Seth shot right back, "I've been with three customers at the same time here. I don't know when I would have had time to clean up the counter."

"It's never your fault, is it, Seth?" Jessie said, straightening and shifting things with almost violent movements.

"Now that all depends on who you ask, doesn't it, Jessie?" Seth asked in silky sarcasm. "According to you, everything that's ever gone wrong in your life is *my* fault."

Before Jessie could shoot back another angry retort, a cry from Hannah could be heard coming from the storeroom.

"Now, look what you've done!" Jessie snarled at him before shooting around the counter and running that way.

Seth stared after her, not sure when anything had made him so angry. He could feel the blood pounding in his temples and thought that if he couldn't get out of this store for a while, he was going to lose his mind.

He ran a distracted hand through his hair while his eyes caught sight of a letter. It had come yesterday and was for him. He didn't receive mail very often. Something—he still didn't know what—had compelled him to put it out of the way on a high shelf and not read it or mention it to Jessie.

The postmark was from Texas.

March 1884
Nearly Eight Years Later

Sheriff Nate Kaderly made his way slowly toward Pastor Rylan and Bri Jarvik's home, the wind calm for the moment. He was bundled up warmly, coat collar to his ears and hat pulled low, but was quite chilled by the time he knocked on the front door. Thankfully Bri took little time to answer, welcoming him into the warmth of the living room.

"Are you frozen?" she asked, seeing that he removed only his hat, not yet willing to give up the coat.

"Just about. The sun is deceiving. It looks warmer out there than it really is."

"Sit close to the fire, Nate. I'll get Rylan."

"Thank you. Where's that little guy?" Nate asked, referring to Rylan and Bri's son, Danny.

"He's napping, but he'll probably be up before you go."

Rylan was not long in joining his friend. Not many weeks ago, he would have been getting his own coat and readying to leave with Nate for some emergency in town, but things had changed when Nate had been shot in the line of duty. Nate's visit today was not an emergency.

"Hello, Nate," Rylan greeted as he entered.

"Hello, Rylan," Nate spoke in return as the men shook hands.

"Are you sure you should be out?" Rylan asked. "I would have come to your house."

"I needed the walk," Nate said quietly, now setting his coat aside.

For a moment he looked older to Rylan than his 41 years, and the pastor was swept back, back to a day just two months earlier that had been life changing for Token Creek's sheriff.

"How is he?" Rylan asked of Doctor Ertz, wanting to head directly to the bedroom but making himself wait.

"Not good. He's lost so much blood, I don't know if he'll make it."

Rylan moved then, heading to the sheriff's bedroom and finding his friend very still. He stood looking down at the white face, pale even amidst the white pillowcases and the two windows that allowed a bit of cloudy light into the room.

Rylan said Nate's name, but that man didn't move or respond in any way. Rylan felt his heart clench and wasted no time going to his knees. With his arms on Nate's mattress and his forehead on his arms, Rylan began to pray.

He's not ready, Lord. He's not ready to meet You. He has never humbled himself before You and seen You for the God that You are, the God who longs to save him and be his Lord. Please Father, give him more time. Please spare him, Lord. Your will is perfect, Father, and if it be Your will, please leave him here to find You and serve You.

Rylan didn't move for more than an hour but prayed, giving Nate over to God and thanking Him for His will. Rylan asked God to help him remember who was in charge and to want His way above all else so that God might be glorified by this incident.

"Rylan?" Nate suddenly asked, bringing the pastor swiftly to his feet.

"I'm right here, Nate," Rylan said, noticing that Nate's eyes were still closed and wondering how he'd known.

"Thirsty," Nate managed, and Rylan dribbled some drops of water into his mouth. Nate tried to talk after that but couldn't manage it. He fell back to sleep for another two hours, but when he woke again, Rylan was still there. This time the sheriff's eyes were open, and he stared at the big man next to his bed.

"Has Ertz been here?"

"Yes. He says it's bad. You've lost a lot of blood."

Nate saw the tears in Rylan's eyes and tried to lift his hand.

"It's all right, Rylan. If it's my time, it's my time."

"It's not all right, Nate," Rylan said in quiet humility. "You're not ready to go. You've heard me talk to so many townsfolk about God's Son, but you've never shown the least bit of interest. I know what God's Word says, Nate, and you're not ready to face Him."

"How do I even know if there is a God?"

"I can answer that question for you, Nate, but let me ask one first. Are you willing to take that chance? Are you willing to leave here not knowing?"

The questions made Nate think for the first time. He couldn't stay awake for very long, but each time he woke, Rylan was there. The men talked off and on for hours. Doctor Ertz came and went again. Nate's deputies checked on him, and still Rylan stayed, determined to do so until Nate threw him out. The sheriff didn't do that. As darkness fell, Nate, feeling as though he was indeed slipping away, listened as Rylan read to him from the book of John. The words were familiar to him as Nate had heard Rylan say these things before. He listened well and after a time believed in the blood of Christ to save him.

Rylan eventually left, fairly certain his friend would not be there in the morning, but the sheriff lived through the night. He was weak and still not out of the woods, but he was alive. And that was only the beginning. Slowly Nate got back on his feet, and it was evident every time he and Rylan talked that his faith was real. It had been the start of a whole new life for the lawman.

"I read those verses in Acts 13 and Romans 3 and 7 you recommended," Nate said, suddenly bringing Rylan back to his own living room. "They make sense. I didn't see it before, but they make sense now."

"What changed for you?"

"I'm not sure. It's just so new. I mean, the aspect of Christ dying for sins that have yet to be committed is hard to wrap my mind around."

"It's easy to put God in our world and limit Him. We can't see past the moment, and so we don't think anyone can."

"I do have one question," Nate said, and Rylan reached for his Bible. "Where are those verses you used to explain it to me?"

"Hebrews 7," Rylan said, and Nate opened his Bible as well.

Rylan explained again about the difference between living under the law in the Old Testament, which required one animal sacrifice after another to atone for sin, and living under grace since Christ's death on the cross, which covered all sin for all time.

The men worked on the verses for close to an hour before the topic changed to Nate's job. The town council had not even hesitated about keeping him on as sheriff, but Nate had not expected his recovery to take so long. He'd been told how much blood he'd lost but not really taken it in until he'd experienced his own weakness firsthand. He was not worried about losing his job, but for the moment things had to be handled differently.

"Are you still happy with Thom's work?" Rylan asked, referring to Thom Koeller, who was Nate's most reliable deputy.

"Yes, and he tells me that Bryce Stanton is doing well."

"That's good news. Will you be putting another man on soon?"

"Yes, as soon as I'm up to holding the interviews. Token Creek is growing fast, and even though it took awhile for the council to decide, the vote was unanimous."

"Am I interrupting?" Bri asked from the edge of the room, Danny in her arms.

"No," Rylan said. "Hey, Danny. Did you have a good nap?"

The still sleepy 14-month-old reached for his father the moment he was close, and Rylan cuddled him closer still.

"Look who's here," Rylan said, turning Danny so he could see Nate, who was smiling at the baby, doing nothing to hide his fondness.

"Hey, Danny."

The little boy smiled at Nate but was clearly happy where he was, his small head pillowed on his father's chest. Bri sat down with the men, her own smile tender. For her, all else could wait when Rylan held Danny. It was a sight she never wearied of.

"It doesn't look like he's coming over here today," Nate said, still smiling at the baby.

"Do you want to go see Sheriff Nate?" Rylan asked the little guy, who gave no protest when his father shifted him over to Nate's lap.

"How are you, Danny?" Nate asked, barely keeping his eyes from filling. Since being shot, whenever he held Danny Jarvik, he wanted to tear up.

Danny smiled up into his face, and Nate hugged him a little closer.

He talked softly into one small, soft ear, saying something that made the baby giggle.

Looking on, Rylan and Bri could only smile and laugh with their son. This man had been a friend of Rylan's for many years, but never had their relationship neared the depth they knew today. God had brought yet another miracle to Token Creek, and at the moment he was sitting right in front of them.

"Shall I admit something to you?" Rylan asked the congregation in the morning. He smiled widely before admitting, "I love looking into my wife's eyes."

Bri smiled from her place in the front pew, as did almost everyone else in the room.

"Now before you think I'm going to bore you with my romantic thoughts, I'll just tell you that even though I find this romantic, I'm also learning things about who I am."

Rylan let the congregation take this in for a moment and then continued.

"I guess I'm becoming a pupil of the pupil. By that I mean I'm learning more about how the eye works because of Sabrina's eyes, and even Danny's. You probably know what I'm talking about. What does the pupil in the eye do when it encounters light? It shrinks. That's right. It diminishes. Unless damaged or impaired by poor health, the pupil gets as small as possible as fast as it can.

"I lived alone for a long time, but with Sabrina and Danny in the house, I've begun to take a new interest in eyes. And I've asked myself what I can learn. How do I respond to light, and by light this time I mean God's light? Do I see my own smallness? Do I grasp how tiny I am in God's light? My mind has run in many directions as I've contemplated this, but it stopped when I compared the shrinking of my pupil to humility and an understanding of its place in my life. When the light shines, I must diminish. I must grow tiny and know my place.

"If I can learn this and remember it always, I will become a true pupil to the pupil. I will see the wonder in the creation of my own eyes and in those of my wife and son, and I will see what I must do. I must shrink when I see how huge and amazing the Creator is who made eyes. Eyes that don't have to be trained to get small when the light comes in. Eyes made exactly as we need them because God is a perfect, Creator God.

"The verses we've been talking about concerning humility in Philippians, Colossians, and First Peter, as well as the verse from James 1 about being hearers of the word who are also doers, have taken on new meaning for me when I think about my shrinking pupil. It might not be a help to you, but I'm reminded of this perfect Creator who saved me, and that helps me to see how important it is that I take His Word so seriously.

"Don't misunderstand me," Rylan added, bringing his sermon to an end. "I'm never to shy away from the light. And by light you know I'm talking about the truth of God's Word. But my heart and attitude need to be small, shrunken, and knowing their places. Only then is God able to help me be the believer I'm meant to be. Only then will I be able to see God for who He is and myself for who I am.

"Please think on these things with me this week. I would welcome any questions or comments as we work together on this topic."

Rylan closed in prayer, and not until that moment did Bri realize that Danny had fallen asleep in her lap, something that suited her very well. Her husband had given her a lot to think about, and she welcomed a few minutes on her own.

Chapter Five

Trace Holden watched his very expectant wife, Cassidy, push food around her plate but didn't say anything just then. She had made it to church that morning, but he could tell she wasn't comfortable. Joey, who was two months past his second birthday, was growing sleepy. As soon as he was down for his nap, all Trace's attention would go to his wife. A small gasp of surprise left Cassidy just then, and Trace made a swift decision.

"I'm going to run him next door for his nap."

"That's probably a good idea," Cassidy said.

"Is it going to be today?" Trace asked, remembering how attuned she'd been to when Joey would be born.

Cassidy could only nod, and Trace cleaned Joey up enough to get him to Brad and Meg's. He knew his brother and sister-in-law's own two children, Savannah and Cathryn, would also be going down for naps and thought this might be the best opportunity. Not even remembering to have Joey say goodbye to Cassidy, he moved swiftly for the door.

"You were quiet during dinner," Rylan said to Bri after Danny was

down for his nap. Bri was settled in the living room, working to mend
a small pair of pants for Danny. Rylan had sat down next to her on
the sofa.

"I'm just thinking."

"Do you want to tell me?"

Bri looked at the man she married, still amazed by the way he
thought. His God was so big, and sometimes she knew she shrank
God to her size.

"I needed to hear what you said today," she finally admitted.

"What exactly?"

"The part about the way I see God and the light He gives me. I need
to shrink. I have too big an opinion of myself."

Rylan didn't witness this in her very often, but he trusted her to
know her own heart.

"Sometimes life is too easy, Ry," Bri went on. "When I was alone
here in Token Creek, knowing hardly anyone and not sure each month
if the money would last, I trusted God more. You take such good care
of Danny and me that I tend to put my faith in the wrong place."

"It's a good problem, isn't it?"

Bri had to smile. It was just the type of thing he would say.

"Do you think you're expecting?" Rylan suddenly asked.

"What made you ask that?"

"I just remember with Danny you craved salt, and during dinner
you added salt to everything but dessert."

"Did I?" Bri asked, her brow furrowed as she tried to think. It didn't
take long for her to realize he was probably right and she'd been too
busy to notice.

Rylan had to smile. She was concentrating on remembering, and
he thought she looked adorable.

"Am I being laughed at?" Bri asked, having caught the look.

"Are you pregnant?" he asked, still smiling at her with a good deal
of humor in his eyes.

"I don't know," Bri replied, deciding to tease him. "I might not tell
someone who laughs at me."

"Would you tell someone who kisses you?"

"I might," Bri answered slowly, a smile stretching her mouth.

Rylan did kiss her but spoke again before she could say anything.

"What do you want, another boy or a girl?"

"I don't care, as long as the baby is healthy."

"What if the baby isn't healthy? Did God make a mistake?"

Bri's mouth opened in surprise. It was true. It didn't matter. Whomever God sent they would love and treasure.

"Oh, Ry," Bri said, setting the sewing aside and cuddling close to him. "I love you."

"Don't misunderstand me, Sabrina," Rylan said, his arms holding her close. "It would be very hard to watch our child struggle with some physical affliction, but just like you had to learn to trust God for everything when you came to Token Creek, we would learn to trust God for the baby's needs as well as our own."

Bri put her arms around her husband and held him right back. She was challenged and encouraged by his words, and she knew what he said was exactly right. She also suspected he was right about her expecting another child and how wonderful that news would be to share.

When they both relaxed enough to doze off, neither one could say, but Danny was suddenly awake, sounds coming from his crib. Rylan went to get him, and Bri started on the hot dish she needed for that night. They were having dinner with Chas Vick, one of the church elders, and his family, and she was taking a dish to share. She would have to ask Rylan if they would be sharing their news as well.

Cassidy watched Trace and Joey leave and then tried to summon the energy to do something about the dishes. She knew it wasn't important, but she enjoyed cleaning and thought it might relax her. She was wrong. She hadn't even had a chance to heat water for the washing when a pain hit. Cassidy held on to the edge of the dining room table and tried to breathe.

Well, now, she said to the Lord, *I think it's going to be today. Every time I think of how long Joey took to arrive, I dread this. Please, Lord, help me to see this as a blessing. Help me not to count the hours until I'm comfortable but to rest in You.*

Cassidy was still praying when the pain eased and she made her way to the living room. She knew Trace would help her upstairs when he returned and for the moment let herself be lazy.

"Cassidy?" Trace suddenly called, having gone to the bottom of the stairs on his return.

"Over here," she said on a laugh. "I don't know how I didn't hear you come in."

"Why are you in here?" Trace asked, sitting on the edge of the sofa.

"Because I'm being lazy and want you to carry me upstairs."

"I can't lift you when you're this big," Trace said, and laughter burst out of Cassidy. It was such an outrageous thing for him to say and completely unexpected. "And besides," he added, eyes twinkling, "you haven't done the dishes."

"I was working on them when I had a contraction."

"How long ago?"

"I don't know," Cassidy said, looking drowsy and content, something that didn't last for more than ten minutes. She didn't end up going directly upstairs as the pains were slow in coming, but Cassidy was right: This was the day. A baby girl was born just before midnight.

Jeanette Fulbright's buggy headed out of Token Creek and to the Holden Ranch first thing Monday morning. She had received word the day before that Cassidy was in labor, and when no word came before bedtime about a birth, she headed that way in the morning.

It was cold out, but the wind was calm and that made a difference. Not until she pulled under the wooden archway that said Holden Ranch did Jeanette realize she would be glad to get indoors. Swinging past

Brad and Meg's house, Jeanette stopped in front of Trace and Cassidy's, pleased when her nephew came right out.

"A girl!" he said, his face beaming.

"Oh, Trace!" Jeanette cried, the two hugging before Trace could even give her a hand down. "How is Cass?"

"Doing great. Settled in the living room under a pile of blankets."

"Already out of bed?" Jeanette asked, looking concerned as the two headed inside.

"She feels good, and I carried her down."

"What does Joey think?"

"You'll have to see for yourself."

Jeanette headed into the living room to find Cassidy on the sofa, her legs on a hassock. Beside her and holding his sister was Joey. Trace followed Jeanette inside, and before she could even greet the family, Cassidy spoke. "Come in and meet Jeanette Theta Holden," she invited.

For several long minutes Jeanette could not speak. She came near to the sofa, her eyes on Cassidy's lovely face, before swinging to Joey and the baby. Even then she couldn't find words.

"Joey, can you tell Grandma what we're going to call the baby?" Cassidy invited, using the name they had decided the children would call Trace's aunt.

"Netty," the little boy said.

Jeanette put her arms around Cassidy and simply held her. Cassidy hugged her back, giving her time to collect herself.

"She crying?" Joey suddenly asked.

"Yes," Trace said, taking this question, "but she's not sad. She's just happy and excited about the baby."

Trace knew that Joey had no idea what that meant, but in time he would learn. He didn't question his father again, but Trace could see he was growing a bit restless. Jeanette was just containing herself when Trace tucked the baby into the crook of one arm.

"Sit here, Jeanette." Trace invited her to take the spot Joey had just vacated. "Someone is waiting to meet you."

Jeanette could not stop smiling as she held the newest family member in her arms. Tiny and adorable, with dark hair and brows, Netty Holden had a rosebud mouth and a round face. Her face was a little red in places, but everyone knew that would fade.

"Netty," her mother spoke softly, "are you going to wake up and meet Grandma Jeanette?"

Everyone smiled when she made absolutely no move of any kind. Jeanette watched her for a moment more and then began to talk to Trace and Cassidy.

"So how was it?"

"Long," Trace said, his voice dry. "I thought the second time around went faster."

"I tried to tell him that wasn't always the case," Cassidy put in.

"It has been with Meg," Trace said, "and she didn't spend much time with Savanna or Cathryn. Brad will be afraid to leave her alone for the next one," Trace said.

"Have they been here?" Jeanette asked.

"Just before you came."

Joey climbed back onto the sofa then, standing in stocking feet next to Jeanette. He had a toy to show to Jeanette, and she was careful to give him her full attention.

Netty never did wake up, but Jeanette stayed for a long time, enjoying each child. She still missed her sister, the real grandmother to these children. But not a day went by that if Theta Holden had to be gone, Jeanette didn't thank God that He'd left her in her place.

"Is Grandma coming?" three-and-a-half-year-old Savanna asked her mother when Jeanette's carriage could still be seen at the other house.

"I'm sure she'll stop in," Meg said, cleaning two-year-old Cathryn's hands and face. She had just given them a late breakfast and was working on the dishes. Brad had already headed to the barn and quite possibly out to the range.

"When will we see Netty more?"

"Maybe this afternoon. I think Joey might come here for his nap again, and then we can see Netty when we take him home."

Savanna went back to the wooden horses she was playing with, and Meg kept an eye on Cathryn to see where she would end up. The toddler's attention was suddenly taken with the butter churn in the corner, and Meg knew that would keep Cathryn busy for a time.

Meg took full advantage, even going so far as to work on dinner and make plans for supper. If Jeanette was coming this morning and Joey this afternoon, she had plenty to get done in the meantime.

"Tell me everything," Heather, who lived with Jeanette, invited as soon as Jeanette arrived home.

"A girl! And wait until you hear the name: Jeanette Theta. They'll call her Netty."

Heather looked as pleased as she felt. She was the woman Jeanette had hired more than ten years ago to see to Brad and Trace's mother. She had even written a book about Theta Holden after she died. So far no one had wanted to publish it, but since it was also a book about the things she learned from caring for Theta and the way she'd grown in her trust of God, it didn't bother her. Just writing it had made for a time of healing, and that was all that mattered to Heather.

"What did I miss?" Becky asked, coming from the kitchen. She had been cooking and taking care of the house for Jeanette for more years than anyone could remember.

"A girl!" Heather said. "Jeanette Theta."

Tears filled Becky's eyes, and that started the other women. Whenever Becky cried it made them all cry as tears were a rather new thing for the cook. Just a few years earlier, Bri Jarvik had come into their lives when she was still Bri Matthews. Her new faith in Christ and love for all had touched Becky in a way she'd never known before. After years of watching Jeanette and Heather go off to church, she suddenly wanted to join them. The change had gone all the way to her heart. For the first time Becky admitted her need for a Savior and repented to God.

"Is Cassie all right?" Becky finally managed.

"Yes. She's already downstairs, comfortable in the living room. And you won't believe how close I came to forgetting the food!" Jeanette remembered. "Trace came out to meet me when I got there, and then I was seeing the baby, and then I went over to Brad and Meg's, and I came within an inch of bringing it all back home."

Heather and Becky laughed at her expression before Becky said that dinner was almost on. Over the meal Jeanette told the women each and every detail, not just about the baby but about Joey and about Brad's girls too. By the time she was finished, they felt almost as if they'd visited the ranch with her.

Bri was at the mercantile first thing Tuesday morning, Danny in tow. Jessie was in the rear but called a greeting. As soon as she heard Bri's voice, she came to the front.

"Hi, Danny," Jessie greeted, wasting no time in taking the baby from his mother. "How are you?" she asked fondly, kissing his round cheek as she removed his hat. "Hi, Bri," Jessie finally remembered to add, and that woman laughed.

"You become invisible when you bring a baby into the room," Bri said dryly. "Have you ever noticed that?"

"Try being Clancy's mother. That child draws attention like flies."

"She's a charmer," Bri agreed.

"Big list today?"

"Not bad, but I'm out of a few things."

"Do you want help?" Jessie offered. Bri had worked for her in the past and knew her way around the store.

"Not if you want to keep holding Danny."

Jessie only smiled, and Bri got busy. She stacked things on the front counter where Jessie kept a list going, and then put them in her bag.

"Do you miss the girls when they're at school?" Bri asked on one trip to the register.

"By the end of the day, yes. It's nice to have the morning to get things cleaned up and organized with no interruptions, but by afternoon I can't wait to see them."

"Summer will be here before we have a chance to blink."

"That's certain. We'll change from cries of 'too cold' to 'too hot!'"

"It's always hard to imagine too hot on a day like this," Bri added, heading back down the aisles.

"The girls are going to be sorry they missed you," Jessie said to Danny as he tried to put a box of yeast cakes into his mouth.

"Come for supper," Bri invited, still gathering items.

"I just put a pot of soup on. Why don't you three come here?"

"All right," Bri said, arriving back with her last item. "What time, and what shall I bring?"

The women put the details together for the night before Bri paid and gathered her son and bag. Much too soon it was time to head back out into the cold.

Before Cassidy married Trace, she had opened a small business in town, Token Creek Apparel. For a time she ran it on her own, but then Jeanette Fulbright came to work for her. Token Creek supported the business well, and when Cassidy got married, Jeanette purchased it from her and took over, opening the shop door to the public four days a week. Heather worked with her now, and on Wednesday morning when the shop opened, both women were busy inside.

They were working on several orders at the moment, but they weren't swamped. Cold weather, they had learned, was not the most conducive to business, but they were busy enough. This is the way Rylan found them when he stopped in on his way to the livery.

"Good morning, ladies."

"Good morning, Rylan. Come in and warm up a bit," Jeanette invited. She was nearest the stove, and Heather was at the sewing machine.

"Thank you, I will. I've got to get to the livery pretty soon, but I thought I'd stop and see how you're doing."

Rylan heard all about Netty's birth, well and truly pleased that Cassidy was doing fine and that Joey had a baby sister.

"Pastor Rylan," Heather suddenly asked, "do you have news of your own?"

Rylan smiled at her, not sure how she knew but very glad she did. These women were very dear to him, and it seemed most fitting that they would know as soon as he could tell them.

"As a matter of fact, I do. It's early yet—we've only told the Vicks—but Sabrina is expecting."

The women were as thrilled about this news as they were about Trace and Cassidy's. Both of them hugged Rylan and nearly made him late for work with their questions. He hadn't been gone ten minutes when Jeanette realized she wanted to see Bri. Heather urged her to go, and it was for this reason that Nate arrived at the shop and found Heather on her own.

"Hello," Heather greeted with a smile. "You just missed Jeanette."

"Actually, I thought I saw Rylan over this way."

"You just missed him too," Heather said, laughing a little.

Nate smiled at her laughter and wondered at the fact that every time he saw Heather Wales, he wanted to find reasons not to end the conversation too swiftly.

"Do you have many orders?" Nate asked, trying not to stare at her hair or eyes, both of which he found very nice.

"Just enough," Heather said. "We expect two to be picked up today—those are done—and then three items were ordered on Friday and Saturday. I'm working on those now."

"Did you make this shirt?" Nate asked, having forced himself not to stare and spotting a man's shirt hanging on a hook.

"I'm not sure. Jeanette might have done that one."

"How do you divide up the work?"

"I just do what Jeanette tells me."

Nate could not stop his smile, his eyes filling with amusement.

"What did I say?" Heather asked, unable to miss how much he wanted to laugh.

"You don't by any chance want to go into law enforcement, do you? Having someone simply do as I tell them would be a dream come true."

Heather laughed with him then, and this is the way Jeanette found them.

"Well, Nate! How good to see you."

"Hello, Jeanette."

"How are the wounds?"

"Healing fast. I'm looking forward to spring."

"It is *cold* out there today!" Jeanette agreed, going close to the stove and keeping her coat on.

"Well, I'd best let you ladies get back to work."

"Thanks for stopping," Heather said as he left. She bent back over the machine. It took some time for her to see that Jeanette was staring at her.

"How is Bri?" Heather asked.

"Doing well. The Jarviks are going to come to supper tonight, so you can see her then."

"Oh, good."

Heather went back to work but then found Jeanette's eyes on her again.

"Is something wrong?"

"I don't think so, but I did wonder if you wanted to tell me something."

Heather glanced around, wondering what she had missed, but then looked back to Jeanette with a shrug.

"Is Nate sweet on you, Heather?" Jeanette finally came out and asked.

Heather blinked at her employer, stared for a moment at the place Nate had been standing, and then looked to Jeanette with a sad shake of her head.

"It's not even spring, Jeanette. What put such thoughts in your head?"

"Well, maybe he's not, but he didn't seem in a hurry to leave either."

"He was probably just cold."

"Heather," Jeanette said patiently, "you're lovely and sweet, and he would be a fool not to notice."

"You're lovely and sweet too," Heather argued.

"But I still love my late husband, and everyone knows that. You're whole of heart and quite available."

Heather could only laugh. *Available* was never a word she would use to describe herself, and while still chuckling, she bent back over the machine, her foot pumping methodically on the treadle.

Jeanette was not so easily put off. She smiled at the bent head, thinking her friend was too precious for words. And then her smile became of an entirely different sort. She eventually removed her coat and went back to work, but her mind was not on sewing. Nate and Heather. Why had she never thought of it before?

Part Two

August 1884

Chapter Six

SETH REDDING STOOD ON the train station platform and breathed in the old sights and sounds of Token Creek. Everything was not the same. New paint could be seen here and there—new buildings too—but the town was still recognizable after all these years. The August heat was oppressive, but he paid little heed, even in his dark suit.

Walking slowly away from the train station, a large satchel in one hand, he took in everything he could see until he arrived on Main Street. It too was a mixture of the familiar and the new. The bank had a new facade, and someone had opened a shop called Token Creek Apparel. The assayer's office was still there, but the sign out front now said Ryan Samz, Attorney.

One thing hadn't changed, however: Wheeler's Mercantile. Seth didn't move closer to the establishment that was still a block down the way but stared at the windows and the name overhead for a long time. When he did move, it was in the opposite direction, his heart beating painfully in his chest. There might be someone in this town who could help him, and until he had that help, the mercantile would have to wait.

Just managing not to laugh, Bri watched 19-month-old Danny make his way into the room. He had found an empty box and was dragging it into the living room. His face was intent, and she knew if she spoke from the kitchen doorway, she would startle him. Instead, she waited for him to spot her.

"Mama!" he said with pleasure, patting the box.

"What did you find?" she asked, now free to laugh with the delight she felt inside.

He patted it again, and then ran to hug her legs. Bri swung him up into her arms just as Rylan came from his office.

"Well, now," he said, having spotted the box. "Did we find a treasure?"

"I think so," Bri agreed before adding dryly, "and since he's such a frail, weak child, he could barely drag it in here."

Rylan reached for his son, who was already showing signs of being as large as his father.

"Did you find a box, Danny?" Rylan asked.

Danny pointed by way of an answer, and Rylan hugged him close.

"I have to head over to the church for a little while," he told Bri, Danny still in his arms. "Do you want him to go along?"

"As a matter of fact, he needs a bath."

"Do you stink?" Rylan asked the toddler, shouting with laughter when Danny smiled and gave a nod. Rylan wasn't sure the nod had been a real answer to the question, but it was still amusing.

A few minutes later, Bri and Danny walked Rylan to the front door, and the pastor headed over to the white church building some yards away. The small flock had saved enough to paint it a few years earlier, and it still looked very good.

Rylan slipped in the door and was headed to the front when he realized he was not alone. A man who had been sitting in the front pew stood to his feet, hat in his hand. Not until he turned did Rylan recognize him.

"Hello, Seth," Rylan spoke quietly, well remembering him from the mercantile, though many years had passed.

"Hello, Rylan. I hope it was all right to come inside."

"Certainly. We leave the door unlocked for that very reason." Rylan put his hand out. "How are you?"

Seth smiled a little. "I'm doing well at the moment, but then I haven't seen Jessie yet."

"You're just into town?"

"The morning train…"

"…that came in past noon," Rylan finished for him, his mouth quirking a bit. "Have a seat. Tell me why you're here."

"In town, or in the church?"

"Both."

"I guess I came here because I don't want to upset Jessie at work."

"She's not expecting you?"

The other man shook his head no, his eyes on the front of the room.

"When was the last time you were in touch?" Rylan asked, trying to remember if Jessie had ever told him.

Seth shook his head in regret but didn't look at the pastor. "I never was," he admitted. "After I left here nearly eight years ago, I never wrote."

"Where have you been?"

"Texas."

And there it started. For the next two hours the story came out. Rylan inserted a question here and there, but mostly he let Seth talk. Some of what he heard was awful, and some was wonderful. All of it was astounding.

"I'm not sure how to go over there. I'm not sure how to go to the store," Seth said at last. "It's not just Jessie—I have my daughter to think of too."

"Daughters," Rylan corrected quietly and watched as the other man grew very, very still.

"What is that?" Nine-year-old Hannah asked Jessie as she stared down into the box they'd just opened.

"It's parts for a clock. Kaleb Heydorn wanted me to order them."

"What will he do with them?"

"His clock must be broken, and he'll use these to fix it. I think it must be hard to run a train station without the correct time."

Hannah frowned down at the parts again, not remembering when she'd seen hands and gears in the catalog, but before she could ask about that, Clancy, her seven-year-old sister, arrived. She also wanted to know about the contents of the small box on the counter. Jessie explained again before sending Hannah to the train station to let Kaleb know his special order had arrived in the larger box he'd just delivered to her.

"Mama," Clancy said. She had climbed onto the counter to get closer to her mother. "My tooth hurts."

"Which one?" Jessie leaned close when Clancy opened her mouth and pointed.

"Right here" sounded more like "rihh herr," but Jessie still got the point. She peered at the small tooth in the front of Clancy's mouth and then wiggled it with her finger.

"It's loose," the mother said at last. "It's probably coming out soon."

"Will it bleed like last time?" Clancy asked, her eyes growing a bit.

"Probably."

"That's good!" she declared fervently, making her mother laugh.

The store was quiet just then—even when Hannah came back with a message from the stationmaster—which suited Jessie just fine. She had an order to sort and accounts to work on. In her opinion, it couldn't stay quiet long enough.

"Come over to the house, Seth," Rylan eventually invited. "You're welcome to stay with me and my family."

"Did you get married, Rylan?"

"Yes, and we have a son."

"Congratulations."

"Thank you."

Rylan heard the sincerity in his voice, but also the quiet. Rylan sympathized. He had sinned many times in his life, and he knew Christ died for each one and that he was forgiven. He believed no less for Seth, but that didn't change the far-reaching consequences of his choices. Rylan believed that God could work a miracle in Jessie's life, but that didn't mean He would. He would go and see Jessie tonight just as he'd told Seth, but his words might not be received all that well. Rylan hoped Jessie would at least agree to see her husband, but even as they entered the house and Rylan introduced Seth to Bri and Danny, he knew the man might be on the train tomorrow and headed back to Texas.

Seth headed out for a walk while Rylan went to the mercantile. Rylan timed his visit just when Jessie would be closing, even knowing she and the girls might be hungry and tired. He slipped in the front door to find Jessie finishing up with a customer, and even before he could greet her, Clancy had launched herself at him.

"Pastor Rylan! I have a loose tooth."

"Show me," Rylan said, having hugged her in return and then hunkered down to her level.

Clancy distorted her mouth in a way that made Rylan laugh, but he was still able to see the tooth.

"It might bleed!" she added when he'd had a proper look.

"They sometimes do."

"You must be hearing about the tooth," Jessie said, having come up behind them.

"I showed Pastor Rylan."

Jessie smiled at her daughter and then turned to Rylan.

"You just caught us in time, Rylan. What can I get you?"

"As a matter of fact," he spoke quietly, "I need to speak with you."

Jessie's eyes met his for a moment before turning back to Clancy.

"Where is Hannah?"

"Upstairs."

"All right. You head up too and set the table. I'll be up when I'm done down here. And Clancy," her mother added when the little girl started to turn away, "don't come looking for me. Tell Hannah that you're both to stay put until I get there."

"Can we eat?" she asked.

"You may split one slice of bread, but I have to heat the gravy and biscuits. Go on now."

Rylan watched the little girl obey and then turned to find Jessie putting up the closed sign and locking the door. Once that was done, she wasted no time in coming back to face Rylan.

"Seth is in town," Rylan did not delay in saying. "He came in on the morning train."

Jessie stared at him. She knew he was serious. Rylan would never tease about this. But a part of her mind wanted him to smile and laugh and say he was joking.

"He came to you?" she finally asked.

"Yes. He didn't want to just show up here during store hours, but he would like to see you."

Jessie slowly shook her head. It took a moment for her to speak, and when she did she said nothing Rylan expected.

"You won't believe the irony, Rylan. If you had come and told me this a week ago, I might have told you to send him packing, but I can't do that."

"What happened a week ago?"

"My eyes were opened to something that's been going on for years." Jessie looked at the pastor, desperate for him to understand. "I realized for the first time how differently the girls respond to men. When women come in to shop, unless it's someone they're very close to, they don't say much at all, but with men..." Jessie stopped trying to find the words.

"Last week," she began again slowly, "Clancy went to the Vicks' to play and have dinner. From the moment she got home, it was Mr. Vick did this, and Mr. Vick said that. She talked nonstop until she went to bed. And even today," Jessie's eyes closed as she remembered, "I sent Hannah with a message for Kaleb at the train station. She left without a word. Had I asked her to go to Jeanette's or Patience's, she would have complained, but both girls are drawn to men, and I know it's because they don't have a father."

"Do they ever ask about him?"

"Never!" the word seemed to burst from the store owner. "I don't know why. They're both so curious, especially Clancy, but they don't say a word."

Rylan frowned in thought. He hadn't expected that, but before he could comment, Jessie went on.

"Did he say what he wanted?"

"Yes, he did. He wants to move back and start again. Even if you don't want him for a husband, he wants to be a father and help you any way he can."

"Why now?"

"He's got good answers to a lot of questions, Jessie, and I think he should be the one to tell you."

"Did he say where he'd been?"

"Yes. He told me everything."

"And do you think he's telling the truth?"

Rylan actually smiled. "As a matter of fact, I do. I don't know him anywhere near as well as you do, but I could tell he knows what he did was wrong. He wants to make it right. I can't tell you how shook up he was to learn about Clancy. It really got to him. I hope you'll at least talk to him."

Jessie stared at nothing for a moment, but when she spoke her voice was thoughtful.

"I feel like I need some time. If he's going to be around—*really around* and not just passing through—he can see the girls, but not right now. I need some time."

"He'll be pleased to hear that you're willing to give him a chance. How much time do you want, Jessie?"

"A week." Jessie had said the first thing that came to mind but then doubted herself. "Do you think I'm being unfair?"

"No. If you need that time, I'm sure he'll honor it. Why don't I check back with you in a week?"

"Yes," Jessie said with a thoughtful nod. "Do that, will you, Rylan? And thanks."

"You're welcome, Jessie. You know that Sabrina and I will do all we can for you."

The two parted company a short time later, Rylan to report back to Seth and Jessie to go upstairs to the girls. The thoughts of each person were many and varied, and at least one of them wished she could see into the future.

"Oh, my," Bri said quietly when Rylan told her Seth's story in their bedroom that night.

"Amazing, isn't it?"

"And you say you knew Seth before he left?" she asked.

"Just briefly. If my memory serves, he and Jessie did a good deal of quarreling. I would stop at the store and find them both looking frustrated, but I remember that he cared about her and Hannah. Along with the store. He cared about the business and seemed to work hard."

"How long after you came before he left?"

"I don't know. Not long."

Husband and wife sat quietly for a while before Rylan reached for Bri's hand. Bri knew what this meant. She closed her eyes and listened to her husband as he prayed, praying along with him for Seth, Jessie, and the girls, who all needed God's mighty saving hand in very different ways.

For the following week Seth stayed completely clear of people and the main streets of town. He was older but still recognizable, and the last thing he wanted to do was start rumors about being seen in town, rumors that might get back to his daughters and upset or embarrass them.

Even on Sunday he slipped in late for the service and listened from the foyer area, staying completely out of sight. He had discussed this decision with Rylan, and the pastor had agreed with his efforts to remain out of sight until he and Jessie talked.

In that time Seth learned the creek line very well. He walked and sat for hours outside, staying out of the house if Rylan wasn't home, praying and gathering his thoughts, the most prominent of which was the fact that he had two daughters. Seth was in a near state of shock over this. During the years away when he would allow himself to think about Jessie, he would picture her raising Hannah alone. Not once did another child enter his mind. He had left Jessie to raise two daughters alone. At times he wondered how he had the nerve to ever show his face in town again. But come evening, when he would sit with Rylan and Bri, he felt better. The three would talk for hours about Scripture, the things Seth doubted, and how to deal with the fears that kept rearing their ugly heads.

Were it not for those times, Seth didn't think he would have survived. He'd been in situations where it seemed that time had come to a halt. He would not go so far as to say that this was also such a time, but it was a long week for him, one that he prayed God would use in his life.

Not once did he waver from his goal when he prayed, knowing that God's will was best. He continually asked God to restore him to his family or at least allow him to be a father once again. He knew there were folks all over the world who had prayed for something for years. If Seth was tempted to grow weary of asking God for his family, he reminded himself that a week was a very short time.

Jessie could not believe she'd told Rylan she needed a week. Not 24 hours into that time, she found herself so curious about her husband that she would have gone back to Rylan and recanted had she not had a store to run.

As the days went by, she watched the girls to see if she had been truly right about their interest in men. What she saw was unmistakable. They seemed captivated by men. They paid more attention to what they did, how they stood and spoke, and whether or not they were noticed by them. For Jessie it was a chilling revelation, knowing how innocent and vulnerable they were.

When she wasn't thinking about the girls, Jessie thought about Seth in a way she hadn't for years. The feelings were so varied that she could barely think straight. Part of her believed she would never let him get close to her, and part of her recalled sweeter times.

She could tell from Rylan's words that he believed Seth had changed. Well, she wasn't the same either. There had been plenty of time to think about what had gone wrong in her marriage, and even though she would never believe that leaving was the right thing to do, a part of her understood.

Another very small part of her had been glad. She had grown up with quarreling parents and did not want that for Hannah. She thought time apart might do them some good. Never did it occur to her that he would stay away. It certainly never entered her mind that she would have their second child in his absence. She still remembered looking down into Clancy's newborn face and realizing that she was going to be raising her alone. She had been forced at that point to put Seth from her mind and carry on.

Jessie continued to mull all of this over during the week she had asked for, thinking at times she was going to take leave of her senses. Had not Bri made a visit one evening, she might have done just that.

"How are you?" Bri asked as soon the girls went to bed. She had been there since the store closed, just waiting for this moment.

"Most of the time I'm fine, and at other times I think he can't possibly be back."

"He's been careful about that," Bri said.

"How exactly?"

"He hasn't wanted to be seen and cause problems for you and the girls if you don't want him in town."

Jessie had all she could do to keep her mouth shut. She been hoping for a glimpse of him, and here he was keeping out of sight.

Bri correctly read her thoughts and asked, "Did you think he would be around when you said to wait a week?"

"I said I didn't want to talk to him for a week, but I thought we might at least spot each other."

Bri nodded with understanding and then asked, "What were you hoping to see?"

"I don't know. Just how he looks, how he seems."

"Well, I certainly don't have a comparison, but he's a good-looking man, and he's been very kind."

"You've met him?" Jessie asked.

Bri blinked. "He's living with us, Jessie. Rylan didn't tell you?"

"No, I guess it didn't come up. I should have figured as much but didn't."

For a moment it was silent in Jessie's living room. Bri watched her friend, well able to imagine what her heart was going through.

"I'm praying for you," Bri decided to tell her just then.

Jessie gave a small smile and didn't comment. This was the one area where she and Bri ran out of things to say to each other. Or rather she ran out of things to say.

"I need to go while it's still light out," Bri said, and both women stood. They hugged, and Jessie thanked her friend for coming. At the storeroom door she watched Bri until she was out of sight, knowing she would be fine, and then returned to the apartment. She felt a need to be near her girls and slipped into the bedroom to sit for a while. She was still sitting there in the dark when she felt tired enough to turn in and sleep. Readying for bed, she willed herself not to dream all night.

Just as Rylan said he would, he returned a week later. It was closing time just like before, and once again he waited for Jessie to send the girls upstairs.

"How are you doing?" Rylan asked as soon as they were alone.

"Fine, I think. I've had lots of questions go through my mind."

"Seth has told me that he wants you to know that he'll answer any of your questions, but he said to warn you that it's not a pretty story."

This had not occurred to Jessie. She thought for a moment before asking, "He's not wanted by the law or anything like that, is he? I wouldn't want the girls subjected to that."

"I'll let him tell you everything."

Jessie nodded but then panicked and grabbed Rylan's arm.

"Rylan, you love my girls—I know you do! Am I doing the right thing? Do you think Seth will hurt them like he hurt me? Will he win their hearts and then leave?"

Rylan looked into her desperate eyes and spoke from his heart. "I don't think so, Jessie. We've spent most of the week together, and he's not the same man who left here. I certainly can't make you any promises, but I don't think Seth Redding is that selfish man anymore. I could tell you why I feel that way, but I think that's for him to do.

"And Jessie," Rylan added to reassure her, "I'll talk to him. I'll make sure he understands that this has to be forever or not at all."

Jessie nodded, relief washing over her. Her friend had understood, and for the moment, that was the most important thing to her.

"I'll let you go," Rylan said next. "Is there a time you want him to come?"

Jessie thought fast, the reality of actually seeing him still hitting her.

"He should come tomorrow. The girls will be at the Rathmans' all day. He and I could talk then."

"I'll tell him."

Jessie nodded, but for a moment they both stood there. Not until Hannah's voice floated down the stairs with a question for her mother did either move.

"Here, Rylan," Jessie said, heading to the storeroom. "Go out the back here. It will be closer for you."

Rylan followed her, glancing up the stairs as he went past them and waving to the girls when he found them sitting at the top.

"Will they have heard us?" Rylan asked at the door, his voice very low.

"No. The upstairs is funny in this building. Sound from down here is almost nonexistent, even on the stairway."

Rylan nodded and stared at her. "Will you be all right?"

"I think so. Thank you, Ry, for everything."

Rylan nodded and said, "I want the best for the three of you. Seth too."

Jessie nodded and thanked Rylan again, her mind on so many different things, even knowing that most of them would have to wait. She had questions, dozens of them, but now was not the time. Rylan went on his way, and Jessie headed upstairs to her girls, glad she had slept dreamlessly the night before. She was sure to get little sleep tonight.

Chapter Seven

SETH HAD RUN OUT of things to see along the creek bank. He didn't want to go back to Rylan and Bri's until Rylan arrived home, but waiting on this last day was turning out to be more than a little painful. Finding a grassy place to sit at the back of the church, he waited for Rylan to come, questions filling his mind. What if Jessie wouldn't even see him? What if he wasn't afforded even a glimpse of the girls?

For a moment, Seth's mind fell back, back to the day he truly saw himself for the first time, the lostness and sinfulness of his heart. He'd been hearing about the cross and the saving blood of Christ, but until that day he hadn't understood how much he needed that blood and the salvation it offered.

"Are you all right?"

Seth started. Rylan was just 15 feet in front of him, but he hadn't seen or heard him approach.

"I think so," Seth spoke truthfully and pushed to his feet. "How is Jessie?"

"She's all right. Come on inside, and I'll tell you what she said," Rylan invited. Before the men could even start toward the house, Franklin Vick, the oldest of the Vick children, ran up.

"Pastor Rylan," he said, panting hard. "My dad needs you. He thinks Jeb Dorn broke his leg."

"Is Jeb at home?"

"Yes, he's in his shop."

"Thanks, Franklin. Tell your dad I'll be right along."

Rylan went inside long enough to tell Bri where he was needed, and then he and Seth started that way. It was not what either man had expected the next few hours to look like, but questions concerning Seth and Jessie would have to wait.

The ankle bone was set. It was not a serious break, but it was certainly going to put Jeb off his feet for some weeks. Jeb was Token Creek's most successful furniture maker. He'd been working on a tall shelf that was a rush order, sanding it smooth for staining, when he'd stepped back and lost his balance. The leg had twisted in an odd way, and his ankle could not bear the weight. Jeb had shouted until an elderly neighbor heard him. The neighbor found Patience, and she had run to the Vicks' house for help. Doctor Ertz had come and gone, and Chas Vick had also gone home.

Rylan and Seth helped a pale and panting Jeb into his bedroom. Patience trailed behind and was there when Jeb addressed Jessie's husband.

"I'm surprised to see you, Seth."

"I've been in town a week but keeping pretty quiet."

"Have you seen Jessie?"

"No. She might see me soon. Rylan spoke with her for me. He hasn't had a chance to tell me what she said."

"She'll see you," Rylan said.

Seth nodded.

"It's been a long time," Jeb put in, no censure in his voice, but his eyes were naturally full of questions.

"Too long," Seth agreed.

"Are you here for a while, Seth?" Patience asked, her voice a little cautious.

"If Jessie will let me, yes."

"When will you see her?"

Seth looked at Rylan.

"She said to come by tomorrow."

Seth nodded, his heart slamming painfully in his chest. He felt afraid and off balance right now, and might have mentioned that to Rylan, but Jeb's comfort was more important.

"Is there anything else we can do for you, Jeb?" Rylan asked.

"No, but thank you, Ry."

"I'll check back tomorrow."

The Dorns thanked their pastor and friend before Patience saw them to the door. It was growing dark out, and Rylan felt as if he hadn't seen Bri all day. Nevertheless, he didn't rush the walk home, but laid things out in plain terms for Seth. Jessie was willing to let him into the lives of her girls, but only if he was there to stay.

Seth listened quietly, working to take it all in. When they arrived at the house, he only visited with his hosts for a few minutes before excusing himself and heading to the room Bri had offered him. He sat on the bed for the next two hours and prayed and thought about the day. It made perfect sense to him that Jessie would not want him involved with the girls if he was only going to disappear again. What she didn't know, and would have to find out in time, was that Seth had no intentions of leaving. His wife and girls were in Token Creek, and if only he was given the chance, he would never be separated from them again.

Jessie thought about Seth from the moment she woke up on Saturday morning, but no one looking at her would have known. She went through her morning routine with the girls, breakfast and cleanup, before heading down to the store. There were a few things she had not done the night before, and she got to them now. The girls were excited about their day with the Rathmans, and when she left them in the large apartment upstairs, they had been talking about the Rathmans' house and cat.

What Jessie hadn't banked on was Seth's early arrival. She opened the door, swinging it wide for the day, and found Seth in one of the rocking chairs out front. He stood, hat in hand, and stared at her.

"Hello, Jessie," he said quietly, his eyes watchful.

"Hello," Jessie said, her voice a bit formal.

"Am I too early?" Seth asked, fearful of making a mistake.

"No, but—"

Whatever Jessie was going to say had to wait. Hannah appeared just then, calling her mother inside. Jessie went that way and Seth followed slowly.

"Clancy says we're not staying all day."

"Where is Clancy?" Jessie asked.

Hannah turned to yell for her sister, but Jessie stopped her with a hand to her arm.

"Do not shout," her mother instructed. "Go and find her, and both of you come back."

Hannah did as she was told. Jessie was aware that Seth had come in behind her but didn't try to engage him. She figured she would get the girls out the door and then deal with this man who wanted back into their lives.

"Hello," Clancy said, having come down ahead of her sister and spotted the tall man inside the door. She approached him, completely forgetting that her mother had wanted to see her. Hannah was just behind her and followed.

"Hello," Seth said, smiling down at the two little girls. He hadn't planned to do anything without Jessie's permission, but they were so beautiful and small that his heart took over.

"Who are you?"

"Clancy," her mother said, using a voice she knew well. "Come here. You too, Hannah."

The girls obeyed without question, and Seth retreated a bit, forcing himself not to stare.

"You are going to the Rathmans' all day. You will not fight with each other or either of the Rathman girls, and you will do everything Mrs. Rathman asks of you. Do I make myself clear?"

The girls nodded.

"Go on now. Have fun."

The girls kissed and hugged her and shot out the front door without giving Seth another glance. Not until Jessie had walked out front to see them go down the street did she step back inside and face her husband.

"They're beautiful, Jessie. You've done an amazing job."

"Thank you," she said, relaxing just slightly. "I didn't want to introduce you until we'd talked."

"I understand."

"But we can't talk now," Jessie went on. "Saturday is my busiest day."

"Of course it is. I'm sorry."

His humility took her by surprise and for a moment Jessie didn't know what to say.

"Is there anything I can do?" Seth offered into the quiet.

"No," Jessie didn't even hesitate. "If I get too busy, I'll ask Jeb to help me."

"He broke his ankle."

Jessie's mouth opened a little before saying, "When was this?"

"Last night. I was with Rylan when someone came for his help."

"Is he going to be all right?"

"I think so, but he'll be laid up for a time."

Jessie was still processing the idea when a woman came in with her son. She wasted no time in telling Jessie what she wanted, and it was obvious she expected it on the spot. Seth watched Jessie in patient action, debating his next move, when someone else entered and went right to the front counter.

Not sure if he was making a huge mistake or not, Seth stepped behind the counter and offered his assistance. The man was looking only for his mail, and Seth found it for him. He didn't plan to hang around, but before he could tell Jessie he was leaving, two more folks entered. Still wondering if he was doing the right thing, Seth assisted them as well, amazed at how familiar it all was and how much he remembered. By the time he and Jessie had the store to themselves again, three hours had passed.

"How have you remembered so much?" Jessie asked when she found Seth down one aisle restacking the pots.

"I don't know," he said, coming to full height and looking down at her. "It just suddenly came back."

Jessie nodded, and Seth knew he could wait no longer to tell her something.

"More than one person recognized me, Jessie. I didn't think about it until it was too late. I don't want my being here to make trouble for you."

Jessie stared at him, weighing her options. She decided to say what she was thinking.

"There are no third chances here, Seth. If you hurt my girls, I'll never let you get near them again."

Seth nodded, not surprised by the strength of her words. Jessie was never a woman to be trifled with, and in truth he deserved far worse.

"When the girls go to sleep tonight, we'll talk."

"What time will that be?"

"Come to the back door at eight. I want to know where you've been and why you didn't come back. After that, I'll tell you what this is going to look like. If you can agree with my terms, I'll introduce you to the girls tomorrow. If not, you can leave on the next train."

Seth had time only to nod before they were interrupted. Jessie assisted a rancher who needed to order a machine part. Seth waited on a small boy who had a penny for candy, able to do so with a hopeful heart. Jessie hadn't kicked him out, and at the moment that was all he cared about.

"You stayed all day and worked at the store?" Rylan confirmed during supper, sure he'd heard wrong.

Seth shrugged. "The store got busy, and it just worked out that way."

"Did you actually remember things?" Bri asked.

"Almost everything," Seth said, still rather amazed.

"And the girls? Did you see them?"

"Not to meet them. I'm to go back tonight so we can talk."

"With Jessie or the girls?"

"Just Jessie. When she's heard my story, she'll tell me what she has in mind."

"Does it seem promising, or are you working not to get your hopes up?" Rylan asked.

"I'm glad she didn't see me to the door, but she spelled it out in plain terms that I'm on my last chance here. I don't need more than one chance, but she couldn't possibly know that."

"Will you discuss the two of you or only your relationship to Hannah and Clancy?" Bri wanted to know.

"I would be very surprised if I was allowed to get near Jessie again. She's done with me, but for some reason she's letting me into the girls' lives."

"Do you hope to have Jessie as your wife again, Seth? I mean, really your wife?" Bri suddenly asked.

"I don't know," Seth said slowly, his face thoughtful. "By leaving and staying away so long, I killed her love for me. I'm sure of that. As for my own feelings, I've become so good at not thinking about her that

I would have said my own love was dead. Then I saw her today and it wasn't quite that simple. She's my wife, and I still feel a lot of things for her."

"Maybe it's best to keep your heart in check for right now," Rylan put in, surprising both of the other adults. "I think you might find your heart and hands full just getting to know the girls. Maybe one relationship at a time is enough."

Seth thought that Rylan had a good point. He had never been a father, not a real one, and was probably in for many surprises. His mind had begun to speculate about the meeting with Jessie and whether he would ever get to know his girls, but he knew that was dangerous territory. Instead he concentrated on the moment and found himself observing the way Rylan and Bri handled Danny. Without warning it occurred to him he didn't have to travel far for a chance to learn about parenting.

Eight o'clock could not come fast enough for Seth. He didn't know where he would stand two hours from then, but at the moment he just wanted to tell Jessie everything and let her decide. Jessie let him in the back door right on time and led him up the stairs. The apartment looked much the way he remembered, but the davenport was new, and Jessie had added a rocking chair to the living room. It was still comfortable and warm.

"You can have the sofa," she offered, taking the stuffed chair to the side. Plenty of light came from the front windows, but Jessie had two lanterns burning. It would be dark soon enough.

"Will we wake the girls, talking this close?"

"No," Jessie said with a shake of her head. "They played at a friend's house all day and are out cold."

Seth looked toward the two bedrooms. The one with the closed door was their bedroom, the one he'd shared with Jessie. For a moment he was swept back to a time when he had been faithful and committed, but before he could get very far, Jessie spoke.

"Where have you been?"

"Texas," Seth said, turning immediately to look at her. "Most recently in Heywood Prison."

Jessie had not been expecting this, and for some reason it wrung her heart. Texas was no surprise, but the mention of prison was. She kept this emotion well hidden, however, and was glad when Seth kept talking.

"I never told you that I'd received a letter from my brother."

"Eliot?" Jessie asked before she remembered that Eliot was Seth's only brother.

"Yes. Just as he had in the past, he wanted me to join him in Texas. At first I wasn't even tempted, but that didn't last for very long." Seth kept his eyes on Jessie, not afraid to admit that he was wrong but knowing she wasn't going to like the next part. "Hannah wasn't crying so much by then, but you and I fought about everything. The letter came in the midst of those times. On a whim, I wrote you that note, packed my bag, and left."

"Eight years is no whim," Jessie said, her voice flat.

"No, it's not, but the farther I went and the longer I was gone, the more impossible it seemed to come back, and so I didn't."

It was quiet between them. Less than a minute passed, but it felt much longer.

"Why were you in jail?"

"Eliot and I took jobs working for a man named Jared Silk. He thought himself above the law. I'm ashamed of the things we did, but the money was blinding. He paid well and we lived well. Then Eliot met a woman and fell in love. We put roots down in the community, and I became very good at not thinking of you and Hannah at all."

Seth was still looking at Jessie so he saw her flinch but kept on.

"It was years before there was enough evidence to put Jared behind bars, but when it happened, we went down with him."

"What had you done?"

Seth's eyes finally dropped, his shame real.

"Jared was a banker. He would loan money to anyone, including the desperate, and if they couldn't pay, he would send Eliot and me. We never killed anyone, but we did hurt people. We dressed well and deluded ourselves into thinking we were businessmen, but we were thugs in nice suits."

Jessie's hand came to her mouth. She would have sworn that Seth was not capable of such actions, but there would be no reason for him to lie.

"And that's not the worst of it," Seth went on. "Jared wanted a woman picked up and talked to. She was a newspaper columnist who kept saying things about Jared in her column, and he hated it." Seth swallowed at the memory but made himself keep going. "He wanted us to make it very clear that she had to stop, and we were prepared to do that, but it was a case of mistaken identity. We brought the wrong woman in. By the time we discovered our mistake, I fancied myself in love with her, so I abducted her."

"Oh, Seth," Jessie whispered before she could stop herself.

"It's awful but all true. I never hurt her, but I kept her against her will."

"What happened?"

"She was rescued and then testified against all of us. Eliot and I served 15 months. Jared is still in."

Jessie could not speak. Her mind reeled with all he had shared, an odd mixture of horror and sympathy.

"Jessie." Seth's voice was hoarse by now, emotion riding him as the memories surfaced. "I'll make no excuses, but I'm not that man anymore. I wasn't in jail for a month before I realized what a fool I'd made of myself. I wasn't in love with that woman. I didn't even know her. I became completely ashamed of who I was.

"I was miserable and stopped eating. I didn't care about anything. But then letters started coming from Eliot's wife. Her name is Cassy. Not long after Eliot and I went to prison, she believed in Jesus Christ for salvation. She wrote to Eliot about the changes going on inside of her, and then she began to write to me. For the first time I began to have hope. About six months into my term, I trusted in Christ to save me.

Up until that time I didn't let myself think about how far I was from Token Creek, but after I believed I told myself if I ever got out alive I would come home and at least tell you how sorry I am."

Jessie had not imagined this. Not even remotely. At first she feared he was dead, and then at times she hoped he was. All sorts of images had run through her mind in the first few years, and then like Seth, she had gotten very good at not thinking of him. But this—this was beyond her wildest dreams.

"What happened to the woman?" Jessie asked.

"She was rescued by a Texas Ranger, whom she eventually married."

"She's all right?"

"Yes. After I got out, I went and saw them at their ranch. They forgave me for what I'd done, and I'm grateful for that."

"She forgave you?"

"Yes," Seth answered, not adding that Darvi and Dakota Rawlings' faith in Christ was amazingly real.

"Would you have come home if you hadn't found God?"

"I doubt it. I was drowning in self-pity over the past. I sometimes wonder if I'd even have survived prison without Christ."

"So you believe the way Rylan believes?"

"Yes."

Jessie nodded. She believed Rylan to be one of the finest men in Token Creek, but she wasn't convinced that God was the reason.

Silence had fallen again, and Seth knew he must be the one to break it.

"I wish I could have met my daughters today, but I understand why you didn't want that. I'm hoping you'll let me know them, but I'll also understand if you don't want the girls to have anything to do with me. All of this is a lot to put on you, but I didn't want you to hear it in pieces. I'm willing to answer for my past, and in the eyes of the law, I've paid for my crimes. I don't expect you to look past them, but I hope you will give me a chance."

Jessie looked at him, her mind registering random things. He was older, but he still looked the same—tall, dark, and good-looking. She was used to seeing him smile when he looked at her, and a small part of her missed that.

With a little shake of her head, Jessie stood up. Seth's heart sank, sure he was about to be sent away, but Jessie didn't speak.

"Is there anything you want to ask me, Jessie? I'll tell you whatever you want to know."

"Tell me again why you left."

"I wanted some time away. I didn't plan to stay away. We had had a big fight about something. I can't remember what. I just remember that leaving felt good. I was young and foolish and didn't think about the consequences of what I was doing."

Jessie nodded, remembering how deserted she felt but also glad to be rid of him for a while. They had fought about things, and on top of that, Hannah had not been an easy baby. Part of her wanted to send him away, but she knew it would be wrong. If she did that, she would forever look at her girls and know she'd cheated them.

"Where are you staying?" Jessie suddenly asked.

"With Rylan and Bri."

"Oh, that's right," Jessie remembered. "Are you welcome there for a while?"

"I believe so."

Jessie nodded, looking thoughtful. She needed time to think. She did want Seth and the girls to know each other, but it was all happening rather fast.

"Why don't you come by tomorrow afternoon, and I'll introduce you to the girls."

"All right," Seth agreed quietly, not sure that meant they would know who he really was. "Did you want to tell me the terms now?"

Jessie frowned and shook her head.

"We'll figure that out as we go."

Seth stood, not sure what to do next. Jessie was staring at the bedroom door, and Seth's eyes went that way.

"What will they think about me showing up like this?" Seth asked.

"I don't know."

"I'm sorry I didn't know about Clancy. I'm sorry I left you to cope on your own."

"She was certainly a surprise," Jessie said, her eyes still on the door.

"Is Clancy her real name?"

"No." Jessie had to laugh. "It's Maryann, after my mother. Somewhere along the line Hannah started calling her Clancy, and it just stuck."

"Did they have fun today?" Seth asked, recalling their excitement when they left.

Jessie nodded, smiling a little more. "The Rathmans have a cat, and they love it. They also love their house."

"Is it pretty nice?"

"It's just a normal house, but we don't have one and that makes it special."

For a moment memories assailed Seth, but he knew that now was not the time to ask Jessie about her dreams.

"I'll get out of your way now. What time should I come by tomorrow?"

"Maybe about one o'clock. The girls will have questions, and I don't want them all stirred up for bedtime."

"Should I come to the back door again?"

"That's fine."

Seth put his hat on and looked at his wife. He wondered if they would ever talk about the two of them, but he remembered Rylan's words and knew it was good for that to wait.

"Thanks, Jessie. Goodnight."

"Goodnight," Jessie said, and then realized that she had to lock the door behind him. They needed the lantern by now as the skies had grown fully dark, and they said their goodbyes again at the door. Jessie went back upstairs and sat just where she'd been, her mind numb. She was a woman used to knowing her job and getting it done. She didn't second guess or doubt herself very often, but at the moment uncertainty filled her.

She sat for the next two hours and tried to make sense of what had just occurred. It didn't look as though she would sleep at all, but then she remembered Rylan's words. He believed Seth was changed, and if the truth be told, Jessie trusted Rylan with all her heart.

Fatigue falling over her like rain, Jessie finally took herself off to bed, sinking into sleep with the relieved thought that tomorrow was Sunday.

Chapter Eight

"THANK YOU," SETH SAID to Danny when he handed him a wooden block on Sunday morning.

The toddler smiled into Seth's eyes before wandering off, and something clenched in his heart. He had missed all of this with the girls. They were both so grown up, no hint of the babies or toddlers they had been. Seth watched Danny toddle off and looked up to find Rylan and Bri's eyes on him.

"Are you going to make it?" Rylan asked.

"I wonder that myself. How do I get past the regret and move on?"

"Thankfulness. You've been given a chance to meet the girls and know them. Nothing can change the past, but you can be determined to make the most of the future."

Seth nodded, but he still looked burdened. After Rylan and Bri exchanged a glance, Bri spoke up.

"I'm not sure anything you've done compares to my past, Seth. There's no point in making it into a competition, but you can trust me when I tell you it was shameful."

"But you found Christ," Seth stated with confidence.

"Exactly. I left that old life and did just what Ry said: I determined to be different in the future. I *was* different. I was no longer that person, and I think it's the same for you."

Seth felt hope surge inside of him. To look at Bri Jarvik, one would never imagine anything but the life she was living. That she had a past that did not glorify God would never have occurred to him.

A small hand patted Seth's leg, and he looked down to see that Danny was back. Seth again took the offered block, but he also lifted the little boy onto his leg. Danny was a natural cuddler and snuggled close, as though he'd known Seth all his life. Seth laid his cheek on Danny's soft little head and prayed. *Please God, make something from this mess I'm in. I meet my own daughters today, and my mind can barely take it in. I have no idea what Jessie really thinks, but I know You can work in her heart. She might never want any part of me, but help us to make a life for the girls, one that includes You.*

"Hello," Jessie called from just inside the back door at the Dorns' house. "Are you here, Jeb?"

"Come on in," Jeb called from the bedroom, and Jessie and the girls went that way. "Well, now," he said when he saw the girls. "This is quite the visiting party."

"What did you do?" Clancy asked, her little brow furrowed with worry.

"I lost my balance and broke my ankle."

"Did it hurt?" Clancy wished to know.

"Yes. It still does."

Jeb forgot about the pain and smiled when Clancy stared at his wrapped ankle. She clearly expected to see something profound as she frowned after a few moments and looked at her mother.

"You can't usually see broken bones, Clance. Thankfully, they're on the inside of the body."

Jeb laughed at Jessie's dry tone as she got comfortable in the room's only chair.

"I figured Patience went ahead to church," Jessie said, "so I thought we would visit."

"I'm glad you did," Jeb replied, and then noticed that the girls were busy with the intricate wooden box that Patience kept on the bedside table. He glanced back at Jessie and found her eyes on him.

"We talked last night," she said quietly, having understood what he wanted to know just from the rise of his brows.

"And?"

"He'll meet the girls today."

"Do they know?" Jeb got out before Hannah turned to him with a question. Jessie was able to shake her head no, and they dropped the conversation.

The guests didn't stay long, but Jeb was glad to have seen them. The girls went out of the room first so Jeb was able to say a little more.

"Are you ready for this?"

"I don't know about me, but I think the girls need him in their lives."

"I'll be praying for you, but then you already know that."

Jessie nodded. She never thanked him for those words, but she didn't argue either.

"He helped me out all day yesterday," Jessie felt a reason to add. "As far as the store is concerned, it was like he'd never left."

"Well, that's nice to hear because I won't be in for at least a month."

"We'll see," Jessie said, and then took her leave.

Jeb wasted no time in doing what he'd promised. He was still praying for his younger cousin when Patience arrived home from church.

"I need to talk to you," Jessie had started when they arrived back at the apartment above the store. But then she found herself strangely tongue-tied. The girls looked expectantly at her, but it took some moments for her to gather her wits.

"Have you ever wondered about your father?" Jessie tried, and to her surprise, both girls gave her their complete attention.

"Do we have a father?" Hannah asked.

"Yes, you do," Jessie answered, actually glad she was able to say this. "I was married a long time ago, before you were born, Hannah."

"Where is he?"

"Well, he's been away, but he wants to come back now and meet you girls."

"He's not dead?" Clancy asked.

"No. Did you think he was?"

"Well, Rosie's father is dead, and I thought ours was, didn't I, Hannah?"

Jessie watched Hannah nod.

"You girls have talked about this?" Jessie asked.

Again Hannah nodded, and Jessie barely got out her next question.

"Why didn't you ask me?"

"We didn't want to make you sad," Hannah said.

Jessie could not believe what she was hearing. She hadn't thought about Seth in a long time and assumed her daughters were no different. She had at least known Seth, but he'd left when Hannah was only 16 months old. The girls hadn't even a memory to fall back on.

"Are you mad at us?" Clancy asked when the silence lasted a little too long.

"No," Jessie was swift to say, but nothing about her face or voice reassured them. "I just need to tell you something, and I'm making a mess of it."

"Just say it," Hannah suggested, having heard her mother say this often enough.

Jessie looked at her and said, "Your father is here. In Token Creek. He wants to meet you."

"We have a father in Token Creek?" Hannah asked, not sure she understood.

"Yes. He's been away for a long time."

"Where has he been?"

"In Texas. He left before you were born, Clancy, and didn't come back until last week."

"Why not?"

"Well," Jessie started but then faltered. What would Seth want her to say? This question had no more formed than Jessie felt a spark of anger. He hadn't had to stay away all these years. He could answer that question himself!

"I'll tell you what," Jessie went on, successfully covering her feelings. "He'll be here this afternoon to meet you, and you can ask him yourself."

"He's coming here today?" Clancy asked.

"Yes."

The girls looked at each other with such excitement that Jessie knew she'd done the right thing. She wasn't sure if she was ready for this, but she knew it was right.

"When?" Clancy asked.

"After lunch."

That the girls were excited was only too obvious. Jessie expected more questions and even some trepidation, but they both looked eager, and Clancy even asked how long it was until lunch. Jessie answered her absently but wouldn't have answered at all if she'd known she was going to be asked at least ten more times.

"This is a fine roast, Becky," Jeanette complimented her cook, and everyone occupying her dining room table agreed.

"Courter had just butchered a steer, and I told him I needed a big piece," Becky said in her indomitable way. "How is that gravy?"

Compliments came from all around for the gravy as well, and Becky finally joined the diners at the table, taking a seat next to Heather.

Jeanette had gathered the family for Sunday dinner. Brad and Meg, who were expecting their third child in December, took one side of the table with Savanna and Cathryn nearby. Trace and Cassidy were also in attendance, with Joey on his father's knee. Five-month-old Netty had been hungry during the service but fallen asleep before her mother could feed her, giving Cassidy time to enjoy the meal.

"Who was the man sitting with Bri this morning?" Cassidy asked Trace.

"That was Seth Redding, Jessie's husband," he told her and in the next few minutes explained what he knew of Jessie's marriage.

"I don't think he's been around since before Clancy was born," Brad added, "and when he was here, he certainly wasn't in church."

"Do you think Jessie knows he's here?" Jeanette asked the table at large.

"I think she must," Trace responded. "It looked to me as if he's staying with Rylan and Bri, and Ry wouldn't do anything to hurt Jessie."

Everyone knew how true this was, and after a few more moments of speculation, the conversation changed to the sermon. Rylan was teaching on the subject of humility through the summer, and nearly everyone at the table had something to share. They were all learning much about their own need to be humble, and that topic didn't vary for the next hour.

"Are you ready for this?" Rylan asked just a few minutes before Seth was ready to leave.

"I think so. I'm working to keep my expectations low."

"I think you're wise not to expect the girls to embrace a stranger, but be careful, Seth, that you don't sell God short. Your expectations of Him should be as high as they can get."

"In what way?"

"He's already brought you an amazing distance, and I don't mean from Texas. You were just saying last night that you'd finished memorizing more than half of Job 23. You would never have even considered doing such a thing two years ago. God will bless you today, Seth. He may not give your daughters back to you or ever restore your marriage, but He will bless you for going there and making this effort."

"Thanks, Rylan," Seth returned sincerely. He would not have thought of it in those terms. He was so busy working not to expect too much from Jessie and the girls that he'd missed all the blessings he had already been given.

Seth thought about this all the way to the back of the store, but he was still feeling more than a little uncertain about meeting the girls when he arrived. He knocked and didn't have long to wait, but suddenly the realization of what he was going to do made his heart feel like lead in his chest.

"Are you all right?" Jessie had to ask the minute she saw Seth. She'd never seen him so pale.

"I think so."

Jessie stared up at him, surprise filling her. He was scared. She would not have believed it possible, but Seth Redding was terrified.

"They're very excited to meet you," Jessie said, shutting the door behind him and finding her arm gripped in his hand.

"Really, Jessie? Are they really?"

"Yes," she said softly, reading the desperation in his eyes. "It's all they've talked about since I told them."

Seth suddenly realized he was touching her and dropped his hand. He pulled at his collar and tried to compose himself, his eyes focused across the storeroom for a moment as he prayed for calm. When he glanced back at Jessie, his look was unreadable, but she knew his calmness was an act. Emotions were surging through him, and he was barely able to function. Jessie led the way upstairs, thinking that all her thoughts had been for her daughters. When it came to this first meeting, she had not given Seth a moment's thought.

Seth was certain his heart was going to pound out of his chest. He followed Jessie, feeling as though he were dreaming. He'd thought about this so much, and now that it was here, he could barely take it in.

"You were in the store," Clancy said the moment Seth stepped into the room.

"Yes, I was," Seth managed with just a small clearing of his throat. The girls were standing not six feet inside the door, both looking adorable and expectant, their faces clean and their hair combed and neat.

"Girls," Jessie stepped in, finding this more emotional than she imagined. "This is your father. His name is Seth Redding."

"Seth Redding?" Hannah asked.

"That's right," Jessie answered, seeing that she was going to have to take control. "Come in, Seth, and sit down. Come, Hannah and Clancy. Come and sit down so we can all talk."

Once seated, the sisters stared at Seth and said nothing. This was the last thing either Seth or Jessie expected, but Seth finally composed himself and found his voice.

"You girls are beautiful, like your mother."

"We look like her," Clancy said, having heard this many times over the years.

"Yes, you do," Seth agreed, smiling for the first time. "I'm glad you have her blonde hair and blue eyes."

"Where do you live?" Hannah asked.

"I just moved back to Token Creek, and I don't have a place of my own yet. I'm staying with Rylan and Bri right now."

"They have a baby!" Hannah said, coming uncorked. As though Seth had never met Danny Jarvik, he heard all about him—how big he was, when he learned to walk, and the last word Hannah had heard him say.

"Why don't you live here with us?" Clancy asked when Hannah paused for breath.

Seth had not been expecting this but was still able to answer.

"I think it's good that I stay at Rylan and Bri's."

"The dads are supposed to live with the moms," Clancy said when he was done, her brow furrowed in thought.

"You're right. They usually do but not always."

"When will we see you?"

"Well, since Jeb broke his ankle, I'll be coming in to help your mom with the store."

Seth was not looking at Jessie, or he would have seen her raise her brows. She had not known this was the plan and would wait until the girls talked themselves out to mention this fact.

The girls were suddenly on their feet, running to the bedroom to find things they wanted to show Seth. Before she had planned on it, Jessie found herself alone with Seth, his eyes on her.

"They're so beautiful, Jessie, and smart and fun. You've done an amazing job."

"Thank you." Jessie smiled a little, her eyes going to the bedroom the girls had disappeared into. "They keep me young."

"You are young."

Jessie shook her head without looking at him, and Seth wondered what she meant. He knew the store was ofttimes backbreaking work and marveled anew at how capable she was and always had been.

"This is my doll," Hannah announced, placing the doll in Seth's hands. She had a porcelain head and black hair, and she wore a yellow and black plaid dress and black, high-buttoned shoes.

"She's very nice. Does she have a name?"

"Dorothy."

"She's looks like a Dorothy. You named her well."

Hannah was looking pleased about this when Clancy came running with a hatbox.

"Oh, Clancy." Hannah rolled her eyes. "You didn't have to bring *everything.*"

"Yes, I did, Hannah," Clancy started to frown and quarrel, but Jessie intervened.

"No arguing, girls."

Clancy managed one more fierce glare at her sister before putting the box next to Seth on the sofa.

"Do you have a hat?" Seth asked her, but Clancy didn't answer. She was too busy unloading her *treasures.* The first thing from the box was a comb for her hair, much too grown up and too large for her fine locks. Next came a small mirror, rather ornate and not very useful. Following these items came a deck of playing cards, a fan, a boy's hat, cufflinks, a trinket box, and a calling card case. Almost everything that came from the box was placed in Seth's hands or lap with Clancy saying, "And look at this."

The new father did look at everything, but when Clancy was distracted by the latch on the trinket box, he looked to Jessie with raised brows.

"Clancy *needed* things a few years ago," Jessie remembered fondly, "including the hatbox."

"Things she spotted in the store, I take?"

"Exactly. I eventually got her slowed down to one a week, but it was still a long summer."

Seth's smile became huge as he turned back to Clancy, and not until that moment did he realize that Hannah was watching him in silence. Seth looked at her, so much regret filling him that he couldn't find a word to say.

"How do you know our names?" Hannah suddenly asked.

"I was here when you were born, Hannah," Seth said, just managing the words.

"How about Clancy?"

"I'm sorry to say that I wasn't here when Clancy was born, but your mother told me you gave her her nickname."

Hannah nodded as a matter of course. "Her real name if Maryann, but I like Clancy."

"My teacher sometimes calls me Maryann," Clancy filled in, "if I'm talking."

"And she's *always* talking," Hannah said, her longsuffering tone evident.

Not sure if he should, Seth laughed. Hannah looked pleased by this and smiled.

"Do you want to see our room?" Clancy asked. "We sleep with Mama, but we keep our things in our room."

"Certainly," Seth agreed, having to calm his heart all over again when Clancy took his hand. He hadn't touched either of them and found that the riot of emotions going on inside of him was making it hard to breathe.

Jessie did not follow. She went to the kitchen and put some coffee on. It was a warm day, but she needed something to do with her hands, and coffee was the only thing she could think of.

She hadn't known what to expect from Seth or her daughters but realized she was surprised at how well they were doing. At the same time, her heart told her it couldn't last. Seth had left before, and no matter how much he loved the girls and got to know them, Jessie was sure it was only a matter of time before he left again. She wanted to protect them from that but had no idea how.

"You're not working on supper, are you?" Seth, who was suddenly next to her, asked quietly.

"Just coffee. Why?"

"I thought I'd take you and the girls to the hotel for supper. If you want," he remembered to add.

"Have you said something to the girls?" Jessie asked just as they came from the bedroom.

"I wouldn't do that without talking to you."

"You don't have to do this, Seth."

"I want to," he said and meant it.

"I mean," she whispered, "you can take the girls on your own."

Seth blinked. He could hear the girls and knew they were almost beside them, but still he asked, keeping his voice low, "Why would I leave you out?"

This time it was Jessie's turn to blink. Why *had* she thought that?

"Are we going to the creek?" Hannah asked, having misinterpreted her parents' conversation.

"I don't know," Jessie said to cover her other thoughts. "Did you want to?"

The agreement on the girls' parts left no doubt in her mind, and so Jessie explained to Seth.

"During the summer it's not unusual for us to go to the creek to cool off. Sometimes we take a picnic."

"We get wet," Clancy said in her matter-of-fact way.

"Sounds fun. Why don't I provide the food?" Seth suggested.

"Do you cook?" Hannah asked.

"With my wallet," Seth said, revealing the first sign of the Seth Jessie first met and married. Not able to help herself, she laughed, and the girls even without knowing why joined her.

Within 30 minutes they were off. It was early yet so there was no need for food, but eventually Seth left his family by the creek and headed to the hotel. By the time he rejoined them, he had amassed a feast that was not wasted. They had played hard in the sun and water and were ready to eat the beef, rolls, applesauce, and berry pie he had coaxed out of the hotel kitchen.

After the meal, when the girls ran to rinse their hands and faces at the creek bank, Seth was able to say what was on his mind.

"Thanks for letting me into their lives, Jessie."

"They need you," Jessie said, not looking at Seth but feeling his eyes on her. She was thankful that the girls were coming right back. She was not in the mood to explain herself.

Chapter Nine

SETH HAD TOLD RYLAN and Bri about his long and wonderful afternoon, his doubts, regrets, and encouragement that the girls seemed to accept him. Bri had taken it all in, pleased that he and Jessie were off to a good start, but she had questions about her friend, questions that could not wait another day. For that reason, Bri stood at the store's back door that very evening, hoping with the windows open to the back of the building that Jessie would hear her knock.

"Well, Bri," Jessie said with obvious surprise but still pleasure, "how are you?"

"That's what I'm here to ask you."

The friends' eyes met for a moment before Jessie said, "Come on up."

"Are the girls asleep?" Bri asked as she trailed Jessie up the stairs.

"They're just down. We'll have to keep our voices low for a while, or they'll be out of bed."

The women got comfortable on the sofa, turning a little to see each other as the light began to fade from the windows.

"How do you feel it went this afternoon?" Bri wasted no time asking the moment the women were settled.

"I think it went well," Jessie started and then stopped. She stared at

Bri, who waited patiently, and then went on. "My mind hasn't taken in that he's really here. Last Friday morning I woke up, and my life was just normal. By Friday at bedtime, things had been turned upside down. Seth came yesterday and ended up working in the store, and I still can't feel the floor beneath me. I think the world has tipped, and I seem to be the only one to notice."

"Maybe the girls have noticed a little too?"

Jessie shook her head in wonder. "They've taken to him so fast, Bri. Almost without question, they've accepted that he's their father. They had talked about him!" Jessie suddenly blurted. "I had no idea that they'd discussed their father, but they told me this morning that they had. They assumed he was dead and never asked me about it so I wouldn't be sad."

Bri was as surprised as Jessie had been. Hannah and Clancy never seemed to hold back about anything. That they'd discussed something as significant as a presumed-dead father and not spoken of it was rather amazing. And Jessie! The calm, steady Jessie Wheeler was as rattled as Bri had ever seen her.

"What now, Jessie?" Bri, thinking fast, asked. "How will you handle all of this?"

"I guess we'll just go on. The girls want him around, and he's not difficult to be with." Jessie stopped and shook her head. "He looks so much the same—just a little older—but he's not the same man, Bri. I keep watching for the real Seth to show up, but he hasn't yet."

"Do you want the old Seth back?" Bri asked carefully, not wanting to speak of Seth's salvation just yet. "I mean, he left you without a word for eight years. You don't want *that* man back, do you?"

"No, but can a person change that much? It's a little hard to believe."

"A person can change, Jessie," Sabrina said with a small smile. "One of these days, when life isn't quite so busy for you, I'll tell you just how much."

Jessie's look became a mix of skepticism and appreciation. Clearly she thought Bri had never done a shameful thing in her life, but at the same time she was grateful for her words.

"Why don't you and the girls come to supper this week," Bri finally offered.

"What night?"

"Just pick one."

"How about Tuesday?"

"Tuesday it is. Seth will be there, but you haven't sounded too uncomfortable with that."

"No, it's fine. What time?"

"Come when you close the store. We'll eat when everyone gets there."

"Thanks, Bri."

"You're welcome. And don't let it slip to the girls about supper."

Jessie had to laugh. When her daughters knew they were going to see Danny, their excitement knew no bounds.

The women talked a bit longer, mostly about how busy the store was and something Bri had read in a recent newspaper article. The conversation did not turn spiritual, but Bri was used to that. Still she prayed and had hope for her friend.

Jessie had completely forgotten that Seth had said he was coming to help with the store, but he was good at his word. Much as he'd done on Saturday, he was on the porch when she opened the store.

"Hello," she said, sounding distinctly cooler than the last time he'd seen her.

"Hello."

"I don't know if there's enough work for you to stay," Jessie said without warning, and Seth nodded, watching her. She turned and went back inside, slipping behind the counter. Seth followed slowly.

Seth glanced around a moment, seeing that things were in good order, but he wasn't willing to leave quite so fast. Instead he said, "I have some memory of you saying there was always something to do."

"For me, yes, but not always for two people."

Again Seth nodded, but he was willing to bide his time.

"I seem to remember that you had a hard time getting to the books," he tried next. "Why don't I watch the store while you do that?"

Jessie gave him a direct look and asked, "Don't you have anything better to do?"

"No."

The one word completely disarmed her. She hadn't expected this. And in truth, she didn't know why she was fighting him. He'd certainly proved on Saturday that he still knew his way around the store.

"I guess I could work on the books," she said after a few minutes, her voice back to normal.

"Okay," Seth agreed, forcing himself not to sound pleased. "If something comes up that I can't handle, I'll come find you."

Jessie stared at him a moment, and Seth stared right back. He wanted to ask why she didn't want him around right now but knew they could be interrupted at any moment. As it was, she didn't give him time. Moving around the edge of the counter, she disappeared into the storeroom without another word.

"What are you doing?" Hannah wanted to know when she found her father behind the counter not ten minutes after he arrived. He was restacking a few piles of mail that had yet to be claimed.

"Good morning, Hannah," Seth said, not sure if her question was directed at the moment or his being there at all.

"Does Mama know you're back there?" Hannah persisted.

"She does. She's working on the books this morning."

"Do you know how to work with the mail?" Hannah asked, coming close enough to climb onto the counter and stare up at him.

"I do. I used to work here a lot."

"I didn't know that," Hannah said, sounding a bit suspicious and a lot like her mother.

"Do you help out around the store?" Seth asked, hoping to change the direction of the conversation.

"All the time."

"That's great. Does Clancy help too?"

"She dusts."

"I'm glad to hear you girls are so helpful."

"When did you work here?" Hannah asked, now sounding like the child she was.

"A long time ago, when your mother and I first met."

"Mama's parents owned the store," Hannah said.

"I remember her telling me about them."

"You didn't know Grandma and Grandpa Wheeler?"

"I'm sorry to say I didn't. I think your Grandpa Wheeler had been dead only about a year when I met your mom."

"Where did you meet her?"

"Right here at the store. She gave me a job."

Seth was certain that Hannah's questions would have continued for the next hour, but a woman came in and Seth was given the excuse to leave his daughter so he could wait on her. He wasn't afraid to tell Hannah the details she wanted to know, but he thought such questions should be asked in front of her mother. Seth knew that Jessie was suspicious of him as it was. He had no intentions of doing anything behind her back or giving her any worry on that account.

In fact, just as soon as he had a chance, he darted into the store-room to talk to her.

"Some of the questions I expected the girls to ask me yesterday came pouring out of Hannah this morning. She wanted to know how we met and if I'd known your parents."

"Is that a problem?" Jessie asked, not sure what she was missing.

"I don't mind telling her any of it, but I wanted you to know that we'd talked some more."

Jessie nodded with understanding, and in her heart she really did appreciate his coming to her, but he need not have worried.

"Actually, as I was falling asleep last night I wished I had warned you. That's how they are sometimes. Give them a few days to think on something, and you won't hear the end of it for a while."

"Do you want me to wait until we're together to tell them things?"

Before he could say anything else, Clancy found them.

"Hey, Seth," she started without preamble. "Hannah says you sorted mail."

"I did, yes. Did I do a good job?"

Clancy did not take the red herring. She questioned Seth until she was sure he was right for the job and then went on her way. Not until Clancy moved off did Seth notice Jessie's face.

"You're enjoying this," he accused.

Jessie tried to look innocent, but Seth could see right through it. He might have had something more to say to her on the topic, but someone was calling from out front.

Jessie didn't allow a full-blown, satisfied smile to stretch her mouth until after he'd left the storeroom.

Seth didn't know when he'd been so tired. There had been no break all morning. If it wasn't a customer, it was one of his daughters asking questions or telling him how to do something. At one point Seth was ready to snap and ask the girls to leave him alone, but then he caught himself. He was going to have to tell Jessie that he needed a dinner break soon, but for the moment he chose to calm down and think about why he'd come back.

Not long after he'd trusted in Christ, Cassy had written to him about a verse in the first chapter of Luke. He'd not committed it to memory, but he recalled that it said something about turning the hearts of fathers to their children. He didn't know why, but it seemed that men often deserted their children. His father had certainly not stayed around to know him.

Now on the job so many months later, Seth remembered Cassy's letter and the verse and began to enjoy the interrogation of his daughters.

That they might not always be respectful was becoming very clear to him, but it was not the first issue that had to be covered. Their love and trust for him was.

"Are you going to dust up there?" Clancy asked. She'd come upon Seth when he was next to a section of very tall shelves. "It's high for Mama."

"I'll tell you what," Seth suggested. "Why don't you run get the feather duster, and I'll lift you up so you can dust it."

Clancy's eyes got huge before she ran to find the duster. Seth was not surprised when she was back in little time, looking up at him expectantly.

"Ready?" Seth asked, looking down into her face with a sensation in his heart he'd not felt before.

"Ready!"

"All right," Seth said, swinging her up onto his arm. "I'm going to set you on my shoulder. If your arm can't reach, I'll lift you higher."

Clancy nodded, breathless with more than just running for the duster.

No small amount of dust came down into their faces, but they were a good team. With Clancy feeling as light as thistledown, Seth simply walked slowly in front of the shelf while she sat comfortably on his shoulder, her arm doing all the work.

"How's it look?" Seth asked at one point, only to hear Hannah come up behind him.

"When you're done there, you should probably sweep the front walk. Mama does that every day."

"What now?"

Hannah and Seth—Clancy still perched on his shoulder—turned to find that Jessie had come into the aisle. She was not looking at all pleased, and Seth quickly but carefully lowered Clancy to the floor.

"Have they been giving you orders?" Jessie asked of the man before her.

Seth looked uncomfortable and was working on a delicate way of saying yes when Jessie speared her daughters with her eyes.

"Have you been giving Seth orders?"

Both girls nodded, guilt written all over them.

"That will end right now," Jessie said in a voice only a fool would argue with. "You are not Seth's boss. If I want something done, I will ask Seth. You are not to boss him around ever again. Do I make myself clear?"

Both small blonde heads bobbed.

"Now apologize to him and remember what I said."

"I'm sorry" came from Clancy and was immediately echoed by Hannah.

"Thank you, girls," Seth barely got out before Jessie spoke again.

"Go upstairs and start working on dinner. Make butter and jam sandwiches. The bread is cut and ready."

Jessie watched them obey and then turned back to Seth.

"Has that been going on all morning?"

"It was my idea to put Clancy on my shoulder," Seth said, not trying to protect the girls if they needed correcting but wanting Jessie to have a full picture.

Jessie stared at him, something occurring to her for the first time. He was afraid to make a wrong move. She had told him there would be no third chance, and he was obviously willing to put up with anything in order to be a part of their lives. This should have given her great satisfaction, but it didn't. She should have wanted to make his life miserable, but it wasn't in her.

"I'm going to go check on the girls," Jessie said. "I'll bring you some lunch."

"You don't have to feed me, Jessie. I can stop over at the hotel."

"I don't mind," Jessie said, and for a moment they looked at each other. "I just realized," Jessie continued after a few seconds, "I forgot to pay you on Saturday night."

Seth looked dreadfully uncomfortable with this, but he knew he was going to have to pay rent as soon as he found a place of his own to live. He had savings he'd just put into the bank in town, but he also had plans for that savings, and those did not include using it for monthly living expenses.

"I'll just cover last Saturday at the end of this week if that's all right," Jessie said. Seth nodded. More regret knifed through him, and he was not able to look at her for the moment. A customer came in, and Seth went to the front counter, using him as an excuse to walk away from his wife.

"How are you doing, Jeb?" Rylan asked. Jeb was sitting in his living room near an open window, his ankle propped up on a pillow.

"Not bad. It only throbs now, and Doc Ertz says that will lessen in a short time."

"It looks like he got everything back into place," Rylan said, coming close to look at but not touch the wrapping.

"I think so. It would be nice to have it work normally when all is said and done. Tell me, Rylan," Jeb suddenly said, "what's going on with Jessie and Seth?"

"Were you surprised to see him?" Rylan asked, smiling a little.

"I could hardly believe it. Do you know how long it's been?"

"He told me eight years."

"How did it go with him and Jessie?"

"Good. She let him meet the girls, and he's working there right now."

"Patience was going to stop in to check on Jessie while she ran errands, but she's not back yet."

"They're coming to supper with us tomorrow night."

Jeb looked thoughtful for a few seconds. He was concerned about his cousin, but he also wanted to talk to Seth. Much as he trusted Rylan, Rylan didn't know Seth like he did.

"I want Seth to come to supper tonight. Do you know if he has plans?"

"I don't know, but I can swing over there and mention it to him."

"I would appreciate it, Rylan. I feel I need to talk to him. I didn't talk to him as much as I should have while he was still living here, and I've regretted that for a long time."

"I'll tell him."

"You might run into Patience, but let me tell her what I have in mind."

"Certainly."

Jeb nodded in satisfaction, reached for his Bible, and said, "I'm ready for my private sermon now."

Rylan laughed but also opened his Bible, ready to tell Jeb what he'd missed on Sunday.

It was Seth's turn in the storeroom, this time to eat lunch. Jessie had brought him a plate some ten minutes past, and he'd taken her place at the worktable in the back room of the store. The account books were still open and waiting for her, but Seth didn't look at them. He was curious as to how she was doing financially and knew her system from when they'd first been married, but he would never have presumed a welcome to that information.

Seth was still deep in thought when he realized he was being watched. Hannah had come to the edge of a tall shelf and stood staring at him. He'd not seen the girls since their mother had sent them upstairs and knew why she was hesitating. Seth had no such qualms.

"Hi, Hannah," he greeted her. "Did you eat dinner?"

That little girl nodded and came forward.

"Was it good?"

Again the nod, but Hannah was still silent.

Seth scrambled for something to say to this suddenly quiet child. It saddened him to think that if she couldn't order him around, she had nothing to say. He thought he would welcome some questions right now and even tried to come up with one for her. His mental gymnastics made him want to laugh and just a hint of a smile came to his lips. Seeing it, Hannah had a small smile of her own. Seth's smile grew a little, as did Hannah's, and before long the two were grinning at each other.

"Come here," Seth invited and Hannah moved close. Seth fixed the turned up collar on her pink gingham dress and smoothed her hair. The action seemed to tell Hannah that all was forgiven, and she asked a question.

"Does Bri feed you at their house?"

"She does."

"What do you eat?"

"Whatever she serves me," Seth said, not admitting that he wasn't at his best in the kitchen and was thankful when anyone offered him food.

"I like chicken," Hannah volunteered.

"So do I. With dumplings."

"What are dumplings?"

"Have you not had dumplings? Your mother makes great dumplings."

Hannah looked surprised and would have moved away, but Seth caught her arm.

"I don't want you to ask your mother why she never makes dumplings. If you haven't had them, then she has a good reason."

"Time."

Both Hannah and Seth looked up to see that Jessie had joined them. Seth sat back in his chair and looked at her.

"Not even on Sundays?" he asked, remembering that's when she would serve them to him.

"I'm tired on Sundays."

"I'll bet you are," he agreed softly, seeing for the first time just how much had changed. The two of them working the store even after Hannah came along was nothing to watching both girls and still keeping track of customers at the same time. For a moment Seth wondered if she looked forward to school starting, but then realized he knew the answer. Jessie would not want her daughters away from her just so things could be easier. It wasn't her way.

"Will you make dumplings sometime, Mama?" Hannah asked, her voice not at all demanding.

"Sometime, yes, but you're not to pester me about it."

Hannah nodded and swiftly left the room. Jessie knew she would tell Clancy about the mystery food and Clancy would demand all the details, but at the moment she let her go.

"I won't tell the girls until I close the store," Jessie said to her husband, "but we're invited to Ry and Bri's tomorrow night for supper."

"Good," Seth said, nodding with satisfaction.

Jessie was opening her mouth to ask why that was good when Hannah came back to the storeroom to tell her that Patience Dorn was looking for her.

Seth went back to work as soon as Jessie left the storeroom. He thought it might be nice to sit for a while longer and relax, but something in Jessie's face had disturbed him. He didn't know how to read her anymore. Some things were the same and some looks were unmistakable, but as angry as she had been with him in the past, there had never been distrust, and he was sure that's what he was seeing now.

A part of him knew he was holding back. His faith in Christ was real, but he was still Seth Redding, a man who loved to tease and have fun with others. In just the few days he'd been back, he'd been tempted to tease Jessie a dozen times but didn't dare. He wanted to do the same with his daughters but didn't know how that would be taken.

Pete Stillwell, the local livery owner, came in looking for shoe polish just then, and Seth had to go out front and put his mind back on the job, but he did so with a prayer that he could someday be himself again. Not the selfish man he had been, but the peaceful man he now was—the one who loved his family but had no idea how to show it.

Chapter Ten

"HOW ARE YOU?" PATIENCE wasted no time in asking Jessie. The women had walked only to the back of the store, but it was private enough. "Jeb wanted me to come yesterday and then decided you might need a little more time."

"It's all right. Seth is good with the girls."

"And with you?"

Jessie put it plainly, "He doesn't have to be good with me."

"Jeb wants to know if he's treating you well."

"Well, tell him I'm fine. We're getting along fine. How is Jeb doing, by the way?"

"It's hard on his back to lie around, but other than that he's doing well."

"Good. The girls and I will come by on Sunday to see you."

"We'll plan on that. Do you want to come for dinner?"

"That sounds good. What shall I bring?"

"Just the girls. I'll take care of everything else."

"What time?"

"Come at noon. If we're running late, just use the back door. Now, Jessie, before I forget, do you have thread in this color?" Patience asked, bringing a piece from the reticule that hung from her wrist.

"I don't know," Jessie said, fingering the small piece of cinnamon-colored thread. "You might have to check with Jeanette."

"Jeanette isn't open on Mondays."

"Well, then, let's go look."

The women found Seth at the front counter, but he was working with a pretty, dark-haired woman who wanted to order something from the catalog. Clancy sat on the counter looking on, and Hannah lingered near the door. The moment the woman had placed her order and walked from the store, Clancy started in.

"Tell me now," she ordered her father.

"Well," Seth said, trying to think. "Dumplings are like wet biscuits."

The look of distaste on Clancy's face caused her mother and Patience to laugh. Not until that point did Seth realize he was being listened to and watched. He turned and leaned one hip on the counter, his arms crossing over his chest and a challenging look covering his face.

"Well, ladies," he said with mild sarcasm, "if you think you can describe dumplings better, be my guest."

Jessie opened her mouth and then shut it. Patience, however, was ready to give it a try.

"The dough for dumplings is a little like biscuit dough, Clancy, but it doesn't bake in a pan. You drop spoonfuls of dough onto the top of the gravy and they cook there. They end up a little wet on the bottom, but the inside is light and fluffy."

"Why are they wet?" Clancy asked, not able to let this go.

Her mother tried to explain, but it didn't go very well. Jessie looked over at one point and found Seth watching her, a more-than-satisfied look on his face that she hadn't had a ready explanation.

"You had to mention dumplings," Jessie muttered, shooting him a look.

Seth did not look the least bit repentant. He shrugged a little and said, "We were talking about foods we liked."

Jessie rolled her eyes at him and realized that if she was going to

settle Clancy on the topic, she was going to have to make dumplings
sometime soon.

"I didn't know," Seth told Jeb that evening near the end of the meal,
"how much I would want to talk to Pastor English. I had so many
questions when I was still in prison. When I lived in his house, I didn't
know there would come a time when I would give anything to have
answers from him."

"Did you actually remember some of the things he said?" Patience
asked.

"Not specifics, but I remembered that he was so open and honest
about praying for me. I might have thanked him, but never once did
I think to ask him why he believed that way." Seth stopped and stared
at the couple and then asked, "Is he dead now?"

"Yes," Patience volunteered. "He was quite ill when he left here and
went back to Denver. I'm not sure he lived another year."

"But he's in heaven," Seth said.

"Yes, he is."

"He's the first person I've ever known who I thought went to heaven.
For a long time I didn't know if heaven was real or not, but now I do,
and I realize I have a friend there in Pastor English. It changes the way
I think about heaven and eternity."

"That's a special gift," Jeb agreed. "For me, it's my father. I want to
talk to Jesus more than anything, but knowing that my father is there,
the man who told me about my need for salvation, means so much to
me."

Seth looked at the couple for a moment and said, "I can't tell you
how much I want to be able to talk to Jessie the way I talk to you and
Rylan and Bri, but I can't do it. She doesn't understand."

"Her father didn't either," Jeb said. "Maryann was a little more
receptive, but never Hiram."

"And Jessie is so much like him," Patience added. She had been a little uncomfortable when she learned that Seth was coming, but was very glad she had listened to her husband and given him a chance.

"She certainly is," Jeb agreed. "How are you doing with the girls?"

"I can tell they like me but don't know quite what to do with me. And Jessie is still very tentative, not that I blame her."

"I'm not condoning what you did, Seth," Jeb offered, "but I hope you know that after Clancy was born it wouldn't have mattered when you returned. I knew better than to even ask if she'd heard from you. After Clancy's birth she was calling herself Jessie Wheeler again. She didn't seem bitter. It was more like you'd never existed."

"I think it was the only way she could survive," Patience guessed.

"I think so too," Jeb agreed. "The Wheelers have always been very good at surviving."

Seth hadn't thought about any of this, but it was true. She was Jessie Wheeler again in nearly every way. Were it not for the girls, it would be hard to find any evidence that he'd even been in Token Creek.

"Have we given you too much to think about, Seth?" Jeb asked, having watched the younger man's face.

"It's a lot to take in, but I'm all right."

"Well, I don't want to pile more on you, Seth, but I do need to repent to you about something," Jeb stated.

Seth had all he could do not to blink in astonishment at his host.

"We didn't have you over enough and befriend you as we should have all those years ago. You might have come to me about the way you were feeling instead of just leaving, and for that I'm sorry."

"Thank you, Jeb," Seth said quietly, his heart overwhelmed.

Patience could feel tears at the back of her eyes and rose long enough to get the cake she had made. She did not make a fuss over it but simply served up large pieces and set them out.

Over dessert, the men continued to talk about the changes God had brought to both of them in the last eight years. Before Seth left for the Jarviks', he knew he would not make the same mistake again. Even if he was tempted to leave, he would come here first.

Jeanette had never seen anyone move more slowly than Sheriff Nate Kaderly. Since commenting to Heather months past about his possible interest, Jeanette had simply kept her eyes open. And she had not been disappointed. Nate was interested in Heather—Jeanette was sure of it—but doing nothing about it.

And as for Heather! She had no clue. Jeanette watched her as well, thinking that the way he lingered in her company whenever he had a chance or the kind way he spoke to her would have to get her attention, but so far it hadn't worked.

"You're not opening today, are you, Jeanette?" Rylan asked, finding her outside the shop.

"No, I just came to get some papers," Jeanette answered in a distracted way, her gaze flicking down the street.

Rylan glanced behind him and then back at Jeanette. He took a moment to study her before saying, "I think you're watching someone."

"Just Nate Kaderly," Jeanette admitted.

"You haven't lost your heart, have you, Jeanette?" Rylan asked, his voice turning serious.

"Of course not!" Jeanette said, an incredulous laugh escaping her.

"That's good since Nate has already lost his."

Jeanette gripped his arm, her face hopeful. "Is it Heather?"

"Of course," Rylan said with a kind smile. "Who else?"

"I knew it!" Jeanette said too loudly, looking triumphant as she worked to keep her voice down. "If he feels that way, why hasn't he said anything?"

"Because the lady herself shows not the least bit of interest."

Jeanette sighed. "I tried to talk to her about this some months ago, and she basically told me I was imagining things."

"You're not, but I know he would not appreciate your being involved."

"No, I don't suppose he would."

She looked so saddened by this that Rylan smiled, but he still had to be getting home.

Jeanette said goodbye, not realizing until he was too far away that she had one last question. Jeanette turned for home herself, almost glad she hadn't had a chance to ask. It would be much too hard if he had said no.

"Is this going to work?" Bri asked Rylan while she worked on dinner Tuesday afternoon. "I mean, I don't really know how they're getting along."

Rylan nodded thoughtfully before saying, "I don't think it can be too bad, or Jessie wouldn't have him working there."

"Oh, that's true."

Danny, who had found his father's ear, continued to poke at it, but Rylan's eyes were on his wife.

"Are you worried?"

"A little. I mean, I know them both in such different capacities. I don't know Seth well, but even if he'd been living here longer, I have no past with him. Jessie and I have a good friendship, but it doesn't include Seth at all."

Rylan found himself thankful that he'd been able to come home early. He worked part-time at the livery for Pete Stillwell. He should have worked until closing, but Pete had shown up and said he could leave anytime. He'd stopped and talked to Jeanette, but that had taken less than ten minutes. Once home he'd cleaned up and gone to the kitchen to take Danny off Bri's hands and found his wife looking tense.

"When I asked Jessie and the girls to join us tonight, we even spoke about the fact that Seth would also be here to eat. She was fine with it, but now I'm suddenly afraid of making them both uncomfortable."

"I can understand your hesitancy, but this is still a good idea. Jessie and the girls have been coming and going since we got married, and

Seth would not expect us to change our habits on hospitality because he was staying here."

"That's true," Bri agreed with a nod, her shoulders relaxing.

"Gently, Danny," Rylan said to his son when he pulled a little too hard on the big man's lobe. "And we'll just take our cue from them," Rylan continued. "If it seems uncomfortable, we'll know what not to do in the future."

Bri's eyes met his and she nodded. Rylan winked at her and went to the living room. Danny had taken all the books off one of the shelves. Rylan was sure Bri hadn't noticed, and that suited him just fine. It gave him a chance to teach his little son to put the shelf to rights before their guests arrived.

Seth ended up walking with Jessie and the girls to the Jarvik home. He hadn't planned one way or the other, but he was done, and they were ready to go. Clancy skipped along beside him, talking all the while, but Hannah was a little quieter.

"Are you all right, Hannah?" Seth asked when they were almost there. She had been silent the entire walk.

"Yes."

Seth didn't press her further, but he felt Jessie's eyes on him. Maybe it was normal for Hannah to fall quiet, but he didn't know her well enough to gauge if all was well. Before he could think of a way to ask, they were at the house.

"How did you two meet?" Bri asked quietly after dinner. The adults were still at the kitchen table, but the girls had taken Danny into the living room to play.

"This is where I found myself out of money," Seth said.

"Where had you been?" Bri asked.

"I had been living in Kingdon, but I was on my way to Texas. I was planning to pass through Token Creek, but someone lifted my money when I fell asleep on the train, and I was broke."

"I wondered for a long time if that story was true," Jessie said, her mind going back.

"What story?" Rylan asked, not sure.

"The one about your money being stolen. I thought it was a line for sympathy."

Seth smiled a little but didn't comment. Bri had another question.

"How did you find out about it, Jessie?"

"He came in looking for a job."

"Why the mercantile?"

"I was well and truly without a cent to my name, but I was also a man, and when I saw a beautiful blonde in a purple dress sweeping the boardwalk in front of the mercantile, I went that way."

Even Jessie had to smile over this.

"Why were you headed to Texas?" Rylan asked.

"My brother lives there, and he had been asking me to come. I had just lost my home in Kingdon and saw no reason to stick around any longer."

The questions might have continued, but Danny and the girls suddenly joined them. Danny made a beeline for Seth, handing him his favorite wooden block.

"Thank you, Danny," Seth said, lifting the baby onto his lap and kissing his small brow. Clancy had come very close, and Seth, without thinking, reached and stroked down her soft, blonde curls.

No one at the table thought anything of this, save Jessie. She watched Seth's hands and his tenderness with Danny, as well as with their daughter, and felt such an ache inside she didn't know what to do. She managed to keep her feelings well hidden, but only until the evening wrapped up. Even before Seth had a chance to offer, she had quietly asked him to walk them back to the store.

Can you walk us home? Seth agreed without hesitation, but there was no comfort in the act. It was clear that Jessie was bothered about something, and it was with a good deal of dread that he walked his family to the rear door of the store.

"Go on up now, girls," Jessie directed when she'd unlocked the door. "Get ready for bed. I'll be right up."

The girls wanted to know what she was going to do, but she stopped them with a stern voice. "That's enough! Now tell Seth goodnight and go get ready for bed. And I'd better not find you sitting at the top of the stairs."

The girls obeyed, but not without a lot of eye rolling and complaining. Jessie ignored them, waiting only until they were out of earshot to speak to Seth.

"Was all of what you told me true? Did you really work for a man and hurt people?"

"Yes," Seth said quietly, wondering where this had come from. "What made you think of that?"

"It's just not who you ever were, Seth. I can't think why you would make such a thing up, but I can't imagine it."

Seth could hear the anger in her voice and understood why she would feel that way. How did he explain what a different person he had been while he was away?

"And then tonight!" Jessie went on. "You held Danny so gently, but you never even saw Clancy at that age. I can't stand the thought right now. It just makes me so angry with you!"

Seth didn't know what to say. It was all true, but it was also in the past. And he didn't know how to fix that.

"I need some time to think," Jessie said. "Don't come in tomorrow. I need to think."

"All right," Seth agreed, his heart constricting with pain.

He watched Jessie move toward the door and thought she looked tired and discouraged. Her shoulders were bent a little and she looked beaten down, not a look that was usual for her.

"Wait, Jessie." Seth stopped her. "Why don't you take the day off tomorrow. That way you'll really have time to think. I'll watch the store, even the girls if you want, and you can have the day to yourself."

Jessie's first thought was to refuse, but something stopped her. She couldn't say that Seth was not experienced enough because he was. In the two days he'd worked, he'd asked her only one question, and it was so insignificant that it hadn't really mattered.

"You can think about it," Seth offered, not sure why he didn't just wait for her to answer. "I can check with you in the morning."

"All right," Jessie agreed, slipping inside without another word.

Seth stood for a while at the door, the sky growing dark fast. When he did turn for Rylan and Bri's, he made the walk back very slowly.

It took some doing to get the girls in bed and settled down. They were wound up from their time with Danny and just wanted to keep talking about him. Jessie finally got them calmed and for a while sat in the living room with one lantern burning.

Her thoughts could not settle on any one thing as her mind went over the evening. She saw the way Rylan treated Bri. It was nothing new to her, but with Seth back in town, it was hard to watch. There had been a time when she had been that happy with Seth, but then the fights had begun. She knew that Rylan and Bri had been married for a while now, and she had never seen them quarrel or be unhappy with each other.

Jessie had a sudden desire to see the girls. Taking the lantern with her, she slipped into the bedroom and looked down at them while they slept. For a moment she wanted life as it had been before Seth returned, but then she remembered Seth with Clancy that night. She saw his hand on her hair and the way she leaned close and looked up at him, her little eyes alight with pleasure just to be near him. Hannah had been the same. Already both girls were more drawn to him than Rylan, and it had just been a few days.

You can stay, Seth Redding, Jessie's heart whispered inside of her, *but only for the girls. Only because they need you.*

Jessie's needs were not on her mind at the moment, but she was being prayed for right then. Seth had gone to his room as soon as he arrived back, lay across the bed, and begun to pray. He didn't know exactly what he'd seen in his wife's face tonight, but Seth knew she needed a Savior. He didn't pray for himself or for the girls, just for Jessie.

For almost two hours he asked God to save Jessie, to open her eyes and soften her heart to her need. When he did rise to ready himself for bed, his heart knew peace. The peace did not hold a guarantee that God would say yes to his prayer, but he knew that Jessie's salvation was out of his hands and he had done all he could by casting his heavy heart on God.

"We're going somewhere today," Jessie told the girls at breakfast.

"Where?" they asked, both rather quiet in light of this revelation.

"Somewhere fun."

"What about the store?" Hannah asked.

"Seth is going to keep the store. The three of us are taking the day off."

"Can't Seth come with us?" Clancy asked.

"No," Jessie said, having anticipated this. "Someone has to mind the store, and he volunteered."

"Where are we going?"

"You'll see. Now finish your breakfasts. We'll be going as soon as Seth arrives."

Thankfully the girls were almost done eating because almost nothing else went in their mouths. They speculated with each other and continued to ask their mother about the destination, but she would not answer them.

Jessie gave them instructions about cleaning the table and their hands and faces before slipping downstairs early. She hoped Seth would be a little early, so it was satisfying to open the door and find him in one of the rockers. The questioning, almost vulnerable look on his face as he stood and came her way was a little hard on her heart, but she made herself stick to business.

"The girls and I will be taking the day off."

"All right," Seth agreed, adopting her formal tone.

"We'll be back at closing, but probably not before then."

Seth nodded and waited for any special instructions she might have. He half-expected to be reminded about not moving things around, but Jessie said nothing. Seth, however, had a question.

"Should I assume you want me to check with you each day about work, or should I just plan on working?"

"You can just come to work," Jessie said, her voice slightly more friendly.

"I'll plan on that."

Seth would have taken his coat off and rolled up his sleeves, but Jessie was staring at him. He stood still, knowing she had more to say but certain they would be interrupted at any moment. He was wrong.

"You shouldn't have left," she said, almost in a whisper.

"No, I shouldn't have. I'm sorry, Jess."

He hadn't called her Jess yet, and certainly not in that tone that used to melt her heart. At the moment it was almost too much for her.

"Maybe I shouldn't have come back," Seth made himself add. "Maybe it's going to be too hard for you."

Jessie shook her head. "I'll get used to it, and the girls do need you, Seth. I mean that."

"I'll do all I can to help you, Jessie. It was never my intent to make things hard or to make you miserable."

Jessie was nodding when the girls arrived.

"We're going somewhere with Mama!" they tried to tell him, each girl talking over the top of the other as well as finishing each other's sentences.

"How fun." Seth got excited with them, seeing the smile on Jessie's face as she watched them. He hunkered down to their level before asking, "Where are you going?"

"We don't know."

"A mystery," Seth said slowly. "That is fun."

"We want you to come," Hannah said.

"I'm sure I would enjoy it, but someone has to mind the store."

"Can you do it by yourself?" Hannah asked.

"I think so," Seth said, realizing she would question him for some time on this topic if he let her. He knew a distraction was needed. "I forgot to tell you that you both look very pretty in your dresses today," Seth said, fixing Hannah's collar. "The next time I see you, you can tell me all about what you did. Have a good time today and take good care of your mother."

"She takes care of us," Clancy said, her brow furrowed in seven-year-old logic.

"Yes, she does, but you can take care of her as well, don't you think?"

The girls didn't know what to do with this. They stared at their father and then looked to Jessie, but she told them only to bid their father goodbye and go wait for her in the rocking chairs out front. Both girls hugged Seth, having no idea the effect this had on him, and then headed out.

"Will you be all right on your own?" Jessie asked him.

"I think so. Have a good time."

Jessie hesitated, not sure how to say what this meant to her. She wasn't altogether happy with his presence, but at the moment this summer day away from the store with the girls was like a dream come true.

"Thanks, Seth."

"You're welcome."

Jessie slipped away before either of them could speak again. Seth walked out behind her to watch them walk away, wishing he could have known exactly what Jessie had been thinking.

Chapter Eleven

"Where are we going?" Hannah asked for the fifth time. Jessie had planned to ignore her but had suddenly had enough.

"First of all," Jessie said as she stopped walking, forcing the girls to stop with her, "you're going to stop asking questions of me. *Any* questions."

"Why?" Hannah asked.

"That's a question, Hannah. I will answer it, but it will be my last one. I want you to just come along with me and enjoy the day. I have plans, but they might change. Whatever we do, we'll have fun, and that's all you need to know. Do I make myself clear?"

The girls nodded, and Jessie continued down the street. They both wanted to ask questions, and a few did slip out, but Jessie kept them on task. The bank was the first stop and then the livery. The Wheeler women were headed out of town.

"How is this, Mrs. Potts?" Heather asked that lady, presenting the skirt they had finished for her.

"Very nice," Mrs. Potts said, fingering the fabric and then taking it to the mirror to hold in front of her. She smiled at what she saw, causing Jeanette and Heather to smile as well. The women finished taking care of that lady and seeing her out the door and then went back to work.

Jeanette had not been lying in wait for Heather, but she had thought long and hard about whether or not she should say something. Telling herself not to have Nate on her mind, she tried to open the conversation.

"Heather, have you ever longed for a husband?"

"I have," Heather admitted, "many times."

"Why have you not married, do you think?"

"I think I'm picky, Jeanette."

"In what way?"

"Well, he would have to be just the right one." Heather stopped suddenly with her sewing, her head tipping in thought. "I'm not sure I'm the marrying kind. Men don't seem to notice me."

"What if someone did?"

"Well, I'd certainly be complimented, but he'd have to be just the right one."

"Tell me about the right one."

Heather was all ready to do this, but someone had come to the door. It was a man this time. Jeanette had seen him around town, but they'd not met. He was looking only for prices on shirts and not ready to order anything that day, but by the time he left, it was time for the women to take turns with their dinner breaks. Not until after Heather left to eat dinner did Jeanette remember they hadn't finished their conversation.

The girls had done a pretty good job. It wasn't often that they went to the bank with their mother, and Jessie didn't think she had ever hired a rig and taken them out. They were wild with excitement as she sent the horse and buggy out of town, and when she turned in under the archway that said Holden Ranch, Jessie was sure their screams of delight could be heard all the way back to town.

"Now, girls," Jessie said, slowing the rig and working to get their attention. "I haven't talked with Meg, so I don't know if she has time for company. This might be a very short visit."

The girls barely looked at her, and she knew it was no use. No matter how long they stayed, the girls would want more.

"Well, Jessie!" Meg was suddenly there to greet her, coming from the house, Cathryn on her hip as the buggy pulled up to the porch.

"Hi, Meg," Jessie called back. "Are you up to a little company?"

"Certainly," Meg said before the two hugged. "I'm working on my baking. Come to the kitchen, and we can visit there. Hi, girls."

Hannah and Clancy did greet her but went right back to making Cathryn smile. The five of them trooped indoors to find Savanna waiting, and in very short order the children were playing in the living room, leaving the women on their own in the kitchen.

Seth could not believe how quiet and lonely the store felt. He had been somewhat busy but not moving nonstop, and this made Jessie and the girls' absence all the more pronounced. He also forgot to ask Bri if he could pack something for dinner. Noon came and went, and he was starting to wish he'd eaten a bit more breakfast.

"Hello, Seth," a male voice suddenly said. Seth turned to find that Trace Holden had come in the door.

"Hello, Trace," Seth said, putting out his hand. The men shook before Trace spoke again.

"It's been a while."

"It has, yes. Too long."

A brief silence fell between them before Seth spoke again.

"I hope you're not looking for Jessie. She's not around today."

"As a matter of fact, I passed her on the road."

"Did you?" Seth said with a smile. "Did she say where she was headed?"

"She said it was a surprise, so I assume they were headed to see Meg."

Seth could not stop his smile. Such a thing never occurred to him, and he knew the girls would love it.

Seeing that smile, Trace relaxed a little. He had been a bit concerned about Jessie, knowing that Seth was back in town, but the smile on the other man's face showed that he was genuinely pleased.

"What can I get for you?" Seth finally remembered to offer.

The men worked together for a time. Trace needed to order an item from a catalog that Seth wasn't familiar with, but they finally managed it. The talk didn't get personal again until Trace was ready to head on his way.

"Will I see you Sunday?" the rancher asked.

"I'm planning on it."

"Do you think Jessie and the girls will join you?"

Seth smiled sadly before saying, "Maybe someday, but I doubt if it will be anytime soon."

"Well," Trace said with quiet sincerity, "it will be good to see you, Seth. Thanks for your help."

"You're welcome, and thanks, Trace."

Seth was on his own just a moment later and for nearly 30 minutes afterward, a state that suited him very well. He had some things to think about.

Seth hadn't planned to stick around and wait for Jessie and the girls, but they arrived back just 20 minutes before he would have closed the doors. The girls were flushed and smiling, and Jessie looked very relaxed.

"Well, now," Seth said, concentrating on his children. "Did you have a good time?"

"We saw Joey and Savanna and Cathryn and *Netty!*" Clancy said.

"And we had dinner on the ranch!" Hannah added.

"That sounds fun," Seth said with a smile, even as he wondered who all those people were.

"What did you do?" Hannah asked, surprising Seth because Clancy was still talking about their day—the barn, the horses, and something about a moose.

"I took care of customers and cleaned a little," Seth told his oldest.

"Was it busy?" she asked next.

"At times, but overall it was quiet." After Seth finished saying this he smiled at her in hope of reassuring her. She seemed worried. Once again he wished he knew what her different looks and silences meant. He didn't dwell on it but went back to their day out.

"Who is going to tell me who Joey and Savanna are?"

"Mama's cousins," Clancy said, and before Seth could look to Jessie for clarification, Hannah cut in.

"Meg is Mama's cousin."

"Who is Meg?"

"She's married to Brad. They have Savanna and Cathryn, and they're going to have another baby before Christmas. I hope it's a boy."

"Well, now," Seth said, remembering again how long he'd been away. "Who is Joey?"

Clancy handled this one, explaining about the little boy and his baby sister.

"Trace was in here today," Seth told them, "and I didn't even know to congratulate him."

"You didn't help him?" Clancy asked, her face showing her shock.

"No," Seth said on a laugh, "I didn't realize his wife had just had a baby. I would have offered congratulations."

Both girls frowned at him, and he looked to Jessie.

"How do I explain that word?"

"Let's see." Jessie frowned a little as she thought. "It means to tell someone you're pleased for them."

The girls looked at their mother for a moment and then back to

Seth, their faces open and interested. Looking into their eyes—at the moment so full of trust—Seth was reminded that at times he didn't know exactly what to do with them. He glanced at Jessie and found her watching her daughters as well. Before he could figure out what she might be thinking, she spoke.

"I can lock up," Jessie offered.

"I'll get out of your way then," Seth said, taking his cue. "Goodbye, girls," he added, and headed to get his coat.

"Seth." Jessie stopped him, and he turned. "Thank you."

"You're welcome," he said but then couldn't turn away. Something in her face stopped him. "Did *you* have a good time?"

"Yes," she said, not able to stop the smile that came to her mouth. "I haven't had a day off since Bri worked for me."

"I didn't know Bri worked here," Seth said, looking as surprised as he felt.

"It was before she and Rylan were married."

"I don't think she's ever mentioned that."

"When she comes in, I play with Danny and she waits on herself."

Seth laughed, not just because the image was funny but because she was unbelievably relaxed. Seth never thought of Jessie as a tense person—she took most things in stride—but her very stance right now spoke of someone who didn't have a care in the world.

Wishing he could find something else to say to any of them, Seth turned for his coat. He was pleased and surprised to find that all three of them waited right where they were and said goodbye to him. Seth walked down the boardwalk in the direction of the Jarvik house, his mind trying to work out if he'd missed something just then or if leaving really had been the best idea.

"What do you think it means?" Meg asked Brad that evening. "I was just so surprised to see Jessie in the middle of the day. She can't have welcomed Seth back with open arms, but she left him in charge of the store."

"Don't forget that he worked there almost from the first moment he came to town," Brad said. "And it wasn't long before they were married. I assume he knew every aspect of the business and still does."

"I guess so," Meg said, still trying to put the pieces together. She was genuinely pleased that Jessie and the girls had come, but it was still a surprise.

"Did it wear you out?"

"Pretty much. Talking to Jessie is no effort, but I wanted to ask questions and didn't feel I could. That was the most draining part."

"She's one independent lady—has been as long as I've known her."

"Yes, she is. Jeb has said she's a lot like her father."

"Did you know Hiram?"

Meg shook her head now. "I came for my first summer visit after he died—after Seth left too."

Brad was thoughtful for a moment, and Meg caught his look and asked about it.

"I was just thinking how much things can change, sometimes very swiftly."

"Were you thinking about that for us or Jessie?"

"At the moment for Jessie. Seth's coming back must have turned things upside down for her."

"Maybe the Lord will use it to get her attention."

"Maybe. I must admit that I haven't really trusted God in that area," Brad said. "I don't pray for her very often."

Brad grew thoughtful again, but this time Meg didn't ask. She suspected he was praying for Jessie, and she took advantage of the quiet to do the same.

"When you didn't come back," Rylan said to Seth over supper, "I assumed she wanted you to stay and work."

"Yes, she did. She and the girls left almost as soon as I arrived and got back right at closing."

"Where had they gone?" Bri asked.

"Holden Ranch. They said something about Jessie's cousin marrying Brad."

"That would be Meg. She's Jeb and Patience's niece."

Seth nodded, still thinking about the interchange.

"Did they have fun?" Bri asked, spooning potatoes onto Danny's plate.

"They did. Jessie looked completely relaxed." Seth paused and suddenly smiled. "She mentioned that you'd worked for her, Bri."

"Before I was married," Bri said with a smile of her own. "I worked part-time for her and part-time for Jeanette."

"You were a busy lady."

"She still managed to find time to get into trouble," Rylan said dryly. Bri laughed.

"I think there's a story I need to hear," Seth said, watching their warm way with each other and feeling envy.

"Let's just say," Rylan worked to put it tactfully, "that Sabrina ran into interesting people in her zeal to share Christ."

Bri smiled in agreement but also said, "There has been some fruit."

"Yes, there has," Rylan agreed with a smile, thinking of the different women whose lives were changed because his wife reached out. Suddenly coming back to the present, Rylan asked, "How are you doing with the girls?"

"I'm not sure. I wish I knew them better. I wish I could tell what they were thinking."

"Did something happen?" Bri asked, hearing his quiet tone.

"Not specifically, but sometimes they look at me and I can't tell what they're thinking."

"They probably don't know themselves," Rylan said. "A man they didn't know existed has come on the scene and is their father. That happened only four days ago, Seth. They're as confused and uncertain as you are."

Seth stared at the other man. That *was* what he was seeing on their faces. Why had he not recognized this?

"Has it been only four days?" Seth finally asked.

"This is Wednesday night, and you met them Sunday afternoon. Even the notion that Jessie would leave you alone with the store this soon is a surprise."

Seth had nothing to say. For him, it felt as if he'd come back to Token Creek weeks ago. So much was familiar—not just the town, people and job, but also the way he felt about things. It was good to be reminded that in the most important things, the things involving his daughters, this was all very new.

"How is it going with Jessie?" Rylan cut into his thoughts.

"That's not as confusing as the girls. It's plain to see there's no trust there. Not that I blame her. I can see the questions in her eyes, and I think it's only a matter of time before she wants to know more than I've told her."

"Did you hold something back?"

"I didn't hold back incidents, but I didn't share all the specifics. The girls are very curious, and I'm sure you know they come by that honestly. Jessie's used to being the center of information in this town. She enjoys knowing what's going and has gone on."

"Will she hold it against you if you tell her more?" Bri asked.

"Jessie is not a mean person—she never has been—but I don't know what she'll do with the details of my life."

"Do you think she'll send you away?"

"Not that. She says the girls need me and she puts them first, but she might put such a wall between the two of us that the girls will hold back, unconsciously taking their cue from her."

That made complete sense to Rylan and Bri. They both wished they could reassure him on Jessie's behalf, but that wasn't possible. On God's behalf, however, it was completely possible.

Rylan spent the rest of the meal reminding Seth that God had a plan and that Seth needed to remember that he had been obedient by returning to Token Creek. Rylan did not promise him that he would have no pain or heartache in the process but that obedience was always blessed.

"And don't forget," Rylan finished, "our actions here are for eternity. We do the right thing and make the right choices here for eternity's sake. We leave the details to God as to what that's all going to look like."

Jessie settled into bed, the little girls already asleep on the other side of the same bed, and thought about the day. It had been wonderful. Somewhere on the ride out of town, it occurred to her that she'd walked away from the store, going so far as to leave it in Seth's care. She'd almost panicked, but the delight of her daughters and the absolutely decadent feeling of being gone during the workday had swiftly crowded all else aside.

She and Meg had always been friends. Meg, the younger of the two, had started making summer-long visits to Jeb and Patience many years ago, and the result had been her staying in Token Creek to marry Brad Holden. And today, somehow Jessie had known that Meg would welcome her. It wasn't that she'd never been to the ranch—she had several times over the years—but never on a weekday.

Jessie sighed a little as sleep crowded in, thinking about Brad and Trace's children and how precious they were. For a moment she thought about having a day like that every week, a day off that wasn't a Sunday. She fell asleep before she could start to wonder where this feeling had come from.

Rylan and Nate met each week but not always at the same time. This week they met on Saturday morning. The August weather was nice, so they had gone down to the edge of the creek and found a stretch of grass to sit on. Each man had his Bible.

"I found a verse from Psalms that I think applies to me," Nate said.

"Which one?"

"Psalm 119:17: 'Deal bountifully with thy servant, that I may live, and keep thy word.'"

"How do you think that applies to you?" Rylan asked.

"I can't remember too much about lying there when I was so weak, but after you told me I wasn't ready I do remember trying to talk to God. I hadn't done that very often, and I realize now that I was trying to make a deal with Him."

Rylan had not heard this before and was quiet as Nate shared.

"I think I said something about 'Just let me live, just let me live,' but I never worked out what my end of the bargain would be if He actually did that."

"And this verse reminds you of that?"

"A little. It almost sounds to me as if the writer is trying to make a deal with God."

"I can see why it might look that way, but don't take this verse out of context. It's from an amazing chapter where all but a handful of verses mention God's Word. That might not seem all that significant, but there are 176 verses in that chapter."

Nate blinked with surprise but kept listening.

"The psalmist is asking to live for a reason, that reason being God's Word. There is nothing self-seeking in this request. God's Word is so great and precious that this writer asks for more time so he can know that Word.

"Also, be sure to keep the next seven verses with it. They're all a plea and a thanksgiving to God for how amazing His Word is and how much we need it."

The men took time to read all the verses that Rylan mentioned and then prayed together. They were just minutes away from Nate heading to work when Rylan asked how Nate was doing with the topic of Heather.

"Most days I'm all right," Nate said. "It's hard not knowing if she doesn't want me or doesn't want *anyone* special in her life."

"I've been meaning to ask you about that. Had you noticed Heather before you came to Christ?"

"Yes, but she didn't get out much before Mrs. Holden died, so I was just drawn to her looks. But now that we've talked and I know how nice she is, the feelings are much stronger."

"This is when trust is so key, Nate. We don't know if God will ever touch Heather's heart concerning you, but we can still trust Him. Memorize Isaiah 26, verses 3 and 4. If ever you're tempted to think that God doesn't know her heart or yours, remember those verses."

Nate looked them up on the spot and had to laugh.

"They're perfect!" he said.

"Yes, they are," Rylan agreed, also laughing.

Moments later Nate thanked him and went on his way, but Rylan didn't hurry home. He sat back down by the creek to pray for his friend. Rylan would never presume to know what God had in mind for Nate, but the pastor did ask God to move and work concerning Heather. He didn't ask for himself but in God's will, knowing that if God wasn't glorified by such a relationship, it would not be worth a moment's time or place in Nate's and Heather's lives.

Clancy hadn't meant to boss Seth, and she certainly hadn't meant to get caught in the act. For a moment, however, the seven-year-old forgot what her mother had said.

"Did you fix those shoe boxes yet?" Clancy asked not long before dinner on the busiest day of the week.

"I haven't had time," Seth told her, working to right a display of kitchen knives.

"Well, they need it and so do those bowls and pitchers on the top shelf."

"Thank you, Clancy," Seth said, having seen Jessie come up behind their daughter.

"Are you giving Seth orders?" Jessie asked, her voice quiet but astounded and angry that she'd been disobeyed.

Clancy spun, her lower lip tucked between her teeth, telling her mother she had heard correctly.

"Head to the stairs and do not move until I get there."

"But it's Saturday!" the little girl argued.

"Go!"

Clancy went off, and Seth waited only for her to disappear to ask about what she'd said.

"I've been known to send the girls to sit on the stairs on a Saturday and been so busy I've forgotten them," Jessie explained.

"How long will you leave her there?"

Jessie was about to answer when she saw what needed to be done.

"Why don't you go to her? Maybe if you tell her you don't want to be bossed, she'll remember."

"All right," Seth agreed, thinking he would never have dared to suggest it. It wasn't that he hadn't given the girls directions, but he never got after them. He figured that would come in time, when the relationship wasn't so new.

"I've been thinking," Jessie said quietly, knowing it wouldn't be long before she was needed elsewhere in the store. "I have some questions."

"For me?"

"Yes."

"All right."

"I don't want the girls to know anything more, but I need to know some things."

"Sure," Seth agreed, glad he'd already anticipated this. "Just let me know when."

There was no time for more. Both husband and wife were needed by customers in the next few seconds.

Chapter Twelve

IT WAS SOME TIME before Seth had time to even go check on Clancy. He found her lying across the second step, looking bored and put out. He sat on the bottom step to be on her level.

"Is Mama coming?" she asked as soon as she spotted him, sitting up in the process.

"No, I'm here to talk to you."

"Not Mama?"

"Not this time," Seth said, working to find brief and simple words for all the things in his heart. "I want to tell you something, and I want you to listen carefully. I think we all have jobs to do. Your job is to be a little girl who listens to her mother and does what she's told. My job is to work and take care of things for your mother here in the store, and do what *she* needs me to do."

Clancy watched him, her eyes intent on his face.

"It's wrong of you to boss me around. But I don't want you to boss me around because your mother said not to. I don't want you giving me orders because it's not *your* job. Do you understand, Clancy?"

"What's my job?"

"Your job is to be seven. You're not an adult, so you don't need to act like one. You need to be seven and listen to what your mother and I tell you, and then obey."

"Are you mad at me?"

"No, but if you forget and boss me around again, I'm not going to wait for your mother to find out. I'll put you on the stairs myself."

Her eyes grew a little over this statement, but Seth did not sense that she was going to argue.

"You can get up from the stairs now," Seth said.

He watched the little girl stand, but she didn't try to move. Seth wasn't sure if she didn't believe he had the right to dismiss her from this place of punishment or if she thought she was still in trouble.

"We call you Seth," Clancy said suddenly.

"Yes, you do," that man agreed, wondering where this had come from.

A moment later, Clancy was gone. Hannah had come looking for her, and she had gone with her sister without a backward glance. Seth went back to work himself, but his mind was not on anything but Clancy. Somehow he thought her last statement might be significant, but for the life of him he couldn't figure out why.

Jeanette, Heather, and Becky walked home from church together on Sunday, each with their own thoughts. They would probably discuss the sermon over dinner as they usually did, but at the moment Jeanette had Nate and Heather on her mind again. That man had sat with Bri, Danny, and Seth. He'd not come anywhere near Heather, but Jeanette had seen him glance her way several times.

Jeanette had run out of patience. She was ready to launch a full-blown investigation of Heather's feelings on the matter and planned to do so as soon as they were home. However, she hadn't counted on Becky, who had some thoughts and ideas of her own.

"Are you ever going to notice Sheriff Nate?" the cook asked the moment Jeanette's front door closed behind them.

"Why would I notice Nate?" Heather asked when she realized Becky was speaking to her.

"Because he notices you. Haven't you seen it?"

Heather stared at Becky in dumbfounded silence and then looked to Jeanette. That lady nodded ever so gently, and Heather looked stunned. She tried to recall even one time when Nate Kaderly had shown her any kind of preference and couldn't think of any. And then that time in the shop when Jeanette asked her about Nate came rushing to mind.

"That day, Jeanette, when you asked me if Nate was sweet on me, what had you seen?"

"Nothing too overt, Heather. He just tends to linger and talk to you if he has a chance."

Heather looked very shaken by this. That had been months ago.

"And you, Becky," she went on, her voice very sober, "what are you seeing?"

"Just that he looks your way," Becky said plainly, almost wishing she'd kept her mouth shut. She hadn't meant to upset anyone.

"I take it you don't want anything to do with him," Jeanette stated without censure.

"It's not that. It's that he must think that I think that."

Jeanette and Becky both took a moment to compute this. The sentence had been a mess, but they did catch her meaning.

"So you do have feelings for him?" Becky asked, deciding to be clear.

"I don't know if I have romantic feelings for him, but I do care. He's so very kind, and he's my brother in Christ. I would hate to think he finds me cold or apathetic. Nothing could be further from the truth."

For a moment Heather looked as helpless as she felt. She had honestly believed she was not the type of woman who attracted men. It was not hard to make this deduction as no one in her 34 years had ever stepped forward in any way.

"What will you do?" Jeanette finally asked.

"I don't know. I don't know what it all means."

"But you might welcome his attention?" Becky again went right to the point.

"I don't know," Heather repeated, sounding confused.

Her friends knew that enough had been said. Without revisiting the subject, the women moved toward the dining room and kitchen. Sunday dinner was not a short meal, but the topic of Nate and Heather did not come up again.

"Good morning," Seth greeted Hannah as she came to the front counter on Tuesday morning.

"Good morning," she repeated, not catching her father's smiling eyes as he watched her.

Her hair was brushed, and she was dressed and ready for the day, but she was not awake. Nevertheless, she climbed up on the counter as she often did and watched her father sort the mail.

"What are you doing today?" Seth asked.

"Nothing."

"When does school start?"

She perked up a little bit with this question, and Seth knew he was onto something.

"In a few weeks. I can read!"

"That's great. What do you like to read?"

"Mama has some books from when she was little. They were Grandma Wheeler's. I don't know all the words, but I like those."

"Maybe you could read to me sometime."

"You want me to?" Hannah asked, her face alight with pleasure.

"I do want you to. Maybe when I stop for dinner today."

"Maybe what?" Clancy asked, coming on the twosome and joining Hannah on the counter. It was something Jessie allowed as long as they weren't in a customer's way.

"Hannah is going to read to me," Seth explained, only to draw a huge frown from his younger daughter. Clancy directed this face at her sister, and Seth wondered what had just happened.

"You'll learn, Clancy," Hannah said with a surprising measure of patience. "I didn't know how to read at your age either."

"This year?" Clancy demanded.

"Yes. I'll even help you."

Clancy turned the frown on Seth, and even though he knew she was being demanding and difficult, he wanted to laugh. The fact that he'd been let in on yet another facet of his children's lives was delightful to him. He couldn't remember how old he was when he'd learned to read, but he did remember the first time he'd read an entire book. The accomplishment had given him such pride that after he blew out his lantern, he smiled into the darkness until he fell asleep.

"I want reading too," Clancy said.

"When Hannah reads to me?" Seth clarified.

"Yes."

"That's fine. If for some reason it doesn't work out today, then we'll plan on tomorrow."

"Which book?" Hannah suddenly asked.

"You can choose."

"I have to ask Mama!" Hannah said, and jumped off the counter in lightning speed, racing for the storeroom where Jessie was working on the books.

Clancy stayed, watching her father in silence, so Seth tried the same line of questioning.

"What are you doing today?"

"Nothing."

"Are you excited for school?"

"Only if Miss Bolton is going to teach me to read and not call me Maryann."

"Why don't you like Maryann?"

"My name is Clancy."

The name Clancy floated through the air just then.

"It sounds like your mother is looking for you," Seth said, impressed when she got right down and went that way. He finished up with the mail and started on a few boxes that had arrived. Jessie had ordered some small items—hair combs and even some jewelry. He was in the midst of putting these away when he noticed a headache starting. Seth didn't get headaches or become ill very often and so did his best to ignore the pain, figuring it would soon pass.

"Do you know where the tin pans are?" The questioning voice caused him to turn.

"Yes, ma'am. Right over here."

Seth saw to the woman's needs, but it was getting harder to ignore the headache. It was starting to throb in his temples, making his head feel ready to explode. By the time he waited on two more customers, even his ears were starting to feel full and miserable. This was the way Jessie found him.

"Seth?" she said quietly, taking in his white face and confused eyes.

"I have a headache," he said, not wasting any time.

"How bad?"

"Bad."

"Come with me," Jessie said, noticing that he moved very slowly and without question. "Hannah," Jessie said when they passed her, "if someone comes in, tell them I'll be right back."

"Where are you going?"

"No questions," her mother said, and Hannah, afraid of what she saw in Seth's face, kept her mouth shut.

"Jessie?" Seth managed very quietly when she began to climb the stairs, but that woman didn't try to answer.

"Come upstairs," she ordered him, albeit softly. "I want you to lie down."

Seth obeyed mindlessly, not remembering much about the next few minutes. He was suddenly in the girls' bedroom, Jessie helping him with his shoes and clothing. When at last his head touched the pillow, he shuddered with pain and worked to let his body relax. He felt covers on his chest and maybe Jessie's hand on his face, but when exactly he sank into blackness he wasn't sure.

"Hannah," her mother spoke quietly when she went back down the stairs. "Go find Doctor Ertz. Tell him he's needed here at the store. If you can't find him," Jessie began and then stopped. "Whether or not you find him, go tell Rylan that Seth is sick. Leave messages for people if you can't talk to them directly. Do you understand?"

Hannah nodded, and Jessie knew she could trust her. Her daughter had been running errands and delivering messages for her for a very long time. She was efficient and serious about such tasks.

Clancy had stayed quiet during the exchange between Jessie and Hannah, but as soon as Hannah left she spoke. "Where is Seth?"

"He's in bed upstairs."

"I want to go up."

"You can, but you must not get near the bed or try to talk to Seth. He's sick."

"What if he needs something?"

"Come and tell me. Do not try to do anything on your own, and *do not* ask him questions."

Clancy, sensing for once that all was not well, slipped quietly up the stairs. She found the bedroom door open and Seth very quiet on the bed. There was a chair by the door, and Clancy sat in it. She willed Seth to wake up and talk to her, but he didn't move. She wanted to talk more about reading and the book Hannah was going to read to them that very day. It didn't occur to her that Seth would not be up for reading for several days to come, so the little girl continued to sit and wait.

"Can you hear me, Seth?" Rylan asked that man about an hour after he climbed into bed.

"Rylan?"

"Yes. How are you?"

"My head hurts."

"Doctor Ertz has been here. He says the sickness could last several days."

"His hands were cold," Seth mumbled and was gone again.

Rylan looked over at Jessie, who stood at the footboard. "Do you want me to try to move him to my house?"

"No, Rylan. The girls and I can keep track of him."

"He might have needs, Jessie," Rylan stated bluntly without elaborating.

Jessie shrugged, and Rylan knew that she would be up for anything. Clancy peeked around the corner where Jessie had sent her when they came up. Rylan spotted the action, and both adults went that way.

"Hannah was going to read to Seth and me," she said, her own interest still very much on her mind.

"Not today she's not. Maybe this evening Hannah can read to you and me, but Seth isn't going to be up for company today."

Clancy did not look pleased over this, but Jessie had been gone from the store long enough and had to get back. Thanking Rylan, who exited through the storeroom, she went downstairs to check on Hannah and found her with Jeanette. They were getting along fine, but as soon as Jeanette left with her purchases, Hannah's next errand was to run to Camille Pallin's home. Lately, if Jeb was not available to help, Jessie sometimes called on Camille. Thinking about the man upstairs, Jessie knew she might very well need her in the next few days.

"I thought you would be in bed," Becky said to Heather when she found that lady in the kitchen much later that evening.

"I'm just having a last cup of tea."

"Can't sleep?"

"Too many thoughts."

"I shouldn't have said to you anything about Sheriff Nate," Becky said, her voice telling of her disgust.

"I'm glad you did."

"Why?"

"I need to think about it. I need to be aware of others and their feelings."

"You never saw it, Heather?" Becky asked again. "You really never noticed?"

"No. I thought you and Jeanette were kidding."

The women fell silent for a moment. Becky had made her own cup of tea, and they sat at the kitchen table, just one lantern burning.

"Are you afraid of getting hurt or giving the hurt?" Becky asked very gently, and Heather turned to stare at her.

"I *am* afraid," Heather whispered, the full realization hitting her. "I'm being governed by fear right now. I just saw it."

Becky's humility since her belief in Christ was obvious to everyone who knew her. That woman now leaned forward a little, her face alive with interest. "What will you do, Heather—just pray or something more?"

"I will pray, Becky, but I also must call the fear by its correct name: sin. I'm sinning against God when I fear in this way."

"What other kind of fear is there?"

"The kind that means awe and respect. The fear I have for God and His authority is all right; it's very good. But the other kind, the one you just put your finger on, is all wrong."

"Let's pray about it right now," Becky suggested, and the women did just that. Their tea forgotten, the hour a nonissue, these two old friends bowed their heads and confessed their great need to God. They did not leave the kitchen to seek their rest until all was repented of and settled.

"Here, Seth," Jessie coaxed that night. "Drink some of this."

Seth complied, but the effort cost him. The doctor had said to keep water in him, and Jessie was doing her best. Seth's eyes opened after he drank. Seeing this, Jessie got a little more water into him.

"How's the head?" she asked, carefully mopping the water from his chin.

"Bad."

"Has this happened before?"

"Never. It's hot in here."

"I think it's you," Jessie said, rolling the covers off his chest a bit. Not until she did this did Jessie notice a scar on the side of his chest that she'd never seen before. Seth's eyes were closed again, so Jessie didn't try to ask him. For a moment she reached out and touched the old wound.

Not wanting to get her mind going on all the possibilities, Jessie blew out the lantern and headed from the room. It might prove to be a short night, but she needed as much sleep as she could manage. Climbing in beside the girls in her own bed, she was asleep in less than a minute.

I can stay all morning had been Camille's words.

Jessie thought they sounded like music. She had sent the girls to be with Bri and then returned to Seth's side. That man had had a pretty good night, but his skin was very warm and Jessie, weary from interrupted sleep, took turns dozing in a chair and bathing Seth's face and chest with cool water.

Rylan visited again, bringing a pot of food Bri had made. Doctor Ertz made another appearance as well with no change in treatment. Not until almost noon did Seth wake and say something.

"Hannah?"

"She's not here," Jessie said, standing so he could see her.

"Did she read to me?"

"Not yet. I'll tell her you're looking forward to it."

"She's so sweet."

"Yes, she is."

"Where?"

"She and Clancy went to Bri's."

Seth managed a smile.

"They love Danny."

When Jessie saw that she was losing him again, she coaxed a bit more water into him. He drank several good swallows before he fell back to sleep. Not until Jessie tried to move to put the water back on the table did she realize Seth had a fistful of her skirt in his hand. It took her fingers to unwrap his, and when she returned his arm to the bed, he rolled to his side and slept deeply.

Jessie sank back into her chair, no longer needing to sleep but weary with wondering what their relationship would be like in the future. Lately it seemed to be all she thought about. She didn't want Seth back in her life, but he was here, and she wanted to make the best of it. Her curiosity over what he'd done and all the places he'd lived was not so she could hold it against him but because she didn't like surprises. She wanted all the details on the table, not coming out in bits and pieces for years.

Years. The word lingered in her mind. Would he be here for years? That was probably his plan. The girls would need him for years; that was certainly true. They were little more than babies right now. When they grew enough to start noticing boys, they would need their father's help in a way she couldn't give.

Even her mother had been wise about that. She had sent Jessie at 13 years of age to have a talk with her father. Some of the things Hiram Wheeler had shared with his daughter had been rather frightening, but they'd also made her aware and wary. It had not been a stroke of luck or coincidence that Seth was the first man she'd ever been involved with. It had been by choice. She had kissed a few boys behind the schoolhouse—only kissed them—and those relationships had not been ongoing or serious. Serious had come many years later, and that was with the man lying sick in the bed. A man she didn't know quite how to handle.

"How are you holding up?" Rylan asked his wife when Danny was down for a nap and the girls were drawing on paper in the living room.

"Fine. They're awfully fun and sweet. I've never been asked so many questions in one day. In fact I plan to find out how glass is made because I don't know either."

Simply delighted by her, Rylan bent and kissed Bri's mouth.

"What was that for?"

"You're still special."

Bri looked at him, working to figure this out but unable to.

"Did I never tell you how often I said that to Chas after you came to town?" Rylan asked.

"I don't think you did."

"I said it just about every time he checked with me."

"That I was special?" Bri clarified.

"Um hm," Rylan said, leaning to kiss her again. "And I was right."

Bri put her arms around her husband and held him close. Rylan held her back, neither one aware of the two sets of small eyes watching them with studied interest from the living room.

"Is Seth all right?" Clancy asked when Rylan delivered the girls back at the end of the day.

"He's still sleeping, but his fever is down."

"Can we see him?"

"Yes, but stay back away from the bed and don't ask questions."

The girls started to run through the store, and Jessie told them to slow down. She then turned to Rylan.

"Please thank Bri for me."

"I'll do that. I know she had fun."

"Did they question her to death?"

"Yes, but she didn't mind." Rylan had to laugh before adding, "She said she's going to find out how glass is made because they wanted to know and now she wants to know too."

Jessie joined Rylan in laughter and then thanked him again. Rylan said he would check on Seth the next day. Jessie locked the door behind him and took a few minutes to put the store to rights. By the time she went upstairs to the apartment, the girls were sharing the chair in Seth's room.

"Has he been awake?" Jessie asked quietly.

"No. He even snored a little."

Jessie had to smile at them. Their faces were serious, and she could see they wanted him to wake up in the worst way.

"Can he live here?" Hannah suddenly asked.

"You mean all the time?" Jessie asked to buy some time to think.

The little girl nodded but didn't look at her mother. Jessie hoped against all odds that meant it was a passing thought. She told the girls she was going to work on supper and was able to leave without gaining comment from either of them.

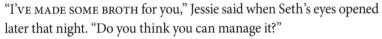

Chapter Thirteen

"I'VE MADE SOME BROTH for you," Jessie said when Seth's eyes opened later that night. "Do you think you can manage it?"

"I'll try."

"Is the pain better?"

"Yes. I'm tired."

"I'll heat the broth and wake you if you fall back to sleep."

"Did I miss the girls again?"

"Yes, they're asleep," Jessie said, leaving without telling him how long they had sat in that chair and waited for him to stir. She went to the kitchen to heat the broth and thought about what Hannah had asked. She remembered that Clancy had said something about Seth living with them the first time she met her father. Seth had handled that very well. Half of her hoped that Hannah would bring the topic up again in Seth's company. She was almost certain to mention it, and some part of Jessie wanted to know what Seth would say.

"Seth." Jessie called his name, holding the mug of warm broth. She ended up having to set it down so she could prop him up on his pillow. This woke him. "Here, drink this."

Seth did as he was told and then thanked her wearily. Jessie got quite a bit into him before he started to fall off again. Jessie was sure she'd seen the last of him, but his eyes suddenly opened and found her.

"I'm sorry for all the trouble, Jessie."

"It's all right. You didn't mean to get sick."

"Tell the girls I miss them."

"I will."

For a moment they looked at each other, and then Jessie asked, "Do you pray at times like this?"

"Yes."

"What did you pray?"

"I just asked for help. The pain was pretty bad, and I didn't know quite what to do with it."

"And do you think God helped you?" Jessie asked, not able to disguise the skepticism in her voice.

"I didn't instantly feel better if that's what you mean, but I had peace. Each time my mind prayed, even in the worst of the pain, I knew peace."

Jessie hadn't expected this and was surprised. She even had more questions she wanted to ask, but Seth's eyes were closed again. Leaving the room, she knew he would have a better night, which meant she would too. But unlike Seth, there was no peace for her. Questions rolled through her mind, and she didn't feel she had answers for any of them.

"You look better," Rylan said when he visited the next afternoon. Seth was awake and sitting up against the pillows and headboard. There was little color in his face, and his messy hair and unshaved face were uncharacteristic for him, but he did look as though he was on the mend.

"I am, thank you. It was a rough one."

"We've been praying for you," Rylan said.

"Thank you," Seth replied, and then realized he'd said that too fast. He wanted to know more. "What did you pray, Rylan?"

"That you would trust God no matter how poorly you felt, and that pleasing Him would be more important even than feeling better."

The look of surprise and then thoughtfulness on Seth's face was not something Rylan could ignore.

"How did you do?" Rylan asked.

"In the midst of it, I just asked for His help, but now that I can tell I'm getting better, I simply want to feel good enough to get out of this bed."

"Well, that's an honest feeling, but why do you want to get out of this bed? If it's simply to mend and get past the inconvenience of being sick, you're missing something."

"There's so much I don't know," Seth admitted quietly. "I still think more about myself than anyone else."

"That's a common temptation. God wants to be in the center and we need to get rid of anything that pushes Him out of the center. He won't stand for any other place."

Seth nodded before saying, "I did remember to thank Him that I was sick, knowing He had a plan."

"That's good. Keep that up. For however long this has you down, keep thanking God for that plan."

Rylan might have had something to add to this, Seth could not be sure, but Clancy took that moment to join them. He enjoyed seeing his daughter, and Rylan left before Clancy did, but Seth determined to get back to the pastor on the topic they'd been on. He knew he had more to learn about thankfulness and God's plan, and he knew Rylan was just the man to teach him.

By the time Jessie got to the apartment on Friday night, the girls were fully ensconced with their father. He was against the headboard of the bed. Hannah had claimed the footboard. Clancy was somewhere in the middle.

"You can walk with us if you want," Hannah was saying.

"I'd like that. What time do you have to be there?"

"Mama always sends us," the older girl answered. "I don't know the time."

"Where do I send you?" Jessie asked.

"To school! Seth is going to walk with us."

"That's nice of him. Does he know you'll talk his ear off?" Jessie teased Hannah, and the little girl smiled.

"Did you talk about it?" Clancy suddenly asked. "Is Seth going to live here?"

Seth's eyes naturally swung to Jessie, but that lady was looking at her daughters. All plans to see what Seth would say flew from her head.

"I'll discuss it with him tonight, and you're not to ask me about it 40 times. Come on now and help me with supper."

Seth found himself alone just moments later, wondering what else he'd missed in the last four days.

"What do I do now?" Heather asked during supper. "Sunday is coming. How do I proceed from here, knowing what I know?"

"What do you want to do?" Becky asked.

"Yes, Heather," Jeanette added. "Are you interested in Nate?"

"If you mean in a personal relationship, I don't know, but I'm not going to be able to find out unless I talk with him." Heather paused and went on. "And that brings up another point. How is he interested in me when he doesn't know me?"

"He's watched you, Heather," Jeanette said, "and your reputation has gone before you. He might find that you don't really share the same likes and interests, but he's willing to get close because he can see how special you are."

"You want her to marry Nate, don't you, Jeanette?" Becky asked.

"If she falls in love with him, yes. I think they would make a wonderful couple."

"But then she'll move from here," Becky added quietly.

No one commented or answered. It was too soon for such thoughts, but the very nature of the conversation meant that it would have to come up again at some point. It simply wasn't a topic that anyone at the supper table wanted to think about.

"I think I can come down in the morning, Jessie," Seth said when all got quiet that evening. Seth had made it to the living room for supper and was still sitting on the sofa. "I might not make it all day, but I can give you a little help."

"Camille is coming in the afternoon, so don't overdo."

"I don't know if I'll have much choice. I feel as weak as a child," Seth said in all sincerity. At the moment he didn't know where the strength would come from to walk to the bedroom, let alone down the stairs come morning.

"I think you should live here."

Seth's mind had been drifting—he'd barely been aware of Jessie's presence—but this certainly brought his eyes to her.

"Where did that come from?" Seth asked quietly, hoping she couldn't see the harsh beating of his heart.

"The girls want you to. They want it very much."

"I admire the way you take care of our daughters and put them first, Jessie, but you have to think of yourself too."

"I think I'll be all right," she said, her mouth even turning up in one corner. "If I need an evening to myself, I'll take a walk or suggest one to you."

Seth waited until her eyes came back to him and then said, "Are you sure?"

"Yes."

"What about the bed?" Seth asked, details coming to mind. "I can't just take the girls' bed from them."

"They sleep with me and have for years. They keep their things in that room but never sleep there."

Seth hadn't known this. He wasn't sure it was such a great idea, but that would be the last thing he could say.

"And I still have questions, Seth," Jessie went on. "I still want to know things."

"I haven't forgotten."

Jessie nodded. She knew what he meant. She didn't want the girls to know that they were talking about things from the past, but short of setting up a time to meet, there was no opportunity during the day to talk. And if she set up a meeting, the girls would know. They missed little that their mother did. Jessie had resigned herself to waiting until they were back in school all day, but it looked as though now she and Seth would be able to talk in the evenings.

For a moment she thought about him being there every night and didn't know if she liked that idea. Knowing that the girls would be thrilled was a huge help. She might need to remind herself of that in the days to come.

"He's going to live with us," Hannah whispered the moment her mother shut the door on Saturday night. "Mama said."

"Seth is?" Clancy whispered back, wondering why no one told her.

"Yes."

"What about Bri and Danny?"

"I don't know. They have to stay with Pastor Rylan, but Seth is going to live here."

The bedroom was silent for a moment, but Clancy wasn't done. "Will they kiss like Bri and Pastor Rylan?" she whispered back.

"I don't think so. I don't think Mama likes kissing."

"She kisses us," Clancy reasoned.

"That's different. Mothers are supposed to kiss."

Clancy had to think on this one, but it was getting hard. Saturdays were big days. The store was always full, and sometimes she had to help.

A jaw-popping yawn escaped her just as she thought of another question for Hannah, but she drifted off before she could voice it.

Seth was nearly out of energy, but he had one thing to take care of before he turned in on Saturday night. Rylan had delivered his satchel to him, and Seth dug into the bottom of it until he'd found something wrapped in the sleeve of an old shirt.

Moving carefully, not wanting to break it after all this time, Seth unwrapped it and studied it in the lamp light. It was just as he remembered. Moving before he could change his mind, he went back to the living room. Jessie was still on the sofa and looked up in surprise when he returned.

"This is for you," Seth said, handing Jessie the item.

Jessie reached without thought and took an exquisite perfume bottle from his hand. Her mouth opened a little. She stared at it and then at him.

"Where did you?" she began and then stopped.

"I was in a small town in Texas and spotted it."

"When?"

"A while ago—maybe five years."

Jessie looked at the bottle again, studying the lovely design. The top was crystal and screwed snugly into place. The glass bottle was surrounded by ornate gold filigree and filled in here and there with precious stones. The sight of it nearly took her breath away.

As she looked at it, the memories came pouring back. They had been married just a few weeks and talking in the bedroom. Jessie had gotten up to close the window and accidentally bumped into the shelf. Her grandmother's perfume bottle had tumbled to the floor and broken. Seth had told her they would replace it, but neither one of them had ever seen another one like it. Until now.

"Thank you," Jessie whispered.

"You're welcome. I'm sorry it took so long."

Seth didn't linger but went back to the bedroom. Jessie watched him, feeling things she did not understand. He wasn't supposed to be thinking of her that long ago. It wasn't what she'd imagined at all. It made staying upset with him and keeping her distance very hard. And on this night it made sleep hard. Jessie sat alone in the living room for much longer than she had planned.

"How do you think they're doing?" Bri asked Rylan as they settled in for the evening, Danny getting sleepy in her lap.

"I was wondering the same thing. Seth said that before he left Jessie to go to Texas, all they did was fight. Seth is not the same person, but if I had to hazard a guess, I would say that unless the things they fought over have changed, they're going to fight again."

"And in front of the girls this time."

Rylan sat quietly for a moment, thinking about what he'd just said. Had he underestimated God and His saving ability by assuming that Seth would still fight with Jessie?

"I didn't mean that quite the way it came out," he decided to add. "I don't automatically think that Seth and Jessie will fight, but in the past they argued, and those topics are going to come up again and cause some type of tension."

"That makes sense. I mean, eight years is a long time. Jessie would have done some growing up over that time, but upsetting situations typically don't go away on their own."

"What will you pray for?" Rylan asked.

"That Seth will be such an example that Jessie will want Christ."

"Maybe the girls will start down the path first."

"Maybe," Bri said with a smile, thinking that God could do the most amazing things in the heart of a child or someone with child-like faith.

"Where are you going?" Hannah asked Seth when he came from the bedroom with his jacket on Sunday morning. He had just helped Jessie with the dishes, his one area of expertise in a house, and then noticed the time was getting late.

"To church," Seth said, his Bible in hand.

"Can I come?"

This question, so artlessly put, stopped Seth in his tracks. He hadn't expected the girls to be the least bit interested and didn't know what to do with this. He stared down at Hannah and then looked to Jessie, who was sitting at the kitchen table with coffee and the newspaper.

"It's up to you," she said, having overheard.

Seth studied his wife a moment and could see she was sincere. As he watched she went back to her paper and coffee.

"Yes, you can," Seth said. "Are you ready to leave right now?"

"Let me brush your hair, Hannah," Jessie got in before the little girl could answer.

Hannah ran for the brush and stood still while her mother worked. Not until she was done did Jessie notice Hannah's dress was not a new one.

"Will that dress be all right?"

"It's fine," Seth said, not having noticed one way or the other, his mind still trying to take in what was happening.

"Off you go," Jessie said, going back to the paper as soon as they disappeared out the door. Not two minutes passed before Clancy came from the bedroom and learned she'd been left out. It was some time before Jessie was able to get back to her paper.

"I'm glad you came with me, Hannah." Seth had finally found words about halfway to the church.

"Me too. Will we sing?" Hannah said, all but skipping along and even going so far as to take his hand.

"We will sing. You might not know all the songs, so just do your best."

"Will you read your Bible?"

"Yes. Pastor Rylan will teach a lesson today that's he's learned from the Bible."

Hannah didn't answer or reply to this, and that gave Seth a moment alone with his thoughts. *Oh, God,* his heart prayed. *You have done this. You have given her interest and curiosity. Her questions might lead to You, Lord. Thank You for this wonderful little girl, this child of mine I don't deserve. Thank You that she wanted to come. Help me with her. Help me to have answers to her questions.*

"Oh, there's Heidi!" Hannah cut into these petitions. "I forgot I would see her."

"Who is Heidi?"

"Heidi Vick. We sometimes go to her house."

"What do you do?" Seth asked, making the connection to Chas Vick, whom he'd met his first week back.

"We play with her dog. His name is Buster. We don't have a dog."

Seth was saved from replying because they were at the building. With Hannah's hand still tucked into his, the two went inside and sat down.

Heather had done it. She had looked at Nate and waited for him to look her way. When he did, she smiled. Now the service was over, and he was headed her way. Heather thought her heart might pound out of her chest.

Nate moved across the church, hoping to just strike up a conversation with Heather, but one look at her face told him this would not work. She looked strained and a little pale as she watched him approach. Thinking fast, he pulled his Bible out as soon as he got to her.

"Heather, may I ask you a question?"

"Yes," she said, realizing it came out in a whisper. She cleared her throat and said, "Certainly."

"Did you get that last reference Rylan gave? I think it was in Romans."

"I did get it," Heather said, opening her Bible as well to check her notes. "It was chapter 13, verses 1 and 2."

"Thank you," Nate said, using a pencil to make note of it.

Heather watched him write, close his Bible, and look up at her.

"Busy week coming up?" he asked.

"I don't think so. We're not overrun with orders right now."

"Does the time ever drag?"

"If it gets too quiet, one of us leaves, and there's always plenty for one to do."

This said, a short silence stretched between them, but Heather was starting to relax.

"How about you, Nate? Busy week?"

"Not that I know of, but you never can tell."

"Are you ever afraid?" Heather asked, swiftly becoming herself and in the process completely forgetting that this man was interested in her.

"At times, yes. Some fear is good. It keeps me on my guard."

"How about when you were shot? Were you afraid then?"

"Things happened too fast for me to feel anything, but when Rylan said I wasn't ready to die, I got scared."

"That would be the good kind," Heather said gently.

"Because I wasn't ready, it was the best kind. Had I died, I would have been lost to God forever."

"I'm glad He had other ideas," Heather said with feeling. She hated the thought of anyone dying outside of Christ.

"So am I."

A silence did fall between them then, Heather suddenly remembering what she knew and becoming tongue-tied.

"Maybe I'll see you around this week," Nate said, thinking another rescue was in order.

"Maybe," Heather agreed and then bid Nate goodbye.

Nate didn't move beyond turning to watch her walk away to join

Jeanette and Becky. He was still standing in the same place when Rylan reached him.

"Progress?" the pastor asked, having witnessed the exchange.

Nate smiled just a little before saying, "Maybe."

"Why did you stand when we singed?" Hannah asked, having been told during the service that her questions would have to wait.

"Sang," Seth corrected automatically. "It's just what we sometimes do."

"I like to sing sitting down," Hannah said.

"Why is that?"

"My legs get tired."

"Well, you did very well. You sat still and stayed quiet when I asked you. So thank you for that."

Hannah managed to look pleased and shy all at the same time. The two finished the walk home in companionable silence, only to gain the apartment and be met by a fiercely frowning Clancy.

"What's the matter?" Seth asked Jessie when his younger daughter glared at both of them from her place at the kitchen table and then deliberately turned her back on the room.

"She didn't realize Hannah was going with you."

"Has she been pouting this whole time?"

"Um hm," Jessie said, sounding unperturbed.

For a moment Seth didn't know what to do, and then Rylan's words from that very morning came back to him. *Do not make the mistake of fearing man over God. Husbands, are you more afraid of your wife and leading in your home than you are of God? Fathers, are you more afraid of doing the hard work as a parent because your child might not like the word no than you are of God?*

Seth took only a moment to decide. Thinking that Jessie might well toss him out on his ear, he went directly to Clancy and sat down in the chair next to her.

"What's going on, Clancy?" Seth spoke to her profile, noticing that her arms were crossed tightly over her chest.

"You and Hannah left me!"

"We didn't sneak out, Clancy. We didn't try to leave you. You were in the bedroom. Had you been out here, you would have known what was going on and been given a chance to go with us."

She turned her frown on him briefly again and then looked away.

"Look at me, Clancy," Seth ordered, his tone firm.

Clancy obeyed, her face growing uncertain.

"The rest of us do not have to watch you pout like a baby, so if you're going to act like this, you can go sit in your room, and you can stay in there until you're ready to be kind."

Clancy made the mistake of looking toward her mother.

"This is between the two of us, Clancy," Seth said, not letting her get away with it. "Now I've explained that we didn't mean to leave you. If you want to come with me next week, that's fine, but you're not going to subject the rest of us to this pouting for one more moment."

This said, Seth stood to his feet.

"What's it going to be? Are you heading into the bedroom, or are you done acting like this?"

"I'm done."

"I'm glad to hear that," Seth said calmly, hoping his voice didn't show his surprise. He expected a huge fight. He turned to the living room and had to force himself not to look at Jessie. If she was angry with him over this, he wasn't sure what he would do.

"Did you sing, Hannah?" Seth heard Clancy ask.

"We did. I had to sit still, but it was better and shorter than school."

"Was Heidi there?"

"She was, but I didn't get to talk to her. But I saw Danny! I sat by them."

"Did you get to hold him?"

"No, he had to stay quiet on Bri's lap."

Seth watched the girls' interchange and then chanced a look at

Jessie. Her eyes were on the girls as well, but he couldn't tell what she was thinking. He took it as a good sign that she was not glaring at him. He could smell dinner cooking and assumed they would eat when it was done. In the meantime Seth reached for the newspaper and tried to relax.

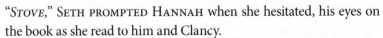

Chapter Fourteen

"*Stove*," Seth prompted Hannah when she hesitated, his eyes on the book as she read to him and Clancy.

"'Stove,'" Hannah repeated, "'where the mother boiled the stew.'"

"Is there a picture for that one?" Clancy asked, just as she'd done every few minutes for the whole story, leaning from her father's lap to see the book in Hannah's.

"Not yet."

"Are you getting tired of reading, Hannah?" Seth asked, having heard the scratch in her voice.

"A little."

"Why don't we stop and do some more tomorrow?"

"Don't you have to work?"

"Not in the evening. Can you read to us then?"

Hannah nodded and shut the book. She would never have admitted it, but she was sleepy. When she thought about how long her teacher could read to the class, she was amazed. She had only read a few pages and felt worn out.

"When is Mama coming back?" Clancy asked, the book having distracted her for only about half an hour.

"I don't know."

"I want her to come now."

"Why?" Seth asked. Clancy blinked at him. He waited, but she didn't answer. "You don't know why you want her?"

"I just want to see her," she said, sounding as young as she was.

Seth nodded and held her a little closer. He didn't see them weary very often, and it was fun to have Clancy willing to sit still and be held. Hannah didn't move either. She was close to his side, the book closed, staring at nothing. At times she even leaned her head against his arm.

Whenever Seth found himself with a few moments of time to himself, he prayed. He did so now, Jessie on his mind. He knew she needed to get out for a time and was glad she felt free to go. He thought he might be part of the reason she needed to get away, and his prayers turned to their marriage.

The thought of God repairing his marriage to the point that they would be in love again did not come to mind just then. His only concern was Jessie's salvation.

Jessie could not remember the last time she had walked along the creek bank by herself. A small part of her heart missed the girls' chatter, and another part felt free as a bird. It was a warm day, hot even, and she decided to sit down and put her feet in the water. She wandered to a quiet spot where she would probably be left alone and slipped her shoes and stockings off without ceremony.

She had no more done this when thoughts of Seth flooded in. One time right after they had married they had come here, and she'd done the same thing. Seth clearly enjoyed the sight of her bare feet and ankles and the occasional glimpse of her calves.

They had been married in August, and this was August. With a start, Jessie realized they'd just passed their eleventh anniversary. At the moment she couldn't remember exactly what day Seth had come back to Token Creek. It might have been on their anniversary. Had he been aware of that?

Jessie lay back, feeling as though a weight had settled on her. He wasn't the same man—she could see that—but that didn't mean much right now. She watched him with the girls. He would not hurt them. Of this she was sure. But what of herself? What if she fell for him all over again, but he was only there for the girls? Or what if he began to love her, but she never felt the same?

Almost wishing it would all go away, Jessie tried not to think about it. This was supposed to be a time alone for her, time to rest and be at peace. Jessie almost shook her head. The last word she would use to describe herself right now was peaceful.

"I keep thinking about the way you lived in Texas," Jessie said that night when the girls were in bed. To Seth's surprise she never did bring up the incident with Clancy from earlier that day. The four of them had had a very peaceful afternoon, even after Jessie got home from her walk.

"Thinking about it in what way?" Seth asked.

"Why you were willing to do this? Why were you willing to live that way?"

Seth nodded, searching for words. "I'm not shifting the blame here, but Eliot was not good company. I was greedy. And the money was very good."

"How good?"

Seth named a figure that made Jessie blink.

"You can't be serious."

"Jared Silk was a rich man and happy to pay the people around him who might make him richer."

"How did you meet him?"

"Eliot met him first. Then I came on the scene, and he said he liked our style."

Jessie could believe that. There had always been something that drew people to Seth. He was suave, but it was more than that. He was also kind and, at one time, there was just a hint of danger about him. Jessie didn't sense that anymore, but she could well imagine what this Jared Silk character saw.

"Tell me more about this woman," Jessie said next.

"Eliot's wife?"

"Actually I wanted to know about the woman you abducted, but I'd forgotten that Eliot was married. Did you say his wife had children?"

"Yes, from the marriage with her late husband. A boy and a girl."

Jessie grew silent for a moment, and Seth waited. When she didn't speak, he did.

"What's troubling you?"

"Eliot's hypocrisy. He had a wife, but he had no problem with you having left yours."

"He didn't know."

The words were said with quiet shame, and Jessie stared at the man she married.

"I didn't try to keep it from you, Jessie. I just forgot."

"That you were married?" she asked with sarcastic anger.

Seth didn't reply. There was no point in defending himself, and she was already angry. The silence between them grew, but Seth could see that Jessie had calmed down again.

"We were in prison when I told him," Seth finally said with quiet remembrance. "I had been getting lots of letters from Cassy, and Eliot and I were talking about the things she was writing. I told him how I'd left you and Hannah and how much I regretted that."

Seth's eyes went to the ceiling in the apartment as the pain of it washed over him. It had been an awful time. He had become good at not thinking about his wife and daughter, but that had stopped once he was behind bars and every memory nearly killed him.

"What did Eliot say?" Jessie had to ask.

"Nothing," Seth confessed. "He was so angry that I would walk out on my wife and child that he didn't speak to me for more than a week. When he did start to talk to me, all he could ask was 'How could you?' He asked it every time he came near me until we nearly came to blows."

This was the last thing Jessie expected. She pictured these men off having the time of their lives, living life without a thought for anyone but themselves. This description of Eliot didn't work with that image at all.

"How long were you in prison after Eliot knew about me?"

"Let me think...maybe ten or eleven months."

"Did you and Eliot get out at the same time?"

"He was released a week earlier."

"Then what happened?"

"He was waiting for me. He took me back to Cassy's ranch where we had all lived, and we made plans from there."

"What kind of plans?"

"He knew that I wanted to tell Darvi and Dakota I was sorry about what happened and that I wanted to try to come home to Token Creek."

Again Jessie did not think of this. She'd heard the word plans and figured he'd meant money or business, not getting back to his family.

"Where did all this come from?" Seth asked. "What made you think of all of this?"

"I don't know. I was all ready to relax by the creek, but all I could think about was you. What day did you come back to town?" Jessie suddenly asked.

"Let me see...I think it was four weeks ago last Friday. What day was that?"

"The first," Jessie said quietly.

"The day before our anniversary," Seth finished, his voice just as quiet.

For several moments the room was silent save the ticking of the clock on the wall. Seth wasn't overly tired, but he sensed Jessie's need to be alone. He could also use some time to himself.

"Anything else you want to ask tonight?"

"No."

"I'll turn in then."

"I'll see you in the morning."

"Goodnight, Jessie."

Seth left the room without another word, and Jessie did nothing to stop him.

It makes no sense, Jessie said to herself after Seth had gone. *I'm supposed to hate this man, but I'm still drawn to him. I got over him years ago. My life has been just fine without him, but he's starting to fill my thoughts again.*

How can this be? He left me! He left Hannah! How can he just waltz in here and pick up where he left off?

As soon as the thoughts materialized, Jessie knew they were unfair. Seth had not waltzed back in. He'd come quietly and humbly and done everything she'd asked of him. Until that very afternoon when he'd corrected Clancy, he'd been very much in the background. And it had not been his idea to move back into the apartment. Jessie had invited him, and it was only fair that she remember that.

Jessie stood and stretched her back. It was early, but she was suddenly tired. She stared at Seth's door and wondered if he was tired too. Times when no door stood between them flooded Jessie's mind. She pushed the thoughts away with an effort and headed into the bedroom with plans to sleep dreamlessly all night.

"Everything all right?" Seth asked softly. He'd come from the bedroom on Monday morning to find Jessie on the sofa, a sleeping Hannah in her arms, both still in their nightgowns.

"She's sick," Jessie said quietly.

"With what I had?" Seth asked, taking the other end of the sofa.

"I don't know. She's warm, but hasn't complained of a headache."

"Why don't you let me take the store today?"

Jessie nodded with relief. She had been awake with Hannah since about three o'clock, and her body felt weighted with fatigue.

"Should I get Clancy up?" Seth asked.

"No, it's all right. If she's not up before you head down, I'll just send her to you."

"All right. I'll head over to the hotel for breakfast."

"Why would you do that?"

"So I won't disturb Hannah."

"She'll be fine. Go ahead and make something for yourself."

As unhandy as Seth was in the kitchen, he did know how to toast bread and butter it. He had several slices, but no coffee, and headed down to ready and open the store.

Watching him go, Jessie could not remember the last time she'd had a sick child and hadn't been forced to divide her time between the store and the apartment. Warm feelings surged through her that she could not bear. She stood with Hannah and put her in Seth's bed. The little girl never woke. Not bothering to dress, she began to make coffee and breakfast, all the time berating herself for the soft feelings she was experiencing.

"Are you full?" Cassidy asked her five-month-old baby daughter. "Have you had enough?"

Netty's big blue eyes were distracted for a moment by something, but as soon as she spotted her mother, she smiled in delight. Cassidy smiled right back, her heart melting with love. Much as she was enjoying this, she was hoping Netty would soon take a nap. Joey was already down, and Cassidy was ready for some quiet time.

She rocked Netty and hummed a little, willing her to sleep. She knew if she put her down she would fall asleep fairly fast, but there was something special for her when her children slept in her arms.

Gaining her wish at last, Cassidy headed out onto the front porch.

The doors were open so she could hear the children if they cried. Trace had been slowly adding furniture to the porch, and Cassidy now took one of the rocking chairs, her eyes taking in the magnificent views of the ranch. The colors of the leaves on the Bur Oak and Quaking Aspen would be changing soon, marking her favorite time of year, and Cassidy tried to remember which of the trees usually turned first.

In the midst of these thoughts, Meg arrived. The window to the girls' bedroom was open at the back of her house a short distance away, allowing her to hear them if they woke. Meg took another rocking chair, and the two settled in to talking.

"How are you feeling?" Cassidy asked Meg, whose baby would be born by the end of the year.

"A little achy, but other than that I'm fine."

"Swollen ankles?"

"Yes."

"Here," Cassidy pushed a little wicker hassock toward her. "Put your feet up."

Meg thanked her and then asked, "What do you hear from your mother?"

"I haven't heard from her in more than a month, so I think she must be busy. I invited her to visit during the cattle drive, but she hasn't answered me yet."

"The drive is coming up fast."

"Yes, it is. I don't know why," Cassidy admitted, "but I'm dreading it this year."

"Some years are worse than others for me. I have a lot I want to do this time."

"Maybe I don't have enough planned."

"I don't know how much planning you can do with Netty at her age," Meg said. "And let's be honest, the older the kids get, the more it impacts them."

"Yes, but the older they get, the busier I am, so that makes the time go faster."

They both laughed a little at their own logic, and then the conversation

turned to their neighbors. The Carlisles owned the next ranch out, and
Marty had not been feeling well. The women were planning to take
some meals to her, so they put their heads together about what to make
and which days to deliver it.

Meg's girls were awake before Cassidy's, so their talk was cut short,
but that gave Cassidy a little more time on her own. She was still
praying for Trace and the children when her own began waking from
their naps.

The woman at the counter could not be termed anything but beautiful. Jessie got down to the store in time to watch Seth filling the woman's
order, a woman Jessie had never seen before. Jessie was able to stand
unnoticed by the folks at the front counter, but she didn't miss a thing.
The woman openly flirted a few times, but Seth didn't even smile. He
was the most businesslike Jessie had ever seen him.

"Is there anything else?" Seth asked.

"Well," the woman began, drawing the word out, her eyes on his
face.

"I'm glad you're all set," Seth said quickly. "Thank you."

This said, Seth came around the counter, not even offering to help
her carry the order. It was small, but he typically made the offer to
most female customers.

Jessie turned away just in time to avoid getting caught watching.
She felt Seth come up beside her and turned to him with myriad con-
flicting emotions.

"How's Hannah?" Seth asked the moment he got to Jessie's side.

"Still warm, but resting."

"Are you getting sick?" Seth asked, thinking she looked tired.

"No, I'm fine," Jessie said, a bit more sharply than she planned.

Seth nodded, wondering what he'd done wrong.

"Hannah wants to see you," Jessie said, making herself say what
she'd come to say.

"Do you want me to go now?" Seth asked, trying to read her.

Jessie nodded, but it bothered her that he felt he had to ask. For the first time in her life, she didn't like being in charge. She didn't like Seth always asking permission. Unwilling to examine where all of this was coming from, Jessie went to the front counter and set to work.

"How are you?" Seth asked the warm child in his bed, her little face flushed.

"Mama says I have a fever."

"I think she's right," Seth said, his hand going to her face.

"Here, Hannah." Clancy came through the door just then with a glass of water. "Hi, Seth," she added when she spotted him.

"Hi, Clancy. It looks like you're taking good care of your sister."

"Mama said I could come down and be with you in the store, but I knew Hannah needed me here."

"I think you made the right decision," Seth said, watching her climb onto the bed and look at her sister.

"Did you miss us?" Hannah asked, her voice wispy.

"I did. It wasn't very busy this morning, and I missed talking to you."

"I should be better soon," Hannah told him, her small face sincere.

"I hope so. I've been praying for you."

"To God?" Clancy asked, moving closer to him and frowning in concentration.

"Yes."

"Did He hear you?"

"I believe He did, Clancy. It's important to agree with God about the things He wants when we pray, and that's the way I prayed."

"What did you say?" Hannah asked.

"Well, I asked Him to heal you if that was His will, but I also asked Him to help you in other ways," Seth said, not wanting to elaborate. He thought it might be fine with Jessie that the girls go to church, but he wanted to be careful as to when he should tell the girls about what he believed. Thankfully Clancy and Hannah let the topic drop, moving on with amazing speed to the subject of school.

"We go in just a few weeks," Clancy said. "What will I wear?"

"Mama will get us new dresses."

"Does she always get you new dresses?" their father asked.

"Every year," Hannah said.

"Do you get to pick them out, or does she?"

"We get to pick out the color we want," Clancy told him.

"I get blue," Hannah said, and for the first time Seth noticed she was looking very tired.

"I like blue too. Clancy," Seth said to that little girl, "I think we need to let Hannah rest a bit."

"Are you leaving?" Hannah said.

"Aren't you tired?" Seth asked.

Hannah nodded with a head that felt weighted. She was tired, but she was also enjoying hearing Seth talk to her and thinking about school.

"Here you go," Seth stood, bending over her to settle the covers around her. "Sleep for a little while." He kissed her forehead before straightening.

Hannah nodded, and Seth could see she had no choice. Her eyes were already closing, and with a finger to his lips, he ushered Clancy out into the living room. He sat in one of the chairs and brought Clancy close to him. She needed no other invitation. She climbed into his lap.

"Do you want to go down to the store or stay here in case Hannah needs something?"

"I'd better stay until Mama comes."

"That sounds like a good idea. I'll head down so she can come up."

Clancy nodded but made no move to get off his lap. Seth did not want to leave Jessie in the store too long, but he thought that sitting here with Clancy, the smell of dinner filling the room, could be comfortable for a long time.

I love you, Clancy, his heart said. He thought it might be all right to tell her that but feared it was too soon. He looked down at her small head, seeing how content she was to sit with him and hoping she would not grow ill with her sister.

"I'd better get downstairs," he made himself say.

Clancy looked up at him, and Seth tried to read her thoughts. For once she didn't say exactly what she was thinking. Kissing her forehead, much as he had Hannah's, he made himself stand and leave the apartment.

He was on the stairs when Clancy changed her mind and came down with him.

"How is Jeb?" Jessie asked Patience when she came in. She had just seen Becky off, and before her was Bret Toben from the saloon across the street.

"He's doing well. He's not putting weight on the ankle yet, but he's definitely doing better."

"Hannah is sick right now, but we'll be over as soon as she's feeling better."

"Is it what Seth had?"

"It might be. She hasn't complained of a headache."

"I would have thought that Seth would watch things for you so you could be with her," Patience said, voicing her thoughts.

"I just came down here. Hannah wanted to see him."

Patience was impressed, and she could see that Jessie was pleased. For the first time, she began to wonder if Jessie might be willing to give her marriage another try. She didn't dare say this but planned to discuss it with Jeb. Jeb could get away with asking, and she hoped he would.

Jessie, completely unaware of Patience's thoughts, helped her with her order, loaded her basket, and sent her on her way. Not until she was done did she begin to wonder what had happened to Seth. He had been gone a long time, and she was ready to check on Hannah.

She had decided to give him a few more minutes when he came down. Clancy was leading the way, and of course she entered the room talking.

"When do I get my new school dress?"

"How is Hannah?" Jessie asked, ignoring the question.

"She's sleeping," the little girl replied.

Jessie looked to Seth, who nodded.

"How was she doing?"

"She was still pretty warm but wanting to talk. Did you want to head back up?"

"I think I will. I'll come back in a bit so you can have dinner."

"It smelled good," Seth told her.

"Chicken and dumplings."

Seth's eyes went to Jessie's, but she would not look at him. On his part, Seth could not look away. Was there a slight softening in his wife? Was she a little less formal and strained with him? In light of her questions from the night before, this made no sense, but he was seeing something different.

"Chicken and dumplings?" Clancy could not help but hear. "The wet ones?"

"You will try them," Jessie said in a voice that meant business, but Clancy's face told them she was not thrilled.

Jessie went on her way, Clancy at her heels, talking all the while about dumplings and school dresses. Seth had to laugh. If that little girl had anything to do with it, she would find a way to get out of eating those dumplings. Seth knew one thing, however: Clancy was strong, but Jessie was stronger. It would be interesting to see how the meal ended.

Chapter Fifteen

BRI STOOD AT THE edge of the livery and watched her husband work. He hadn't seen her yet, and since a livery could be very unsafe for a woman in a long skirt, she kept her distance until he noticed.

When he did, it was worth it. Rylan Jarvik froze at the unexpected sight of his wife and stared. Moving deliberately, he set his tools down and wiped his hands. Not willing to rush, the big man walked slowly to the other end of the livery, his eyes on her all the while. Bri was blushing by the time he stopped in front of her, causing him to smile.

"Well, now," he said softly. "This is a nice surprise."

"Heather said she needed to get out of the house and came to watch Danny."

"I'll have to thank her."

Bri smiled up at him, looking as pleased as she felt. Rylan bent to kiss her, careful not to touch her with anything but his lips.

"What are you up to?" Rylan asked, having already read the situation.

"Well, since I suddenly have a bit of time, I thought I might walk down to Willow Street and see if I know anyone."

"No," Rylan said without hesitation and with no heat.

"Just for a few minutes," Bri tried again.

Rylan shook his head in denial and also chagrin. Willow Street was the area where Token Creek's most disreputable citizens lived. When she first moved to Token Creek, Bri had not been able to find an apartment and lived on Willow Street. It was not without some serious mishaps, but it had led to three different women turning their lives over to Jesus Christ, all of whom left lifestyles of prostitution. Two of them had left town to start over or return to family. The other was working for the foundry office, met with Bri each week, and never missed a Sunday morning with the church family.

"I haven't been down there for months," Bri tried this time. "And you're working."

"Why don't we go this evening when I'm done," Rylan said, not able to flat-out deny her.

"Heather won't be with Danny then."

"We'll take Danny up to Jeanette's. You know one of them will be free to look after him, and even if they're all busy, Becky will want him."

Bri smiled in pleasure, and Rylan leaned to kiss her again.

"What am I going to do with you?" he said, remembering well her desire to help others while taking little thought to her own needs and safety.

"I don't know." Bri gave her standard answer, her tone always saying something else.

They kissed goodbye, and Rylan stepped outside long enough to watch her walk on her way. Her condition was beginning to be obvious, but other than her waist expanding, she looked very much like she had the day he'd first seen her. Rylan smiled with the memory.

Heather had not forgotten her conversation with Nate, but when he arrived at the shop within an hour of its opening on Wednesday, she was surprised. She was also pleased. She had thought about him a good deal the last few days and realized how kind he had been on Sunday.

"Good morning," Jeanette greeted the town's sheriff, noticing a shirt in his hands.

"Good morning, ladies. Can one of you look at this shirt and tell me if it can be fixed?"

"Certainly," Jeanette said, working not to hand it directly to Heather. That woman had stayed at the sewing machine but turned to see Nate. She was not looking strained, but she didn't seem to be full of words either.

Nate waited only for Jeanette to take the shirt before he turned to address Heather.

"How are you today?"

"I'm doing well. How are you?"

"I'm fine. I can tell that August is over. It feels like fall out there this morning."

"I wore a sweater," Heather said in agreement.

"This one?" Nate asked, pointing to the one on the back of her chair.

"Oh, yes. I forgot I hung it there."

"Did you make it?"

Heather nodded and smiled. "A neighbor taught me how to knit when I was still in my teens."

Nate could not imagine making something like that with his own hands, so for a moment he ran out of words.

"I think I can fix this, Nate," Jeanette spoke up. "Are you in a hurry?"

"No. I can't even remember when I did that, but it's not a very old shirt, and I thought it might be worth fixing."

Jeanette had handed it to Heather, who inspected the tear.

"The fabric is like new," Heather agreed. "I think if we take the pocket off and then fix the hole, we can shift the pocket and hide just about all the seams underneath."

Nate had taken that opportunity to move a little closer. Heather looked up and smiled at him.

"I would appreciate it," he said quietly, looking back at Heather and wondering how anyone could be so sweet.

"We'll let you know as soon as it's done."

"Thank you. Heather," Nate made himself add, "if I came by after supper on Friday night, would you have time to go on a walk with me?"

"I would have time, yes," Heather said.

"Is six-thirty too early?"

"No."

"I'll see you then."

Heather nodded, and Nate bid the ladies goodbye. The shop was quiet on his exit. Heather didn't say anything. She sat and stared at the wall in front of the sewing machine, and Jeanette stared at her.

"Are you all right?" Jeanette asked after a long silence.

"I think so."

"Are you a little afraid?"

"A little. A man's never asked me on a walk."

"Never, Heather?"

Heather shook her head no.

"You've never been out alone with a man?" Jeanette had to ask it another way.

"Never," Heather said simply. "I told you, Jeanette. I'm not the type of woman that men fall for."

"Until now."

Heather laughed at her tone and the way Jeanette's eyebrows rose so high. She went back to sewing with her mind only half on the job.

As the week moved on and Seth went through the daily routine, he found a letter from his brother in the mail. He had kept the last letter he received in this mercantile a secret from his wife. He did not plan to make that mistake again. He slipped it into his pocket. Over supper that evening or in plain view in the living room, he would bring it out and read it. He was still working on the post when Rylan walked in.

"Hello, stranger," the bigger man greeted.

"Hello, yourself. It's good to see you."

"I was hoping you'd feel that way," Rylan said.

Seth laughed before asking why.

"It's occurred to me that with you living at my house, we had plenty of time to talk. I think we need to keep meeting together."

Seth felt relief flood through him. He had so many questions, and much as he enjoyed being with Jessie and the girls, he missed Rylan's calm presence each evening. It had never once occurred to him to ask Rylan if they could meet together.

With all these thoughts running through his mind, Seth simply said, "I would like that."

"Should we try to pick a time or just take each week as it comes?" Rylan asked.

"I think I'd prefer a set time."

"I can manage Monday nights or just about any morning."

Seth had to think about this. He would not have considered a morning meeting had Rylan not mentioned it. They bandied about the time and day, and before Rylan left, the two men had a plan.

When the store was busy, Seth and Jessie were rarely in the same place at the same time, but this Thursday things were a bit quiet. Jessie said she was behind on her orders and spent most of her time at the table in the storeroom poring over catalogs. Seth was not very busy out front, which led him to the storeroom off and on all day. It was for this reason that he knew the exact moment something was wrong. He heard a gasp and then a shuffle and went toward the table.

"Jessie?" Seth said, finding her kneeling on the worktable.

"I think there was a mouse," she whispered, her eyes on the spot.

"Where?" Seth asked, having been through this many years before. His remarkably independent, confident wife was afraid of mice.

"Right there by the rice sacks."

Seth went that way and began to dislodge things. Not only did he not find a mouse, he found no signs of one. He knew it was still too warm for them to be indoors but didn't mention that. He moved and checked everything in the area, Jessie watching him all the while.

"Nothing, Jess," Seth said, going back to her. In the past he might have teased her a little, but not today.

"You're sure?"

"I checked," he stated calmly, his eyes watching her.

It took Jessie a moment to become convinced, and when she looked away from the spot, she found Seth's eyes on hers. It took some seconds to read his look, and then Jessie remembered with him. He used to sit on this table, effectively dropping the difference in their heights, and hold her in his arms and kiss her. It was in the early days, before fights and before Hannah, and the memory was sweet.

Seth made himself look away from Jessie, but much to his chagrin he spotted a box of women's undergarments. His mind didn't need much prompting. His gaze swung back to his wife.

"Do you still wear camisoles?" he asked quietly.

"Yes," Jessie whispered.

"With ribbons?"

Jessie could only nod, and Seth's eyes closed. He took a moment to compose himself and then spoke without looking at her.

"Are you all right about mice now?"

"Yes," Jessie said, even going so far as to get off the table and sit down again, watching her husband all the while. This was the reason she knew he did little more than nod before taking himself back out front to the store.

"What's that?" Clancy asked that evening when she found Seth in the living room with the letter. Hannah had been invited to Deena Rathman's house, and she was still not home.

"This is a letter from my brother."

"You have a brother?"

"Yes. His name is Eliot. He lives in Texas."

Jessie, who had just claimed one of the living room chairs, was all ears, but Seth didn't look at her.

"What does he say?"

"Shall I read it to you?" Seth offered.

Clancy nodded and Seth began.

> Dear Seth,
>
> I thought of you today and knew it was time to write. I think of you most days, but as you know, I rarely put ink to paper. Nate and I were talking today, and he was trying to figure out how God could be forever. Do you remember our discussions about that when we were still in Heywood? I remember how amazed you were. Your mind couldn't take it in. Nate was the same way today, and for the first time I felt the same thing. It was special. I'm glad it hadn't happened before now. Knowing what I know about the cross and forgiveness makes it even more amazing.
>
> How are you doing? Have you seen your wife and daughters? Cassy and I would like to meet them.

"Eliot knows about Clancy?" Jessie cut in softly.

"I wrote to him after I arrived."

"Before or after we talked?"

"Before."

"When you didn't even know if you could stay?"

"Yes. I told him I would write even if I was coming right back on the train."

"Who is Nate?" Clancy asked.

"My brother's son. He would be your cousin."

Clancy looked at her mother, who nodded, her face inscrutable. The little girl looked back to her father, and Seth had to force his eyes away from Jessie.

"Did you want to hear the rest of the letter?"

"Um hm," Clancy said, coming close to look with him as he continued in the same paragraph.

> *How are you doing? Have you seen your wife and daughters? Cassy and I would like to meet them. Have you needed to find work, or are you back at the mercantile? As you can see, I have many questions. Write soon and let me know. Most importantly, did the pastor you wrote about turn out to be a true man of God? Is he helping you?*
>
> *If this does not find you well in your new faith, you know you are welcome here with us as we walk this journey. The church family here is working hard. We are learning to have no regrets and no more wasted years. I hope you can sense my love and prayers for you across the miles.*
>
> *Eliot*

"Eliot prays too?" Clancy asked the moment Seth put the letter down.

"Yes, he does."

These words were no more out of Seth's mouth when they all heard the banging.

"Clancy, please run down and let Hannah in," Jessie said, and then added, "and don't forget to lock the door."

As soon as Clancy exited the apartment, Seth addressed his wife.

"What are we going to do with the fact that I pray and you don't?"

"Do you think it matters all that much?" Jessie asked, not seeing a problem.

"Our believing completely different things is going to eventually be an issue. Maybe not for a long time, but eventually."

"I guess we'll handle it when it happens," Jessie said, her mind still on the letter itself. She knew why Seth read it in the living room. He wasn't trying to hide things, and she found that she appreciated his efforts.

"You're different," Jessie said, even as she heard the girls on the stairs.

"Good different or bad different?"

"Good."

Seth heard the girls as well and had to work not to be frustrated. This was the very thing he wanted to talk to her about, but in a moment they would not be alone. There was nothing slow about Jessie, but Seth wondered about her blindness on some issues. She could see that he had changed but not that their different beliefs were an issue to be addressed now and not later.

"Hey, you," Jessie was saying to Hannah, who came in with a hug for both her parents.

In the next ten minutes, they heard all about her time at the Rathman home. Clancy pouted from time to time until Seth noticed and told her to be done with that. The younger girl responded fairly well, and as before, Jessie did not seem to mind.

"I think it's late enough that you two should wash up for bed," their mother told them.

This was met with loud protests that Seth didn't remember hearing before. He wasn't going to put up with it.

"Girls," he said quietly. He hadn't been sharp or loud, but they both stopped and looked at him. "I want you to obey your mother without arguing."

The faces they made were almost as bad, but they went off without a word. Seth got ready for battle with Jessie, and he was even willing to start. The girls had left the bedroom door open, so he kept his voice low.

"Why do you allow me to do that? Why are you not getting angry at me for stepping in?"

"I've been thinking about that, and I think it's because of Rylan and Bri."

"In what way?"

"Rylan always steps in with Danny, and that little boy is the most obedient toddler I've ever known."

Seth was so surprised by this that for a few moments he couldn't say a word. Was she saying that she wanted him to help? Was she saying she saw value in a father being involved?

"What happened to us, Jessie?" Seth had to ask, his heart aching. "Why did we go from loving each other to fighting all the time?"

"I don't know. You made me so angry."

"What did I do?"

"You wanted to change everything."

"Would that have been so bad?" Seth asked.

"Not from here—not from this side of things—but at the time I couldn't cope with it."

Seth nodded, and for a few moments silence fell between them.

"Are you coming to kiss us?" Hannah called from the bedroom.

Both Seth and Jessie laughed a little but did as they'd done for the past few nights and went to the bedroom to kiss their daughters. It was never a drawn-out affair. Both girls were usually tired, and tonight it was just as fast.

When Jessie shut the door on the girls, Seth stayed on his feet with a question.

"Do you need me to go for a walk tonight?"

"No, but I don't feel very talkative."

Seth nodded and sat as far down the sofa as he could, reaching for the newspaper. He had just started on an article when Jessie spoke.

"Were there many women?"

Seth looked her square in the eye and said, "Yes."

"Right away?" Jessie whispered.

"No, not for a long time."

"But then a lot?"

"One other is too many, Jessie, but I did get involved with other women over the years."

"But not the woman you took?"

"I'm thankful to say she wouldn't let me touch her."

"And then you went to jail," Jessie checked.

"Yes."

"So it's been a long time for you too." It was a statement, not a question.

"Yes." Seth was quiet a moment and then found he had to know as well. "Did you have others?"

"A few times I wanted to, but I could never do that to the girls. I never left them in the evening, and I never wanted anyone enough to bring him up here."

"I'm sorry you've been alone all this time. It's not the way it should have been."

Jessie nodded, not looking angry or upset. As he watched, she turned away from him in her seat. Seth knew that she was *now* done talking.

"A cousin?" Hannah whispered from her pillow when the door was shut.

"That's what Seth said. He told me, and Mama was there."

"What's his name?"

"Nate. And Seth's brother is Ellie."

"Ellie is a girl's name."

"That's what he said!"

"Shh," Hannah shushed her. "You're going to get us in trouble."

"That's what he said," she repeated in a softer tone, and both girls heard footsteps. They lay very still with their eyes closed in case their mother opened the door. She didn't, however, and the girls were able to get in a few more words.

"Seth had a letter. I saw it, and Ellie prays like Seth does."

"To God?"

"I think so."

Hannah had to think about this. Clancy was saying something else, but Hannah was still thinking about Seth and his brother praying. She wished Clancy would stop talking so she could think, and then she didn't hear her anymore. All was quiet. The day was catching up to Hannah, and sleep claimed her.

Chapter Sixteen

"ARE YOU FEELING BETTER, Hannah?" Jeb asked her on Friday evening, as this was the first time he'd seen her.

That little girl nodded, and Jeb smiled at the smile she gave him. There wasn't much to either of the girls, so Jeb was glad to see Hannah back on her feet.

"How are *you* feeling?" Jessie asked her cousin.

"Pretty good. I'm moving around some. The cane helps."

"Are you able to work at all?"

"Some. Mostly sanding, which I can sometimes do without having to stand."

"When does school start?" Patience asked the girls and received the normal response. They talked all over each other in their excitement, and none of the adults had the heart to stop them.

"My dress is blue," Hannah got in finally.

"And mine is green," Clancy said. "It has a piyna-fore."

"Pinafore," Jessie corrected patiently, not sure her youngest would ever get it right.

"What color is the pinafore?" Patience asked and heard all about that.

The adults let the children have the floor for a bit longer, and then

Patience headed to the kitchen to get some cookies. When the girls followed, Jeb had some minutes alone with Jessie.

"How are you doing with Seth living there?" was Jeb's first question.

"It's going well. The girls like him so much."

"And you?"

"I don't mind."

Jeb looked at her. Some of the hardness that had been in her eyes in the past was gone.

"Are you going to fall for him again?" Jeb asked, not sure where this had come from.

"If I do, I'll be the biggest fool in town."

"So you still think he's here to hurt you all?"

"I don't know," Jessie admitted. "He's changed. I can see that, but that doesn't mean he'll stay, and I'll be raising a third child by myself."

Jeb was quite sure that no such thing would happen, but Jessie would never understand why he believed that.

"Where is he tonight?"

"He said he needed to talk to Rylan about something, and I forgot to tell him we were coming here."

"Are you getting along?"

"Is that your way of asking if we're fighting?"

"Yes."

"We're not."

"Why aren't you?" Jeb asked, surprising Jessie into silence. She knew the answer, but it hadn't fully hit her until just now.

"What's the matter?" Jeb went on, hoping he hadn't pushed too far.

"I'm just thinking."

"Then I'll be done asking questions."

"It's all right," Jessie said, truly wanting him to know, but Jeb was finished. He and Jessie talked on a range of other topics, but the older cousin did not continue to press her about Seth. Jeb hoped to catch Seth on Sunday and see how he thought things were going, but for now he just wanted to keep his relationship with Jessie as open as he could. Something had struck her, and he wanted to be wise about how much he pushed in.

Patience and the girls returned with a plateful of cookies and mugs of coffee at just the right time. Jeb began to tell Patience about something that had happened to Meg's folks, and Jessie was more than ready to stop thinking about Seth for a few minutes. The threesome stayed for more than two hours. It was just what the mother of two girls needed.

"Did you see Danny?" This was the first question the girls had for their father on Saturday morning. They had gone to bed before he got home.

"I didn't see him. I went to the house, but no one was home."

"Rylan didn't know you were coming?" Jessie asked. For some reason this was important to her.

"No. I just needed to ask him a question."

"We saw Patience," Clancy cut in. "She gave us cookies."

"That was nice. How is Jeb?"

"He has a cane."

Seth looked to Jessie, who explained how he was healing. The two adults talked about it for several minutes before they both realized the girls were watching them.

"What did you do?" Hannah asked.

"I went for a long walk," Seth said. "It was a nice evening, and I even talked with a man I worked with a long time ago."

"Worked where?" Jessie asked.

"At the foundry. Remember that week?"

Jessie's mouth opened in surprise. "You remembered each other from that long ago?"

"Yes," Seth said on a laugh. "It was a long time ago, but we worked side by side for those days. He still works there. He even said they're hiring, so if you're ready to kick me out, I'll head there."

"Since it's Saturday, I won't do that until at least five o'clock," Jessie told him, willing to tease right back.

Seth's warm gray eyes twinkled at her, and Jessie felt that old, odd sensation in her chest. The girls had to be told that their parents were only kidding about Jessie kicking Seth out, but had Jessie known it, Seth was just about floating.

With Rylan not at home, he had been forced to work out his thoughts on his own, and they had been about Jessie. How should he act? How should he treat her? What did some of the things she said mean?

He knew Rylan would not have all the answers, but he desperately wished he knew how to proceed. The conclusion he came to was to be himself. He still loved his wife and would care for her and act that way. If at some point it seemed she would welcome his love, he would act accordingly on that too.

The same with the girls. He didn't know much about being a father, but he would be a father to them to the best of his ability. Jessie was not fighting him on that issue and that gave him great confidence and hope.

The four of them ended up heading downstairs to the store together. If it was a typical Saturday, they would not stop moving for the next nine hours. In that time he would be more of a store worker than a husband or father, but come evening when they were back upstairs as a family again, he knew that's when his real job would start.

"Will you be warm enough?" Nate asked when Heather stepped outside the door on Saturday evening. She had her sweater with her, but the evenings and nights were cooling fast.

"I think so, but you don't have a jacket," Heather noticed.

"It's a heavy shirt."

"Can you wear whatever you like when you work?" Heather asked. With that the two began to talk about Nate's life in law enforcement.

Heather was a great listener, but at one point Nate realized he was doing all the talking.

"How did your week finish up?" he stopped reporting to ask.

"It was fine. We were busier than I expected, so both of us worked all week."

"Is that normal?"

"It's never the same twice. For several weeks in the summer, Jeanette considered opening even fewer days, but then business picked up again."

The silence between them got a little long this time, and seeing that Heather looked a tad uncertain, Nate decided to be honest about what he was thinking.

"Do I make you nervous, Heather?"

"Well," she said softly, not able to look at him as she admitted this, "I haven't done too much of this."

"Too much of what?"

"Walking with men."

Nate could only stare at her lovely profile and creamy complexion, thinking this was impossible.

"This is my first time," Heather nearly blurted.

Nate came to a halt, much the way Jeanette had. Heather's look became even more uncertain, and every ounce of compassion Nate possessed welled up within him.

"I would never hurt you, Heather, or let anyone else hurt you."

"I think I knew that. Have you..." Heather started, and stopped to clear her throat. "Have you been on many walks?"

"I was married, Heather."

"I didn't know that. Where is your wife?"

"She and our daughter died in a hotel fire."

"I'm sorry, Nate," Heather said, willing herself not to cry. "How awful for you."

"It was awful, but it was also a long time ago. I was just a young man in my early twenties."

There was a bench ahead of them. It sat outside the fence at Mrs.

Kuster's house, and the two sat down. For a time Nate did even more talking. He told about the way he met his wife and how old their daughter would have been today. Heather listened to every word, her head tipped a little to look up into his face.

"There hasn't been anyone else, Heather. It's not that I was against marrying again, but no one was the right one. I think you need to know that I've been noticing you for a long time. I didn't understand why you are the person you are until I understood what you believe. For a long time I just thought you were sweet and kind, but now I know it goes much deeper than that.

"It's a lot to put on you, but I think it only fair for you to know where I stand. I'll never hold it against you if you don't want to take walks with me anymore. Or if you need to think about some of what I've said. I'll understand completely."

"I didn't know you were interested. Becky told me."

"How did she know?"

"She said she saw you. I don't know what she meant."

Nate had to smile.

"Are you wanting to laugh?"

"Not laugh exactly, but it's not often that I meet someone so inexperienced."

"What do you mean?"

"I've been throwing myself in your way for months, but you never noticed my interest."

"Why couldn't I see it?" Heather asked, searching her mind for the times he'd done that and coming up blank.

"I don't know if you knew what to look for."

"Why do some women?"

"They must have experienced that type of interaction some other place."

"I told Jeanette that I'm not the type of woman that men fall for. I think that must be why."

"Could it be that men have been interested and you never knew?"

The look of surprise on Heather's face caused Sheriff Nate Kaderly to laugh. His head went back as the laughter burst out of him. Heather laughed a little with him, shaking her head and trying to make sense of it all, but it was Nate who spoke when he got his breath back.

"Well, for myself I'm glad no one else gained your notice."

"You're really interested in me?" Heather had to ask, slightly amazed.

"I'm really interested."

"I don't know much about this," Heather began.

"I'm not going to rush you."

"You'll probably get tired of explaining what everything means."

Nate had to smile at her again. Heather smiled too, but Nate could also read the chagrin in her eyes. They eventually continued their walk, and Nate was good at his word. With no thoughts to rush her in any way, they simply talked about themselves. Nate had her home long before dark, and before he left Jeanette's ornate front porch, he asked if he could see her again. Heather said yes.

"How are you?" Bri asked Jessie on Sunday afternoon. The pastor's wife had made a deliberate effort to go over to see her friend, and the two were on a walk.

"I'm all right. A little confused at times."

"Confused about what?"

"Seth and me."

"Your own feelings, or what you think he's feeling?"

"Both, I think. I was all ready to hate him and keep him at arm's length, but I don't feel that way anymore, and I don't know why."

"Are you saying that you would welcome a relationship with him?"

"I don't know," Jessie said slowly, and then all but snapped. "See, Bri, it's even that! When he first came back I would have said no as fast as I could get that word out of my mouth, but now I'm actually considering it!"

"What are you more afraid of—that he'll leave or that he'll stay for the next 40 years?"

Jessie stopped and looked at her friend. It was a good question. If he stayed, things would not look the way she planned. Was she all right with that? She had never planned to be alone forever, but she was going to wait until the girls were older before she made room for a man in her life. Now her husband was back, the man who walked out on her, and she wasn't able to hate him. Everything was changing.

"Did I ask the wrong question?" Bri tried this time. Jessie had stopped as though she had something to say but then was quiet.

"No, but I don't have an answer. I had things somewhat planned out in my mind. I thought I knew what my life would look like. Having Seth here changes it all."

"And what exactly do you object to, Jessie? Is it just because he left you, or is some of it who he is now?"

"What do you mean?"

"Well, he's not the same man, is he? Can you love this man?"

"That's just the problem, Bri. I think I could love him so easily. I'm still angry at him at times, but I didn't expect to be this drawn."

"Tell me why that's such a bad thing. Is it because of his faith in God?"

"No," Jessie said with a shrug. "That doesn't bother me."

"What do you have against God, Jessie?" Bri asked in a completely nonthreatening voice. "I don't think I've ever asked you."

"I just don't think He exists."

"How did all of this and all of us come into being?"

"Not everything can be explained, Bri. Some things just are."

"But you have such respect for Rylan, and you know he believes very strongly in God. Why is he the man he is?"

"He was just raised well, the way I'm trying to do with my girls."

"But what about Seth? What changed him?"

Jessie was at a loss there. He was something of a mystery to her. Since he'd come back, he'd displayed tendencies of patience and kindness she didn't think were possible. He had been patient and kind in the past, but only to a point. This time he was taking everything she threw at him without so much as a hint of retaliation or irritation.

"You didn't know me before, Jessie," Bri said quietly when the silence lengthened. "If you want to hear my whole story, I'll tell you. I'm living proof that God can completely change a person. You and I would not have a friendship if it weren't for God's intervention in my life."

This was not the first time Bri had hinted at this topic. In the past Jessie told herself that Bri had never done a thing wrong in her life, but that was foolish. Bri had lived most of her life in Denver, and Jessie knew nothing about that time.

"I would like to hear it sometime, Bri."

"Certainly, Jessie," Bri agreed, knowing that now was not the time. "Just let me know."

The women didn't stay out much longer, but when Bri left Jessie at the back door of the store, Jessie stood outside on her own for a few minutes. It had just occurred to her that good people cared for her. Jeb had checked with her on Friday. Now Bri had made a specific visit to check on her.

It also did not escape her notice that these two folks believed in God. Jessie shook her head a little. Was it possible to be wrong after all these years? Had her father been wrong? What about her mother? Jessie didn't know what that woman believed. She was not sure if Maryann Wheeler had ever said.

Jessie knew if she kept this up she would have a headache, and that was the last thing she needed. She was living with a man who was her husband in name only, and she had two girls whose lively minds were a lot of work. Jessie deliberately put all other thoughts aside and went indoors to her family.

"Was it any problem to come this morning?" Rylan asked Seth when he let him into the house early Tuesday morning.

"No. I told Jessie last night that I wouldn't be around until the store opened. If Bri hadn't come on Sunday to see her, she might not have understood, but I think she just sees this as one friend checking on another." Seth's mouth quirked a little before he added, "When she finds out I want to do this every week, she might not understand, but for the moment it's fine."

"Why wouldn't she understand?" Rylan asked as the men got comfortable in the living room.

"Jessie doesn't ask for a lot of help. For extra hands in the store, yes, but not for personal things. I think the only reason she ever has input is because others check in with her."

This made complete sense to Rylan. Bri had been checking on Jessie since their friendship began, but Seth was right, Jessie didn't appear to need anyone. He was thankful that this was not the case with Seth. That man was humble and honest about what he didn't know.

The two prayed together and then talked about the sermon. Seth stayed for more than an hour, but managed to be on time when the store opened. He started work thinking about the letter he needed to write to his brother. It was an amazing thing to be able to assure Eliot that someone in Token Creek was looking out for him and that the pastor he remembered was still a blameless man of God.

"Hold still," Jessie said to Clancy on the first day of school. That little girl was getting her hair brushed and could barely contain herself.

"When do we eat?" Clancy asked Hannah. "I can't remember."

"At noon."

"Where is our dinner tin?"

"You'll have it," Jessie said patiently. "Hold still, please."

"Seth," Hannah went to the man watching all of this in silence and asked, "are you going to walk with us?"

"I would like that," he said. "Does your mother usually take you?"

"Just on the first day. She puts a sign on the door."

Seth's eyes swung to Jessie, who only glanced at him and kept brushing. He had never known her to do this, and his expression said as much.

"It happens once in a while," she said, her tone not inviting further comment, but Seth found himself smiling. "You think you know so much, Seth Redding, but you've been gone a long time," Jessie added.

"True," he agreed, his tone affable. "Very true."

Jessie fought the smile that threatened her own mouth and finished Clancy's hair. Had the girls not been distracted by their thoughts of school, they would have wanted to know exactly what was going on, but this time the adults got away with it.

"All right, girls, do you have everything?" Jessie asked, her eyes scanning them for every detail.

"Do I have to walk home with Hannah?" Clancy asked.

"Yes. Stay with her all the way back to the store."

"What if Clara wants to walk with me?"

"As long as Hannah is with you, that's fine."

"But sometimes Hannah walks with Vera, and Clara is littler like me."

"Clancy," Seth spoke up. "You're worrying about a lot of things, and the day hasn't even started. Plan to obey your mother. After you've walked with Hannah a few days, you can ask questions about changes you want to make."

"I think about things," she said, her voice not demanding and expectant as it often was.

"Yes, you do, and most of the time that's good, but sometimes you worry, and that's not good."

"Will you pray for us today, Seth?" Hannah came close to ask.

"Yes, I will," he said, smoothing the hair away from her face. "You look very pretty, Hannah."

"Do I look pretty?" Clancy asked, voice back in full form.

"Yes, you do. You both look ready to start school."

"And read," Clancy said, her frown in place.

Neither parent responded to this, but both smiled. Moments later they started toward the schoolhouse.

"Are you all right?" Seth asked when they were far enough away from the schoolhouse not to be heard.

"Why do you ask?"

"You just look a little sad."

Jessie didn't say anything. She wasn't used to having an adult around who could read each nuance. She was sad, but she didn't know why. The girls were excited, and she would not lack things to do until they arrived home.

On Seth's part, he let it go. She didn't answer him, which could mean any number of things. He didn't think she was upset with him, but on the chance that his question felt intrusive, he kept his peace.

"Why did you ask that?" Jessie suddenly asked again.

"You just looked a little pensive."

Jessie didn't stop walking, but she had slowed quite a bit. Seth matched his longer steps to her shorter ones and waited, shooting the occasional glance in her direction.

"I don't know why," Jessie said, and Seth knew she meant it. "It just feels odd, as if part of me is missing."

"The store will certainly be different," Seth commented, having just realized how much this would affect him. He wished he had the right words for Jessie, but he didn't.

"I'm always ready to see them at three o'clock," she added.

"Is that when they come?"

"About that time, yes."

The store came into view just then, and Seth asked a question that had been on his mind since he returned.

"What happened to your dream to build a house?"

Jessie laughed before saying, "Who has time?"

"Is that all that's stopping you?"

"Isn't that enough?"

They reached the store and the conversation was dropped, but enough had been said. A solid plan was forming in Seth's mind.

Chapter Seventeen

"WHAT IF HE DOESN'T like what we're fixing?" Heather said to Becky on Monday afternoon.

"He'll like it," Becky said in her unflappable way.

"How do you know?"

"He's a bachelor. He'll like anything."

At just about any other time Heather would have laughed, but at this moment it was lost on her. She went to work on the dining room table, hours too early, wanting it to be just right. She had taken another walk with Nate on Friday evening and then seen him the day before at church. Jeanette had asked him to supper tonight, and Heather suddenly found herself all nerves. At some point she got ahold of herself and made herself calm down, but it didn't last long. Nate Kaderly was coming to supper, and Heather didn't know the last time she'd been so excited.

"I walked with Hannah" were the first words from Clancy's mouth to her mother.

"I'm glad. How was your day?"

Seth hung back and listened to the girls talk to their mother. He was fairly certain he was seeing their daily routine. Jessie had come up front to work at about quarter to three. A woman had come in looking for something, and Jessie only directed her to the aisle, holding her place at the front. When the girls came through the front door, she was right there. Everyone hugged, and much as Seth would have enjoyed being part of it, he enjoyed watching as well.

"My seat is by Deena's," Hannah said.

"That must be fun. Did you talk when you weren't supposed to?"

"Only once."

"I didn't learn to read," Clancy said, a small frown in place.

"Well," Jessie said slowly, fighting laughter, "I think it might take more than one day."

"Our teacher is reading *Black Beauty* to us," Hannah put in. "I like it."

Without warning, the girls turned to Seth. They told him everything they'd told their mother, and it was Jessie's turn to watch. She expected to feel a little jealous over sharing them, but she didn't. It was just as fun to watch them as it was to be a part of it, and if the truth be told, the look on Seth's face made it all worthwhile.

He loved his daughters. There would be no way to miss this fact. They had climbed onto the counter, and he put his arms on the counter to lean close to their faces as they talked. As usual the girls' words tumbled all over each other, and it was fun for Jessie to see how she must look to Seth as she tried to follow each one.

"What was your favorite part?" Seth asked just as a man came into the store. He saw that Jessie was taking care of him and stayed with the girls. "Wait a minute," he had to cut back in. "Hannah, you go first."

"I like sitting by Deena. She's nice."

"I don't think I know her."

"She goes to church," Hannah informed him, as though this explained everything. "I'm going to ask Mama if she can come and play."

"That would be fun. Okay, Clancy, what was your favorite part?"

"We get to play outside after dinner. I ran with Clara, but she was faster."

"Is she older?"

"A little, I think."

"Where do you eat dinner, outside or at your desk?"

"Outside, as long as we eat before we play."

"And what's your teacher's name?"

Seth had to laugh when it started them both again. He knew at some point they were going to have to be taught not to interrupt each other, but for the moment, this was simply too much fun.

Heather went to the front door for the third time to see if he was coming. Becky kept on with her work, which included a huge effort not to laugh. Heather had helped with most of the meal, but for right now Becky was on her own. Jeanette came down to find Heather looking tense, and for a moment Becky stopped to listen.

"How are you?" Jeanette asked.

"I'm fine," Heather said with her mouth, but nothing else about her agreed. Jeanette took pity on her and didn't say anything else. As it was, they were out of time. The man himself was at the door, and Heather looked like she was going to faint. Thankfully Nate was a man of keen awareness, and he saw instantly that Heather was not relaxed.

"How was your day?" he asked when he'd been let inside. Jeanette and Becky had greeted him but then moved toward the dining room.

"It was fine," Heather said, but her voice was pitched higher than usual. "How was yours?"

Nate smiled before saying, "Fine. Tell me something, Heather. Are you worried about my being here?"

"A little," she said, obviously embarrassed.

"What did you think would be a problem?"

"It occurred to me that you might not like the food," Heather answered truthfully, but she was mentally adding to the list, *or my dress and hair.*

"I'll like it," Nate said with a surety that Heather could not miss. It immediately brought her out of herself.

"How can you be so sure?"

"Because I've tasted my own cooking and enough of Becky's to know what I'm in for."

Heather smiled, relaxing a little more.

"That's better," Nate said, wanting to take her hand but resisting.

"I suppose I was being silly."

"No, you weren't. Just kind."

The two shared another smile, and this time Heather's was real. She led the way to the dining room, believing for the first time that this was a good idea.

As for Nate, he thought if he had to wait much longer to tell this woman that he loved her, he was not going to survive. He made himself concentrate on the meal and the wonderful company, all the while reminding himself that Heather was worth any amount of time he needed to wait.

"Well, Seth, come on in," Rylan invited on Monday night when he found him at the front door.

"Thank you, but I've just come with a question. Hi, Bri."

"Hi, Seth. Can you sit down?"

"Thank you, but I need to keep moving if I'm going to be home before the girls go to bed."

"Go ahead, Seth," Rylan invited. "Ask your question."

"Thank you. Who builds houses in town?"

"Chas Vick."

Seth frowned before saying, "I thought he built furniture like Jeb."

"No, Chas builds houses."

Seth smiled before saying, "That's perfect."

"Are you building?" Rylan asked, smiling at Seth's expression.

"If I have anything to say about it, but I have to get around Jessie."

Rylan laughed. "That should be fun."

"We'll see," Seth said before thanking the Jarviks and heading on his way. He was pretty sure he knew which house belonged to the Vicks and wasted no time getting there. This would be his fourth stop of the night. He hoped after this he would have something to tell Jessie.

"Thank you for supper," Nate said to Jeanette and Becky.

"You're welcome, Nate. We hope you'll join us again."

"I'd like that," he said before the women took their leave. In a matter of seconds it was just he and Heather. "Would you like that?" he asked the woman in front of him.

"For you to join us again? Yes."

Nate looked at her, wanting to say what was on his mind but not sure how. Something had happened tonight. He didn't know exactly what, but Heather was looking at him differently.

"You look like you want to say something," Heather said when the silence lengthened.

"I was just thinking about the evening. I had a good time."

"I did too. You fit in with us very well," Heather said, laughing a little. "I hope that wasn't an insult."

"I'm not insulted at all. My men probably wouldn't believe I could enjoy such an evening, but I do."

"Have you told anyone that we take walks?" Heather asked, her term for seeing this man.

"Rylan and I talk about it, but I've not spoken to anyone else about it. How about you?"

"Just Jeanette and Becky, mostly Becky."

"Is Becky a help?"

"She's very practical."

"Let me guess. She tells you to relax and enjoy yourself."

Heather smiled. "That just about sums it up."

"And have you been able to do that?"

"I think so. I tried very hard tonight."

"Why do you suppose it's so hard?" Nate asked innocently, only to have Heather's eyes grow huge.

"Men are so hard! I don't know anything about them. You've been married, but I don't know a thing!"

Nate had never seen her quite so animated. The longing to take her into his arms and kiss her almost got the best of him, but he held off.

"I'm glad you told me," Nate said, thinking the words sounded inadequate.

He knew they were inadequate when Heather looked uncomfortable, her eyes dropping to the floor. Only then did Nate decide to act. He picked up her hand and held it, watching to make sure he wasn't overstepping. The way Heather's eyes met his and softened did much for his heart. He kept her hand in his and spoke.

"Walk me to the door?"

Heather nodded, her mind centered on the hand holding hers. They walked slowly through Jeanette's large home and finally arrived at the front door.

"I have to work tomorrow night, but I'll come on Wednesday to the shop to see you."

"I'll watch for you."

"Goodnight, Heather," Nate said, giving her hand a squeeze.

"Goodnight, Nate."

Nate grabbed his hat and was out the door just seconds later, but Heather didn't move. She stood by the door, working to take in the new things she was feeling. She even looked down at her hand, still able to feel Nate's. She didn't join Becky in the kitchen until that woman came to check on her, and even then she had very little to say.

"Where were you?" Clancy asked Seth as her parents came to the bedroom to tuck the girls into bed. Seth had been home for only about ten minutes.

"I had some business I needed to attend to."

"Where?" Clancy pressed.

"A few different places."

"Did you and Hannah wash your faces?" Jessie asked to divert the child. She was just as curious, but clearly Seth was not going to say where he'd been.

"Yes," the girls chorused.

"Do you kiss?" Clancy asked suddenly.

"We used to," Jessie said calmly, not looking at Seth, whose eyes had gone directly to her. "We haven't for a long time."

"Why don't you now?" Hannah asked next.

"Well, Seth and I haven't seen each other for a long time, and sometimes waiting is best."

"Pastor Rylan and Bri kiss," Clancy informed her mother. "I've seen them."

"Yes, they do," Jessie agreed, sounding quite calm.

"Will you kiss again?" Hannah asked.

"Maybe we will," Jessie said, her voice still calm. "If we decide we want that, we'll tell you, but you should not ask again."

Jessie kissed both girls goodnight and then moved so Seth could get to them. He took his time, kissing them gently, his heart feeling things he didn't know how to process.

"Sleep well," he said to them. "I'll see you in the morning."

"Are you going to Pastor Rylan's?"

"Not tomorrow," Seth said, glad that Hannah had asked. "I'll be here."

"Next time will you tell us?"

"I will tell you if you want me to. Goodnight, girls."

The lantern was blown out, and Seth and Jessie left the room. Seth waited only until the door was shut to speak.

"Did you anticipate that question?"

"Oh, yes," Jessie said, a small hint of laughter in her voice. "How?"

"I just know my daughters, and I knew it would come up."

"What did you mean by your answer?"

"Just what I said," Jessie spoke the words from the sofa she'd sat on. Seth took a chair, debating his next question. The couple looked at each other for long moments.

"Do we know what we're doing?" Seth had to ask.

Jessie did not immediately answer. When she did her voice was thoughtful. "I think with the girls we do but not with each other."

Seth nodded his head in agreement before asking, "You don't always know what to do with me, do you?"

Jessie looked surprised but admitted that she didn't.

"I think at times I'm still angry with you."

"And trust comes hard after what I've done."

"I don't plan to hold that against you forever," Jessie said, frowning a little and not looking at him.

"Might you want a relationship with me again, or do you know right now that you never will?"

"What made you ask that?"

"I can't always read the situation. Sometimes it seems like you might be giving me a chance, and other times you keep me away."

"What do you want?" Jessie asked, not willing to admit how confused her thinking was these days.

"I wish I'd never left," Seth admitted quietly, his eyes holding hers.

Jessie had all she could do to keep her mouth shut. Why in all of their conversations had this not occurred to her? She scrambled for something to say and only one thing came to mind.

"What about this thing you have with God? I thought you'd be glad of that."

"I am glad of that, but I believe that God would have found me in Token Creek," Seth said, successfully hiding his surprise that she would even ask. "My conversion might not have looked the same way, but not for a moment am I glad that I left you and the girls the way I did."

Jessie had nothing to say. In her heart she knew this, but the truth of it had not really sunk in. Without warning she knew why she had never entertained these thoughts. It softened her toward her husband. It made her more forgiving and willing to allow him in. When this happened the fear always followed, the fear that as soon as she let him get close, he would crush her again.

"Are you all right?" Seth asked, having watched her struggle.

"Yes," Jessie answered too swiftly, and Seth knew the conversation was over. He had no idea what he'd said or what she'd realized, but a wall had appeared between them. Seth reached for the newspaper, but he didn't see many of the words. He prayed for Jessie, and he prayed for himself. He knew only God could fix his marriage.

"Is something wrong?" Jessie asked, finding Seth at the rear of the storeroom. He'd headed into that room as soon as the girls left and had been there quite a while. When she checked on him, she found him just standing and looking out the window.

"No," Seth said without turning. "I'm just looking at these lots out here."

Not able to help herself, Jessie joined him. Seth spoke as soon as she did.

"This would be a great place for a house."

Jessie turned her head to look up at him, but Seth didn't look at her. His eyes scanned the lots outside and the placement of the other houses, his mind planning and thinking. Not for a few more seconds did he look at her.

"Don't you think?"

Jessie looked out the window again, wondering what he was seeing. The lots were convenient to the store; that was certainly true. The girls sometimes even played out there. She was about to speculate aloud as to who might own them when they both heard someone come in the front.

"I'll get that," Seth said congenially and headed that way.

Jessie turned to watch him leave, wondering what she had just been witnessing.

"I'm going to be out tonight," Jessie told Seth before the girls got home from school a few days later. "I'm going to see Jeb and Patience, but if the girls know, they'll not understand why they can't come."

"Are Jeb and Patience planning on your visiting tonight?"

"No, I'm just dropping in."

"Why not go now before the girls get here?"

Jessie stared at him. Not be here when the girls arrived home? Could she do that? But he was right. It would make things easier.

On Seth's part, he wanted to ask Jessie why she let the girls have so much control over her actions. Having to sneak off to the Dorns' so they wouldn't want to come was ridiculous to him. He felt she needed to tell her daughters exactly where she was going and then expect them to be perfectly content with not always accompanying her.

"If I do that, what will you tell them?" Jessie asked next.

"That you've gone to visit the Dorns," Seth said simply.

"Good luck with that."

"Jessie," Seth began, his voice not harsh, "I think their expectations need to change. They can't expect to do everything you do and know everything you know. They need to be more thankful for what they have."

"You make them sound impossible," Jessie said, her face showing she wasn't happy with him.

"That was not my intent."

Jessie blinked, not expecting this, but still said, "What was your intent?"

"That they not run your life. And also that they see themselves as the children they are, which sometimes means they don't know everything and they don't get to go all the places their parents go."

Jessie thought if she had one more revelation in her life, she would scream, but he was right. Most of the time she did treat them like equal adults, and in turn they acted that way.

"Let me know if you want me to watch things while you're gone or stay with the girls tonight," Seth said as he moved away.

Jessie watched him a moment and then glanced at the clock. She would go see Jeb and Patience now, at least see if they were home, and when she arrived back... The thought came to a halt in her mind. When she arrived back, the girls would be unhappy with her for not waiting for them.

Not wanting to think about it anymore, Jessie told Seth she was leaving. She would deal with the maelstrom when it happened.

Jeanette stared at Heather after Nate left, wondering if her friend knew how much Token Creek's sheriff cared. The shop proprietress had just watched the two of them talk, and Jeanette knew that she had just witnessed a man in love. She thought Heather might be on her way there as well, but also that it was all new to her.

"Are you all right?" Heather asked.

"Oh," Jeanette said, not sure what she was supposed to be doing. "Yes, I'm fine."

"You looked a little upset."

"No, just thinking. Do you enjoy it when Nate visits?"

Heather's smile was softer than usual. "I do enjoy it, very much."

Jeanette smiled at her.

"What are you thinking about?" Heather said, seeing the sparkle in her friend's eye.

"You and Nate. I'm wondering if there's going to be a wedding."

All Heather's euphoria evaporated; she looked worried. She said in a quiet voice, "Jeanette, I don't know if Nate wants to be married again. He doesn't say things like that, and I would never want to pressure him."

"Nate was married before?"

"Yes, many years ago. He's a widower."

"I'm sorry to hear that, Heather. Do you feel that he hasn't gotten over his first wife?"

"No, I don't think that's it, but I don't like to presume anything either."

Once again Jeanette was reminded of how inexperienced Heather was. The man who had just visited the shop was not there out of casual feelings. Jeanette would be amazed if Nate hadn't already considered marriage to Heather. In Jeanette's mind, if he hadn't talked about it, it was probably because he wasn't sure of Heather's feelings, not because he doubted his own.

"If he did wish to marry," Jeanette tried this time, "would you consider it, Heather?"

"I think so. I can't imagine that happening, so it's a little hard."

Jeanette was ready to ask exactly what she meant by that, but Ingrid Stillwell chose that moment to come into the shop. She was looking to buy only thread, but as it worked out, the women were not alone for more than a few minutes the rest of the afternoon.

"Your mother's beliefs?" Patience questioned Jessie when the two were comfortable in the living room. Jeb was not home just then, but Patience expected him back soon.

"Yes. Do you remember if she believed differently from my father?"

"About God or other things, Jessie?"

Jessie wanted to know about her mother's belief, or lack of it, in God, but she couldn't ignore this question and asked, "What else are you thinking of?"

"I thought you might have been referring to the way your father ran the store or raised you."

Jessie thought about this a moment and suddenly realized why Patience would need clarification. Her parents had argued on nearly every issue from the running of the store to the way she was handled, just to name two.

"Jessie?" Patience said, wondering if she'd misspoken.

"I'm just thinking. I'm sorry."

"It's all right. Why don't you tell me what's going on?"

"I don't know," Jessie admitted, knowing that coming here was not normal, not like this. "Maybe I just needed to get out of the store for a time."

"Are you and Seth having trouble?"

Jessie's laugh was mirthless before saying, "That's just it. He's kind and attentive and treats the girls and me very well."

"And you expected different?"

"Yes. He doesn't say a word about the way I run the store or try to change a thing. He goes along with nearly everything I say."

"And that means what?"

"That he's changed."

Patience looked into the younger woman's face and saw many things, but mostly fatigue. She waited for Jessie to speak again, but she just sat there. Patience prayed and debated what to do, but before she could decide, Jessie's head was nodding. When the mercantile owner dropped off to sleep, Patience moved to the door that Jeb would enter. She wanted to catch him before he made too much noise. It seemed that Jessie needed answers, but she also needed sleep.

Chapter Eighteen

"HOW WILL SHE GET in?" Hannah asked when she watched her father lock the store for the night.

"She'll come to the back door and knock, and we'll let her in."

Hannah stared that way, but Seth's voice stopped her.

"We're going upstairs to see what we can find for supper."

"But Mama," Hannah began, Clancy next to her.

"What did I tell you, Hannah?" Seth began to repeat his speech from earlier in the afternoon.

"Not to ask."

"That's right, and I don't want you to worry either. She'll be back when she gets here, and she'll find us working hard on supper and doing fine. Upstairs now."

The girls clearly didn't want to obey, and for a moment they stood there. Seth's brows rose, and they got the message. On the way upstairs, however, he looked at their small backs and heads and felt no end of compassion. This was not common for them. Coming home from school to find their mother missing and then still gone more than two hours later was almost more than they could take.

"Okay, girls, I really need your help," Seth said as soon as they entered the apartment, hoping they would be excited about working on supper together. "What do I do with this stuff your mother has in the pot here on the stove?"

"Don't you know?" Clancy asked, her brow furrowed.

"No, I'm afraid not. What would your mother do?"

"Is it very hot or just a little hot?" This came from Hannah.

Seth swiftly touched the side of the pot.

"A little hot."

"Build up the fire," Hannah said. "Clancy and I will set the table. Get the bread, Clancy."

They weren't overly excited, but they were cooperating, possibly from hunger. The whole room smelled delicious.

When they sat down to eat 15 minutes later, Seth had nothing but praise for them. He watched them relax under his approval, and they even asked him about prayer after he gave thanks for the food. Seth was also starting to wonder what had happened to Jessie, but for the moment he and the girls were getting along.

"I can't believe I fell asleep," Jessie kept saying to her hosts, her hand on the knob.

"Your life is wearing you out, Jessie," Jeb said with compassion. "Are you sure you found out what you wanted to know?"

Jessie looked at him, still trying to work the sleep from her brain, but she had learned what she'd come to ask. "I didn't expect to remember so much so fast," she admitted, having just told them some of the things she'd recalled from her childhood. "Something Patience said brought it all back."

"You know where to come if there's anything else we can do."

Jessie thanked Jeb and slipped out the door. Walking home she realized she'd never fallen asleep at someone's house before. If she didn't know better, she'd have suspected she was pregnant.

A moment later her mind was solely on the girls and what they must think. Jessie walked swiftly home and went to the back door. She banged twice when she found it locked and was not surprised when Seth came swiftly.

"Are you all right?" he asked quietly.

"I'll tell you later," Jessie said, already moving toward the stairs. "How are the girls?"

"Fine, but missing you."

"Mama!" both girls cried when they saw her from the top of the stairs.

"Hi," Jessie said, scooping them both up for a hug. Four arms tried to strangle her, and all she could do was laugh.

"We made supper."

"Good girls! Did you leave some for me?"

"Yes! Your place is all set."

"With coffee!"

"Don't get overly excited about the coffee," Seth said behind her, and Jessie threw a smile over her shoulder.

The evening progressed in the usual fashion from there, but Seth sensed a need in Jessie. As soon as the girls saw their mother, they relaxed and became normal again, which meant both parents were busy with questions and games until bedtime. Seth knew, however, that as soon as the girls were down, Jessie had something to say.

As they came from the bedroom, Seth wondered how the conversation would start, but Jessie was ahead of him. She took the sofa and spoke in a thoughtful voice.

"You have turned my whole world upside down, Seth Redding. I can't even think straight."

Seth didn't know what to say. This was the last thing he expected. He was on the verge of offering to move out when she went on.

"I didn't even spend that much time talking to Jeb or Patience. I went over there and fell asleep. They woke me after two hours."

"Were you feeling sick?" Seth asked with real concern.

"No, I'm just worn out from everything."

"Take the day off tomorrow," Seth offered. "Lie around here in the apartment or go back to Meg's."

"It's not the store, Seth," Jessie said.

"I'll go, Jessie. I'll explain to the girls in the morning, and I'll go back to Rylan's until I can find a place."

Seth was startled to see tears in his wife's eyes. It was so unusual that for a moment he didn't know what to do. When she still didn't speak, he tried once again. "Please tell me what I can do for you, Jessie. Please tell me how to help you."

A sob broke in her throat at that point, and Seth could no longer keep his distance. He had been sitting on the chair but now moved to the sofa and took Jessie very carefully into his arms, expecting her to pull away at any moment. He was wrong. Jessie turned her face into his chest and cried.

Seth held her without pressure, one arm holding her close, his free hand gently rubbing her back. Jessie had taken hold of the front of his shirt and showed no signs of moving. She cried for some time and then just lay against him, her cheek against his chest. Seth didn't speak. Much came to mind, but he kept it all to himself.

"You still smell good," Jessie said after a long silence, her voice rough from the tears.

"So do you."

"If I let something happen, I'd be raising a third baby by myself."

"No, you wouldn't," Seth argued without heat, "but we still can't let anything happen until we work out how we feel about each other."

Jessie tipped her head back and looked up at him. Seth knew he would kiss her—maybe even that night—but not yet, not until he knew what she was thinking.

"Why did you cry?" he asked.

"I don't know if I know."

"Does it have something to do with seeing Jeb and Patience?"

"I went to find out what my mother believed, and Patience said something that got me to thinking about both of my parents."

"Bad memories?"

"Yes," Jessie said, not wanting to admit she had realized she was just like her difficult father.

"Then what happened?"

"That's when I fell asleep."

Seth pushed her head back against his chest. If she kept looking up at him, they were going to start kissing, and at the moment that was sure to lead to more.

"Why have you let me back into your life?" Seth asked.

Jessie sighed before saying, "At first it was for the girls, but lately it's been for me too. It's nice to have someone else who knows the store like I do."

"Do you think I'm leaving again?"

"I don't know. I know you don't plan on it, but still it happened once before."

Seth just held her, not sure what to say. He wanted to know more about her conversation with Patience and if any of it led to talk about Jessie's beliefs, but he had no idea how to ask.

Without warning he felt Jessie's hands on his face. He looked down to find her looking up at him again. The first kiss was tentative; the second a little more familiar. From there they grew urgent with need as old memories surfaced. They were wrapped in each other's arms when they both heard a thud and a small cry.

"That's Clancy," Jessie said breathlessly. "She's fallen out of bed."

Seth could hardly think straight, but Jessie was already on the move. She rose from the sofa and went to the bedroom. Seth kept his place in the living room. It was not a good time for interruptions. His mind tried to tell him that maybe it was for the best, but he couldn't quite believe it. Jessie came back and didn't immediately join him on the sofa. They stared at each other before Seth spoke.

"Is Clancy all right?"

"Yes. She does that every once in a while and doesn't even fully wake up."

They continued to stare at each other, and when Jessie kept her place by the wall, Seth rescued her.

"Do you need to get some sleep?"

"I think I do," Jessie agreed, no longer tired but seeing the offer for the lifeline it was.

"I'll see you in the morning."

Jessie nodded and almost left, but suddenly feelings of insecurity covered her.

"Are you angry with me?"

"No. Why would I be?"

"I started something and now I'm walking away."

Seth nodded slowly before saying, "We both know what would have happened tonight had Clancy stayed in bed. Maybe we need to both decide if that's what we want right now."

"What if only one of us wants that right now?"

"Then that other person will have to care enough to wait."

It was not the reply she expected, but then lately nothing was. Jessie said goodnight and went into the bedroom. Seth stayed where he was and tried not to remember how wonderful it had been to hold her. After a time he blew the lantern out and went to bed, but sleep was a long time in coming.

"Good morning," Seth said when he came from the bedroom the next morning.

"Good morning," Jessie returned, working on coffee. Her back was to him, but that didn't stop his next move. He came up and put an arm around his wife's shoulders.

"How are you?"

For just a split second Jessie stiffened, but then she heard his tone and realized the arm around her was undemanding. She turned her head to look at him and found his eyes on her.

"I'm doing fine. Are you all right?"

"I think so. I hope we can keep talking."

"And kissing?" Jessie asked.

"That was my next question. Are you telling the girls?"

Jessie looked into his eyes and felt herself melt. She should have been angry and scolding herself for her weakness, but instead she saw the truth for what it was. The kiss was going to happen again, and if Clancy stayed in bed this time, she wouldn't be sleeping with the girls.

Seth saw the answer in her face and bent enough to kiss her temple. Jessie could not stop the sigh that escaped her.

"I hate myself for wanting you," she admitted.

"It's not a weakness to want a relationship with the man who never should have left."

Jessie knew she would have to think about that. At the same moment they both heard small feet hitting the floor. Seth leaned down long enough to kiss her cheek, his hand tenderly caressing her back before he stepped completely away. Jessie, however, kept watching him. Her daughters came from the bedroom at the same time she faced the truth: She was still in love with Seth Redding.

"Mama," Danny Jarvik said quietly and a little tearfully.

"It's all right," his father said. "You don't need to cry. Mama is still sleeping so we're going to be very quiet."

Rylan smiled with great tenderness when Danny sighed hugely and put his head on the big man's chest. Bri was not feeling the best at the moment, and naturally Danny could tell something was wrong. Bri had been sick in the night, and Rylan thought it important that she not hear Danny and get up.

"Are you hungry?" Rylan asked his son, who perked up at the word.

Rylan stood and started toward the kitchen, and Danny began to talk.

"Shh," his father said, putting a few fingers over the baby's mouth. "We don't want to wake Mama."

"Mama," he whispered, and Rylan praised him for being quiet. The two Jarvik males raided the kitchen for an early morning breakfast,

Rylan working hard to be silent. The kitchen floor creaked more loudly than the other floors in the house, so as soon as he could manage it, he sat at the kitchen table, Danny in his arms. They had a hodgepodge of food in front of them—bread, some applesauce, and even some leftover pie. Quiet as they'd been, this was the way Bri found them.

She came to the edge of the room and smiled at the sight of them. Rylan took one look at her and wasted no time. He put Danny on the floor and went to her.

"Sabrina," he said calmly and quietly, "there's blood on the front of your nightgown."

An "oh" formed on Bri's mouth, but no sound came out. This was the last thing she expected. She hadn't been feeling well, but there had been no pain, just some queasiness.

"Get back into bed while I find Doc Ertz," Rylan continued.

"All right."

"Mama!" Danny had made his way over and captured his mother's leg.

"Come here, Buddy," Rylan lifted the little guy so he could hug his mother without Bri actually holding him. She kissed him and talked to him for a few minutes before turning her attention to Rylan.

"What does it mean?"

"I don't know. We'll let the doctor tell us, all right?"

"I'm only seven months along, Rylan," Bri said next, and the pastor could see his wife was working to make sense of it.

"It might not be a lot of blood since you weren't even aware of it, so just lie back down and rest until we can get some answers."

Rylan and Danny accompanied Bri back to the bedroom. She changed her gown and got into bed while Rylan finished getting dressed. He was not in a panic, but neither was he going to take his time going for the doctor.

"Here we go, Danny. Tell Mama goodbye."

Her little boy waving at her from his father's arms, Bri watched Rylan start toward the door. The pastor looked back long enough to catch her eyes and smile into them. Bri returned the smile as they left. Her eyes then went to the ceiling as she began to pray.

"Do you think it's too forward of me to make Nate a shirt?" Heather asked Jeanette and Becky over breakfast.

Jeanette could not stop her smile. Becky had coffee headed to her mouth but stopped short. Heather watched their reactions, a bit bemused.

"What did I say?"

"Well," Jeanette began, but Becky cut her off.

"Are you in love with the man, Heather?"

"I don't know. Does my wanting to make a shirt mean I'm in love?"

"Well," Jeanette tried again, "it means you have some type of feelings, doesn't it?"

"I like him," Heather said softly. "I like him very much."

The other women smiled at her, and then all fell to discussing if the shirt was a good idea, and if so, what kind the sheriff would like. None of them realized that their pastor was within an hour of knocking on their door and asking for help. The shirt would not be on anyone's mind for quite some time.

"What's this?" Jessie shot at Seth not long after dinner. A catalog was open on the counter, and she was frowning at it.

"An order I haven't finished. I didn't want to lose my place."

"We haven't been that busy," Jessie said tightly, putting it off to one side but not closing the book.

Seth stared at her, realizing he'd been in trouble all day. The first hour had gone fairly well, but the longer the day went, the shorter Jessie became with him. He'd kept his mouth shut, but no longer. The store had three customers. As soon as they cleared out, he was going to find his wife.

"How much is this cup?" a woman asked him, and Seth dragged his mind back to the moment. He waited on the woman and then turned to see Jessie finishing with a young couple. Seth slipped into the back to work on some shelves, hoping Jessie would wander along. It took some time. Things seemed to be pretty quiet out front, but eventually Jessie came to the storeroom.

"Do you have a customer you're working with?" Seth asked.

"No, I just need some cans of fruit," she said, still not sounding like herself.

"What time is it?" Seth asked, not wanting the girls to interrupt.

"It's one-thirty. Where's your watch?"

"You've been trying to pick a fight with me all day."

The words were out, and Jessie froze where she was, a few cans in her arms. She stared at the shelf in front of her for a moment and then forced herself to turn and face him. The old Seth was not there. The man before her looked as calm and patient as his voice.

"I'm afraid you've gotten it into your mind that I have some sort of agenda because I asked you this morning if you were going to talk to the girls. I don't have an agenda. You can stop fighting with me to keep me away. If you don't want me near you, I won't touch you." The temptation to remind her that she was the one to start the kissing was strong, but he made himself stop and wait.

"I don't know what I want," Jessie admitted.

Seth nodded, thinking that she had known a short time ago. He said only, "It sounds like we need to keep talking."

Jessie nodded, feeling miserable. She hadn't meant to do this. Seth was as far away from her as he could manage, and she remembered his tenderness of last night and even this morning.

"I'm sorry," she said quietly.

"It's all right," Seth said, but he came no closer.

Jessie looked as miserable as she felt. Seth would have been blind to miss it.

"What's wrong, Jessie?"

They both heard someone enter the store. Jessie, feeling defeated, started that way, but Seth caught her hand.

"I'll take care of it. We'll talk tonight when the girls are in bed."

Jessie looked up at him, so many things running through her mind. She only nodded and then stood still when Seth tenderly touched her face. He didn't speak again, but Jessie had to ask herself if a man could touch a woman with that much tenderness and not still have feelings for her.

Jessie was suddenly tired of snapping at Seth and feeling confused and sorry for herself. Tonight she would tell Seth what she was thinking and find out his thoughts. Since he had arrived, her life had felt out of control, and that was something she could no longer allow.

Rylan made his way into the bedroom a few hours later to check on his wife. She lay still and watched him approach.

"How is Danny?"

"He's doing fine. When he asks about you, Becky tells him you're resting. How are you?"

"I'm doing some thinking."

Rylan sat on his side of the bed and asked, "Do you feel like you've missed something?"

Bri shook her head no and then said, "I did for a little while, but I've examined my heart and asked God to make me aware of anything that wasn't right between Him and me or between you and me. It's hard, but I'm thankful for this reminder to check my heart. I know God doesn't hide from us, Rylan, so I'm trusting that this is what He has for me right now."

"I had some of the same thoughts. I've asked Him to show me in any way He chooses if I've failed Him in some way. I'm working to stay humble. It's the only way we're going to know if God is getting our attention over sin, or if this is simply a different way He wishes to glorify Himself."

"I do want this little person, Rylan," Bri admitted, her eyes meeting his.

"I want you both," the pastor said, thinking his wife was a treasure beyond compare.

Rylan then reached for Bri's hand, and he prayed for them. He repeated his need to God to make sure their hearts were humble, and before he said amen, he gave his wife and baby to the Lord to do as He willed, confident that God would sustain all of them for every day He had planned.

"I ate with Bertha. She's new," Clancy told her father from her place on the counter.

"New at school?"

"Yes. She used to live in Helena."

"That's a long way from here."

"She doesn't like it here, but I told her I would be her friend."

"That was very nice of you."

"Can you pray for her?" Clancy said.

"I can pray for her," Seth said, hiding his surprise over the request. "What would you like me to pray?"

"Well, you prayed for us when we went to school, and Hannah and me liked it."

"Hannah and I," Seth corrected her automatically, staring into her precious face. "Do you know what, Clancy?"

"What?"

"God loves you very much."

"And that's who you pray to, isn't it?"

"Yes, it is. I have to check with that man who just came in, but at some point I can tell you more about God's love and about prayer."

Clancy, who grew up with interruptions, took this in stride. Things were just busy enough that Seth did not get back to her. Clancy thought nothing of this, unaware of the way Seth prayed and asked God to give him an opportunity to share Christ with his youngest daughter.

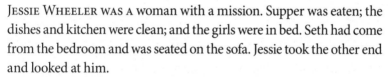

Chapter Nineteen

Jessie Wheeler was a woman with a mission. Supper was eaten; the dishes and kitchen were clean; and the girls were in bed. Seth had come from the bedroom and was seated on the sofa. Jessie took the other end and looked at him.

"How are you doing?" he asked.

"I'm fine. I have some questions for you."

Seth nodded, thinking that she sounded as though she were addressing a business meeting. Gone was the miserable woman in the storeroom. The *in charge* Jessie sat across from him.

"Go ahead," Seth said, trying not to sound like he was dreading this.

"How do you feel about me?"

Seth blinked a little and then caught on. He was not angry, but he was hurt and didn't want her to know it. He kept his voice as even as he could. "I don't want to fight with you, Jessie. I've admitted I did the wrong thing."

Jessie looked startled by this, but Seth didn't notice.

"If I tell you I love you, you're only going to remind me that I haven't been acting like a man in love or ask me how I could have stayed away for so long."

Jessie knew she deserved that. She had snapped at him all day and then sat on the sofa and demanded to know his feelings.

"I'm not doing a very good job with this," Jessie said, sounding less sure of herself and unconsciously making herself more approachable. "I don't know how to start this, and I thought it would help to know how you feel."

"I'm sorry I assumed the worst. If you really want to know how I feel, I'll tell you."

"I do want to know," Jessie said and all but held her breath.

"I've fallen in love with you all over again. I won't insult you and say that I knew exactly how I felt when I came back to town, but I'm learning every day that I'm still in love with my wife."

"I realized just this morning that I still loved you. I could almost hate myself for it, but that's how I feel."

"So it's love mixed with a lot of fear?" Seth asked, his heart slamming in his chest.

"Terror is a better word. I don't want to be hurt again."

"I can't promise that I'll never hurt you, but I'm not leaving again. That I can promise you."

Jessie's eyes closed. He made her feel so vulnerable, but then he always had. This was nothing new. She hadn't felt that way at the end when they fought all the time, but when it was good between them, she had felt things she'd never felt with anyone else.

"Were there other questions you wanted to ask?" Seth said into the silence, wanting her much closer than she was. His wife still loved him, and he needed to touch her.

"I can't remember right now."

"Where do we go from here?"

Jessie didn't mean for her eyes to flick to the bedroom door, but they did. And Seth saw it. The look he gave her was unmistakable. Jessie began to rise, moving away from him, but Seth was too fast. He had her hand in a lightning fast move and was pulling her close.

"Come over here, Jessica," he invited. "We can talk on my end of the sofa."

"You don't want to talk," Jessie said, all the while allowing herself to be pulled into his arms.

"I don't want to *only* talk, that's very true. A certain woman started something last night and didn't finish it."

When she was in his arms, they looked at each other. Their eyes met and held until Jessie had to tell him more.

"I missed you so much."

"I missed you too."

"I had to make myself forget, or I would never have survived."

"Forget what?"

"All that we had at the beginning. How sweet it was."

"It was sweet, but we didn't work as hard on our marriage as we did on everything else. That has to be different this time."

Jessie nodded.

"I love you, Jess," he said softly, just before his lips claimed hers. Jessie kissed him right back with all the abandon she felt, knowing this time they would not leave things undone.

Jessie woke on her back to the weight of a large arm across her middle. For a moment she was disoriented and then remembered she was not in with the girls. She moved her head to look at Seth, who was on his side facing her and still asleep.

For the next several heartbeats she let herself be amazed that they were living again as husband and wife. It was the last thing she'd expected two months ago when Seth came into town, but then that was her way of doing things. She and Seth had married less than two months after meeting each other. She could only hope they would do better this time.

"What are you frowning about?" Seth asked, his voice low with a morning growl.

"The past."

"How far past?"

Jessie looked at him and then rolled to face him.

"I was thinking about what you were saying last night that we didn't do well the first time."

Seth put his arms around her and drew her close, his heart praying. *I'm not that same man, Lord. Please let it be different this time. Maybe Jess will never want You, but let our marriage be all it can be because of Your death for me.*

"I'd better get up," Jessie said.

"What time is it?"

"I think it's early, but until I tell the girls we're kissing again, I don't want them to find me in here."

Seth laughed a little at the wording before asking, "Do they ever wake up ahead of you?"

"Not often," Jessie said and then came close to kiss him. She had no desire to get up, but caring for her daughters kept her on task.

"Why don't you teach me how to make your coffee," Seth offered, and Jessie's mouth swung open as she slipped into her robe.

"Are you serious?"

"Yes," he said on a laugh. "I thought it might help you some mornings if I knew how."

"Seth I'm-Useless-in-the-Kitchen Redding wants to learn to make coffee. I think I might be beyond surprises."

The look he gave her told her she had gone too far. Jessie shot out of the bedroom with Seth on her trail.

"Oh, you're going to pay for that, Jessica," Seth said when he came from the bedroom to find Jessie across the room and still moving. "Now hold still. I'm not 23 anymore."

Stifling laughter all the while, Jessie skirted the furniture while Seth came after her. It didn't take long for them to get loud. She let herself be caught a short time later, and the two were still kissing when they heard the girls' feet coming out of bed and onto the floor. Seth went back to the bedroom to dress, and Jessie started the coffee herself. It was during breakfast that she told the girls about the changes with Seth while he quietly listened.

"Do you remember asking me if Seth and I kiss?" Jessie asked Clancy.

"Um hm. You said you would tell us."

"Well, Seth and I do kiss now."

"Can we watch?" Hannah asked.

"Well…" Jessie had to fight laughter and didn't dare look at Seth.

"This is what we'll do," Seth cut in, his voice also laughter-filled. "If we're kissing and you're in the room, you can watch. How will that be?"

"Today? Will you kiss today?" Clancy asked.

"Why is this so important?" Seth wished to know.

"I don't know," Clancy shrugged, and Seth was certain he'd get no more out of her. Hannah, however, had something to say.

"We want Mama to like you."

"Your mother does like me," Seth said, his heart sinking when he saw how aware his young daughters had been.

Hannah looked to Jessie, who nodded. The nine-year-old managed to look relieved and excited all at the same time.

"Finish your breakfast now," Jessie urged them. "It's almost time to get downstairs."

Taking the conversation in stride, the girls finished and were out the door for school not ten minutes later. Seth and Jessie stood on the boardwalk and watched their daughters walk toward the schoolhouse before heading back inside. It wasn't quite time to open the store, so Seth took the opportunity to talk to Jessie about a house.

"Come here," Seth said to her, taking her hand and leading her to the storeroom. Jessie thought he wanted to kiss her and was surprised when he walked all the way to the rear door and opened it.

"I've been thinking and doing some checking. What do you think of this piece of land back here?"

"What am I supposed to think of it?" Jessie asked, remembering his actions from earlier in the week.

"Isn't that a good place to build a house?"

The face Jessie turned to him was a mixture of incredulous and excited.

"Are you serious?" she asked in a voice that sounded as though she didn't dare to hope.

"I'm very serious. We can buy it and build."

"When did this start?"

"That's what I was doing on Monday night—checking into it."

Before we ever touched each other was all Jessie could think. She was so surprised that she didn't know what to say. Seth took the silence as negative.

"I haven't done anything that can't be undone. If you don't like it, Jessie, I'll drop the whole idea."

"That's not it," she was swift to tell him. "I just didn't know."

"Didn't know what?"

Jessie looked at him, unable to put her feelings into words. He was the same man and yet so different.

"I didn't know what you were doing on Monday night. I speculated on some things, but this never once came to mind."

"And now that it has, what do you think?"

Jessie looked back out at the land. The store sat on Main Street, and the lot directly behind it on Corbin Street was empty. A house sat to the right of the lot Seth was looking at, but to the left was another empty lot. None of them was huge, but there was plenty of room for a house. A home.

"I think it would be wonderful," Jessie finally said, still unable to believe it might happen. "I don't know about the money, though."

"I have enough to buy the land and pay for about half of the house," Seth said.

Jessie's heart sank. "Money from working for that banker?"

"As a matter of fact, no. I did make good money on that job, but I was also into investing. The money I have put away is from money I've invested over the years. I cashed almost everything out before coming back to Token Creek. I still have one investment in Texas that Cassy takes care of for me."

Jessie could barely keep her mouth shut. She had no idea that he had that type of business acumen. She would have said more, but Seth suddenly looked at his watch.

"I've got to open up," he said, bending to kiss her. "Think about it and let me know."

Jessie stayed where she was, still looking out the back, a dozen questions shooting through her mind. She studied the lot with its proximity to the store and began to imagine. What she saw in her mind brought a smile to her face.

"I stopped by the shop, and Jeanette said you were home," Nate said to Heather on Friday afternoon. "How is he doing?"

"He just fell asleep," Heather said, glancing at the child who occupied the love seat, his blanket clutched in one fist. "He misses Bri terribly, but he's holding up well."

"How is she doing?"

"I haven't talked to her since last night, but she was doing well then."

"What did Ertz say?"

"That she needs to be still until they're sure she's not starting labor. It's too soon for that."

"When is she due?"

"Not until November."

Nate's mind was swept back to the baby his wife lost the first year they were married. She had not been seven months along, but it had still been hard.

"Are you all right?" Heather asked.

"Yes, I'm just thinking about babies," Nate admitted and then looked at Danny. "That one is special."

"I think that might start with special parents."

"I'm sure you're right," Nate agreed in a no-nonsense voice.

"You must meet so many people who didn't have a Rylan and Bri as they grew up," Heather said as she realized that fact.

"That's very true. I think many of them didn't have anyone at all when they were growing up."

"I remember Bri telling me about her friend, Crystal. Crystal's father taught her to steal," Heather said, recalling the conversation. "She didn't like going to jail, and that was how she turned to prostitution."

"I remember Crystal. Do you know if Bri has heard from her lately?"

"I don't. I'll have to ask."

Danny shifted around just then, and before Heather could move, Nate stood and made sure the boy didn't roll from the seat. He shifted him a little toward the back, something Danny slept through.

"I'd better go so I don't wake him."

"I'm glad you came."

"Maybe we can go for a walk this evening," Nate offered.

"I'll plan on it."

The two looked at each other a moment before Nate said goodbye and left. He'd never told Heather that he loved her, but she was starting to see it in everything he did. She could also see it in herself. She was starting to love Nate Kaderly.

"I came as soon as I heard," Jessie said to Bri, having let herself into the house on Friday afternoon when no one answered the door.

"I'm glad you did. Is Seth watching the store?"

"Yes, with the girls. They wanted to come until they found out that Danny wasn't here."

Bri smiled. "I simply don't rate as high as Danny."

"It's the bane of every parent. I have some customers who deliberately shop when they know the girls will be there."

Bri chuckled but then grew serious. "How are you?"

"I'm doing well."

"That's good to hear. How is Seth coming along with the girls?"

"It's amazing. I knew they needed a man in their lives, but not until I watched it every day did I realize how much. They respond so quickly to his authority. I didn't think it would last. I thought at first they obeyed out of fear of not knowing what he would do, but it hasn't worn off. Not yet, anyway." Jessie hesitated before adding, "Seth and I are even doing well."

"What brought that about?"

"He said some things I couldn't ignore, and that changed how I felt about him." Jessie knew that wasn't all of it, but she couldn't find the words. Her feelings had been changing for him for the past month. "Enough about me!" she said before Bri could ask anything else. "Tell me more about you."

"I'm fine. I miss Danny, but I'm fine."

"Do you believe God planned this for you?" Jessie asked, not sure why.

"That's exactly what I believe."

"And what if something happens, Bri, and you never have this baby in your family? Did God plan that too?"

"He did. There's great comfort in knowing that nothing is out of His will."

"Why is that a comfort?"

"I didn't believe in God for a long time. I was scared about a lot of things."

"But you don't have any more control over things now," Jessie argued.

"That's true, but God is in charge of everything and loved me enough to die for me. He won't let me go through any of it without Him."

Jessie wasn't sure this made sense to her, but she did her best not to show it. She didn't think there was any point in discussing it further but didn't know how to say this.

She would have been surprised to know that Bri could read this in her, and that's why she changed the subject. The women talked about various things in the next 30 minutes but never ventured back to spiritual topics. Nevertheless, Bri had plenty to say on spiritual topics, and said them all in prayer as soon as her friend left.

"What's going on?" Seth asked when he found the girls in the corner of the storeroom, both sporting murderous expressions. Years ago he had set up a play area for Hannah, and although no longer partitioned off, the girls still used it for their dolls and some of their toys.

"Hannah said I could have the baby carriage, and now she won't share."

"Is that right, Hannah?"

"I just changed my mind," Hannah said defensively, wanting more than believing that this was fair.

"How would you feel if I said I was taking you to see Danny and then just changed my mind?" Seth asked her.

"I wouldn't like it," Hannah admitted in a much smaller voice.

To the girls' surprise, Seth then turned to his youngest daughter.

"You could do better right now as well, Clancy," he told her. "It was wrong of Hannah to offer the carriage and then change her mind, but your getting all angry and upset about a toy is just as selfish."

"But she said—" Clancy began to disagree, but Seth cut her off.

"And you're arguing with me right now, and that's selfish too."

Both girls stared up at him, and Seth made a swift decision.

"Come to the front and do some small jobs for me right now. When I say you can come back and play, I'll expect you to do a better job."

The girls didn't argue about this. Young as Clancy was, she had not liked being told she was selfish. As for Hannah, the example of Seth telling her something and then changing his mind had hit home. She knew that was a wrong way to act, and there was no excuse she could give. Without a murmur of protest, she went to do whatever Seth asked of her, knowing she deserved the punishment.

"How is Bri?" Seth asked when the girls were in bed that night and he finally had his wife to himself.

"She has no idea when she'll be out of that bed, but she's taking it very well." Jessie suddenly frowned. "She talked about God the way you do with the girls."

"Did that bother you?"

"No, I just don't understand it. I don't know how any of you can believe in something you can't see."

"I can see how you might feel that way," Seth said. "You're a very hardworking person. It would be easy to have strong reasons for believing in all the things you've accomplished with that hard work."

Jessie suddenly didn't want to talk about this. He had not sounded mean, but she felt as though all of her hard work meant little. If she kept thinking about it, she knew they would end up quarreling.

"Tell me everything you did on Monday night for the house," Jessie said, remembering they hadn't talked about it again. Seth didn't try to change the topic back. He had decided long ago with Rylan's help that shoving his belief at his wife was one of the worst things he could do.

Seth did go over what he'd done Monday night with her, and she laughed as he described going from place to place and asking the questions he did. When he was finished, they talked about what they wanted in the house, what they could afford, and how soon they could meet with Chas. Jessie was starting to believe this was truly going to happen. It made sleeping that night almost impossible.

"Thank you for your questions and concerns about Sabrina," Rylan began at the front of the congregation on Sunday morning. "Sabrina is doing well, but she won't be getting out of bed until the doctor is sure she's not going into labor too soon. Thank you for the prayers, the food, and seeing to Danny. Sabrina and I can't tell you what a blessing you all are.

"I had my sermon ready early this week," Rylan went on. "That would seem like good news since the week didn't end as I expected, but instead of the sermon I planned for this morning I need to tell you some thoughts I had on Thursday morning when I realized Sabrina needed the doctor.

"I was not frantic to get out the door, but I didn't take my time either. I didn't think Sabrina should be up and around at all, so I took Danny with me. As I was walking toward Doctor Ertz's home, I felt the first signs of anxiety. You know the ones I mean, the feeling of helplessness in your chest, that sensation of dread that someone you love might be hurt or die.

"Interestingly enough, at the same time I also felt the weight of my son in my arms, and it came to me that it would *never once* occur to Danny that I would drop him. He felt as secure and comfortable as any child could. If any of you have lifted my son, you know he's not a small boy," Rylan added, catching smiles on many faces. "But as you might also imagine, he weighs next to nothing to me when I lift him.

"As I thought about this type of trust, it put my worry in a new light. Why did I think God would drop me? Why would I imagine God not taking care of Sabrina in a way that would glorify Him? If I think my son weighs nothing in my arms, I can barely imagine how light I am in the arms of God. God would never drop me or Sabrina. Here I was, anxious for her when the God of the universe is holding all of this in His hands. I saw my worry for what it was. I called it the sin that it was, and I repented of it.

"I can tell you what a relief that was. I hated my worry for what it was. Sin against God. And then I stopped. I didn't think that I'd better think about it or that I needed to work on it. I stopped. When sin becomes clear to me, I must stop.

"Let me go through the process for you again. You might not be worrying. It might be something else. But if it's sin, it has to be dealt with. Call it what it is: sin. Hate it for the sin that it is. And stop it. How many excuses do we have? 'I've always been that way.' 'My dad was hot-tempered and I'm the same way.' 'I'm just having a bad time right now.' 'You don't know how hard this is for me.' How many of those have we said and given ourselves permission to go on sinning?

"I want us to be done with that today. Do we believe that a mighty and holy God died for our sins? I'm looking around this room, and I know that every adult in here believes that very thing. Then what are we doing living in the sin Christ died for? There is no excuse. Call it what it is, hate it, and stop it.

"This is normally the time I would close us in prayer, but I'm not going to do that today. My sermon is done, but I'm not going to dismiss you. Take as much time as you need. If you want to visit with one another, head to the foyer or outside. Today we're going to keep this room quiet. If someone is sitting quietly, please allow them that time."

Rylan moved to the front row then and took Danny from Becky's arms. He sat down with the rest of his congregation and prayed, asking God to humble him and his wife so that they might raise a humble son to serve Him.

It took some time for the room to empty. Most people stayed and prayed for quite a while. Rylan prayed that their hearts would be genuine and that God would bless this flock. When he finally headed for home, Danny in his arms, he did so praying the same thing. Someone had delivered food for their dinner, but Rylan did not fill plates for the three of them just yet. He had to tell Bri about the morning, and that couldn't wait.

Chapter Twenty

JESSIE WAS SUPPOSED TO be enjoying these hours on her own Sunday mornings. The girls had gone to church with Seth, and she was free to do as she pleased. Why then did she feel so discontent and restless? Seth had not asked her to join them, but why would he? And if she understood that he wouldn't feel free to ask her, why was she put out?

She paced the confines of the apartment and even debated going down and working on the account books. It was strictly against her policy to do such work on Sunday, knowing she needed a full day's break from the store, but she gave in.

She was on her way down the stairs when she remembered the house. She turned around and went back to the kitchen table. Using paper and pencil, she began to draw some ideas she'd always dreamed of and that she and Seth had talked about the night before. She had no idea what was affordable, but doing this almost took her mind off of Seth, the girls, and the quietness of the apartment. Almost.

"Did you pray?" Hannah asked her father as soon as they walked away from the church building.

"Yes, I did."

"I prayed too," Hannah said.

"Did you?" Seth asked, slowing his steps to a crawl. "What did you pray, Hannah?"

"Oh, look at the bird! It's blue!" Clancy said, and Seth brought their small group to a halt.

"Clancy," Seth said, speaking with his hands on both of her shoulders. "I'm going to talk to Hannah about this morning, and I want you not to interrupt. Do you understand?"

The younger girl nodded, and Seth turned back to Hannah.

"Can you tell me what you prayed?"

"Well, I told Him that my name was Hannah and that I like going to church."

"Why do you like it?"

"I like it when Pastor Rylan talks about Jesus."

"Do you know who Jesus is?" Seth asked.

"I think so."

"Who is He?"

"He's God's Son."

"That's right, and He did something for all of us. Do you know what I'm talking about?"

"You mean when He died on the cross?"

"Yes. Why did He have to do that?"

"I don't know. I don't like that part. What did you pray?" Hannah asked.

"I confessed some sins I had done. I repented of them. And then I prayed for you, Clancy, and your mother."

"Mama doesn't believe in God," Hannah said.

"What do you believe, Hannah?"

Hannah stared up at her father, afraid to say. Clancy was standing not far from them, probably listening to every word. Hannah didn't want her mother to know that she believed in God and had for a few weeks now. If she said the words aloud, her mother might find out and be hurt.

"Can we go now?" Hannah asked, and Seth nodded. He smiled to reassure her, but it hadn't been hard to see what she was thinking. He'd seen the way she looked to Clancy and then back at him. He thought Hannah might be having moments of clear understanding about God, but discussing that would have to wait.

As they finished the walk home, Seth was praying yet again. This time he asked that God would give him uninterrupted time alone with Hannah, time when she could freely say what was on her heart.

The little girls were in a tight circle, as they were most days. The older girls ate dinner together on the south side of the schoolhouse, and naturally the little girls, their ages ranging from six to ten, formed their own group a ways away from them. They had eaten and played for a while, but now they sat in a circle to talk.

"We went to my grandma's on Saturday," Clara said.

"We went to the creek and got wet," Clancy put in, not to be topped.

"You got wet?" Clara asked in surprise.

"Seth said we could," Hannah added.

"Who is Seth?" one little girl asked.

"He's our father," Clancy put in.

"You call him Seth?" Vera asked; she was the bossy girl in the group and also the oldest. "He can't really be your father if you call him Seth."

"He is too our father," Hannah defended quickly.

"Seth Wheeler," Vera went on. "I've never heard of him."

"It's Seth Redding, Vera! So there!" Clancy said, sure this would be the last word.

"Now I know he's not your father." Vera gave the final stab. "Your last name is Wheeler."

Miss Bolton was calling them in. Hannah was ready to do more battle on the topic, but she shut her mouth when she heard Miss Bolton's voice. She went back to her desk, too angry to cry or speak to anyone. Clancy looked at her face and wondered about it, but not until they started for home did she understand all was not well.

"What's wrong, Hannah?"

"I have to talk to Mama and Seth."

"About what?"

But Hannah wasn't willing to say more. She walked in the front door of the store and stood staring at Seth.

"Hi, Hannah," he greeted innocently.

"I want to be Hannah Redding."

Jessie was not far away and came the moment she heard this. She found her daughter looking defiant, but there were tears on her lower lids.

"What happened today?" Jessie asked.

Before Hannah could find words, Clancy told her version of the meeting. Seth took it all in. He knew that Jessie was ready to take Hannah off and talk to her on her own, but that was the last thing he wanted. He came to his daughter and hunkered down on her level.

"I know you're upset, but we're going to wait to talk about this. As soon as we close the store, the three of us will talk."

"Not Clancy?"

"Not this time. Until then, don't worry about it."

Seth could see that Hannah was tempted to argue, but she didn't. He gave her a quick hug to reassure her and that almost started the tears again. Seth looked at the clock. It was already after three o'clock. In less than two hours they could talk.

"I feel you're old enough to know some things, Hannah," Seth said to his oldest daughter after they'd all had a quick supper. The evening was warm and beautiful so they had gone to a spot on Token Creek to talk. They had dropped Clancy off at Jeb and Patience's, something she wasn't overly happy about, but Seth had put his foot down.

"About what?" the child asked.

"About why I left. You need to understand that was sin on my part. It was sin against God and also against you and your mother."

"Why did you?" Hannah asked.

"Do you know how you and Clancy sometimes argue about things?"

Hannah nodded.

"Your mother and I argued about everything. We were not very kind to each other, and rather than stay and work it out, I left. That's the reason there's confusion about your name. That's why I'm Seth to you and not Papa. We can't expect those other girls to understand all of this, but it's important to me that you understand. It's your heart I'm concerned about."

"And Clancy's?"

"Clancy's too, but for right now, I wanted you to know the facts."

"Your last name *is* Redding, Hannah," Jessie put in, seeing again how much she was to blame. "I married your father, and all of our last names are Redding."

"Why are you Jessie Wheeler?" Hannah asked, feeling more confused than ever.

"I was angry and hurt when your father left, and I took back the name I was born with. You always heard the name Wheeler, and when you started using it, I didn't correct you."

Hannah was not aware that Seth was hearing some of this for the first time.

"Can I be Hannah Redding?" the little girl asked, working to understand.

"You are Hannah Redding," Seth said simply and watched some of the tension leave her. She smiled a little, and Seth could not believe how much it hurt him to know that his actions had caused her distress. For a moment he could barely breathe with the pain of it all. Then he remembered that he had come back, something his own father had never done.

"What about my teacher?" Hannah asked while Seth was still thinking. "What about Miss Bolton?"

"I'll speak with her," Jessie offered, knowing it was her place.

"Thank you, Mama," the little girl said, looking relieved all over again.

"I need to tell you something I love about God, Hannah," Seth said quietly, not wanting this chance to slip away and praying that his daughter would understand. "He's a God of second chances. I did the wrong thing and left, but He's allowed me to come back to all of you. I'm very thankful for that. I don't deserve a daughter as wonderful as you."

From the corner of his eyes he saw Jessie's hand go to her mouth. He knew if he looked at her they would all be crying.

"We're going to go get Clancy now and head back to the apartment to talk to her."

"Can I be there?"

Seth looked to Jessie, who said, "As long as you give Clancy a chance to ask all of her questions."

Hannah was more than agreeable, but before they could even get to the topic at hand, Seth had to speak sternly to Clancy, who was still pouting about being left with the Dorns. He was on the verge of sending her to bed without the discussion, but he knew the girls talked when they were on their own and couldn't risk Clancy getting only Hannah's version on all of this.

It made for a draining evening. When he and Jessie fell into bed a few hours later, they were both exhausted. Seth wanted to ask her how she was doing, but beyond pulling her close and feeling her cuddle against him, they shared nothing else.

"He's coming more and more," Becky said to Jeanette when Heather walked him to the front door after supper.

"Did you expect something different?"

"No, but one of these days he's going to ask our Heather to marry him, and then she'll be moving out."

Jeanette had certainly thought of this, but for some reason Becky's voice putting it in plain terms got her attention. She stared at Becky and was still staring when Heather returned to them. Feeling utterly impulsive, Jeanette spoke her mind.

"Has Nate asked you to marry him?"

"No."

"Do you think he will?"

"I think so. I think he's waiting for me."

"What is he waiting for exactly?"

"Maybe he thinks I'm still unsure."

"Are you?"

"No, but I'm not good at showing or telling such things."

"Will you say yes?"

"Certainly."

The look on Jeanette's face so surprised Heather that she had to speak.

"What is it? Have I made a mistake?"

"No, nothing like that. We just don't want you to move away."

"Well, I don't want to move away either," Heather said in a confused voice and then caught herself. She looked utterly stunned but didn't immediately speak. Her mouth open a little, she lowered herself slowly into the nearest chair. Her voice was just above a whisper when she continued. "If he asks me to marry him, I'll be moving out of this house."

"You don't have to," Jeanette said, knowing she meant it with all her heart. "You can both live here."

"We want you to," Becky added in her need to erase all doubts.

Heather looked between them and saw every bit of truth in their eyes. Why she'd not thought this through, she didn't know. It was true that it had been a busy time, what with the shop and Danny, but at some point she should have considered this. She came to her feet, her face serious.

"I have to think about this," she said. "I'll see you in the morning."

Jeanette and Becky wished her a good night, even though it was a little early. They knew it unlikely that she would be downstairs again. Becky finished washing the dishes, and Jeanette dried. Neither woman had much to say.

"You're awfully quiet," Seth said to Jessie after the girls were down that night.

"Just thinking."

"Do you want to talk about it?"

"You'll only disagree with me," Jessie said.

"I might disagree with you, Jess, but I hope I would do so respectfully."

Jessie knew she couldn't argue with that, so she tried to put into words what she felt. "I just don't think the girls sin. They're too young to know what that is."

Seth thought about this. He didn't know Jessie believed in sin of any kind, and thought this might be progress.

"Do you think I upset them?"

Jessie had to think about this and realized he hadn't. What she couldn't figure out was why not.

"Jessie?" Seth tried again, not wanting this conversation to end too soon.

"I don't think you upset them," Jessie admitted, "but I think what you said should, and I'm trying to figure out why it doesn't."

"We all know when we've done wrong, Jessie," Seth said, his voice even and matter-of-fact. "And the girls are too bright not to be included in that, even at their young age."

Jessie looked thoughtful but not angry. Doing his best to be tactful, Seth went on.

"I've been reading in the Gospel of John lately. The amount of times belief is mentioned is amazing. Even when the word isn't used, belief runs all through those chapters. Chapter five talks about a pool in Bethesda. It says that at certain times an angel comes to the pool and disturbs the waters. When that happens the first person into the water is healed. As you can imagine, many ill people are sitting there waiting to be healed. There's a man who sits by the pool, and he's seen the waters move, but others always get in before him."

"What's wrong with him?" Jessie asked.

"It doesn't say exactly, but I have to assume that his legs don't work very well because when he talks with Jesus, he tells Him that someone else always steps in faster. Oh, I remember now. It is his legs because later Jesus tells him to take up his bed and walk. Jesus ends up healing him.

"But that's not why I told you the story," Seth swiftly added. "I told you because it occurred to me that we live what we believe. That man believed the pool would heal him, and he stayed nearby. It's the same with me. At one time I believed I had the right to walk away from my marriage, and I did that. If the girls believe they can get away with something, they'll do it. You run this store a certain way because you believe it works. We all live by our beliefs, day in and day out, whatever they may be."

Jessie had honestly never looked at it that way, but it made perfect sense. She also realized for the first time that she had never read the Bible. Not once had she looked at a single page.

"Why do you read the Bible?" she asked her husband.

"Oh, that's a good question," Seth said in surprise and then looked thoughtful. "I guess the first thing that comes to mind is that I love it. I love reading about Christ and seeing how God works. I was also taught right after I believed that I can't live for Christ if I don't know what God thinks and expects. It's not always easy—sometimes it seems impossible—but I want to know what God thinks, and the only way to know that is to study His Book."

"I've never read the Bible," Jessie admitted.

"Your parents never took you to church at all?" Seth asked because he couldn't remember.

"No. I guess I have heard the Bible read at funerals, but I never listened."

"Why is that?"

"When I attended funerals with my parents, on the way home my father would use words like 'ridiculous' and 'rubbish,' and that's how I began to see the Bible."

"Is that the way you still feel?"

"I don't know."

"Tell me this, Jessie. Why are you even willing to discuss it at this point?"

"Because the things you say to the girls don't sound like rubbish to me," she admitted soberly. "The reason I had to obey my parents was because my father said so. To any question I asked, the answer was always the same, 'I'm your father and I know what's best.' That might have been easier to believe if he'd treated my mother with kindness. Not until after she died did I even catch a hint of remorse about the way he'd treated her, and then it was too late."

Seth had never heard any of this and was amazed at the amount of thinking she'd been doing.

"Can you scratch my back?" Jessie asked, her voice sounding tired.

"Sure," Seth said and shifted over as Jessie angled herself toward him on the sofa. Seth scratched and massaged her back until she grew limp. When he put his arms around her and pulled her back against his chest, she was nearly asleep. Seth simply held her and prayed until he needed his own rest.

With gentle hands and voice he got them both up and coaxed Jessie out of her dress and into bed. Jessie dropped right back to sleep the moment her head was on the pillow, but sleep took a little longer for Seth. He had never seen his wife this way, and at the moment it was more than his mind could even take in.

Tears flooded Bri's eyes as Rylan left the bedroom with Danny in his arms. Her boy was home in the evening and at night, but first thing in the morning he went directly back to Jeanette's. Bri could not have been more thankful for the help of Jeanette, Heather, and Becky, but there was no getting around the fact that she missed her son.

She heard the door open again downstairs and assumed Rylan had forgotten something. She waited for him to call up and tell her what it was, but instead she heard him on the stairs. A moment later, he and Danny stood in the doorway.

"What's wrong?" Bri asked, but Rylan didn't answer. He sat down on the edge of the bed and watched his son scramble for his mother's arms. Bri turned on her side to hold him, and Rylan felt so emotional he could barely watch.

"Rylan?" Bri tried again.

"I just can't take him away from you again," the pastor said hoarsely.

Bri turned her face into her son's small shoulder and sobbed. Danny looked at her strangely, but quite naturally didn't catch the import of what was wrong.

"You don't complain," Rylan said softly after a few minutes. "You don't utter a word of discontent, and you even wave goodbye to him every day as though you're happy for him. I couldn't do it again."

Bri had reached for his hand and the big man held hers tightly with both of his. Danny was unaware of the emotion going on around him. He was just happy to have his parents to himself for a little longer.

"What about your sermon?" Bri finally managed.

"I'll get done as much as I can. The congregation will understand."

With that Rylan lay down on the bed facing his wife, their precious small son between them. They laughed and played with him until he fell asleep for his morning nap, his head against Bri's round stomach. And while he slept, Rylan and Bri talked, whispering together about the future and the blessings they knew each day because of God's saving grace and goodness in their lives.

"I have to ask you something," Heather said to Nate when they went for their walk on Friday evening. The nights were cool these days, but there was a hint of Indian summer in the air.

"I can hardly wait," Nate teased her, since he'd heard this many times and never knew what she would come up with.

"If you followed your heart right now, would you have already asked me to marry you?"

Nate was so surprised by this that he stopped walking. Since he was holding Heather's hand, she stopped with him.

"I'm sorry," Heather said in a hurry, stealing her hand away. "I didn't mean to ask that."

"I'm not upset, Heather—not at all," Nate said, hearing the panic in her voice and taking her hand back. "Do you really want me to answer?"

Heather wished she'd kept her mouth shut but forced herself to nod.

"Yes," Nate said simply. "I would have."

Heather took a huge breath and said, "And have you thought about where you would want us to live?"

"I don't know if I had. My place is small, but I didn't think that would bother you."

"It doesn't," Heather was swift to say, but she was looking uncertain again.

"But something about this does," Nate said, knowing she would eventually tell him.

"So you can picture us married?" Heather asked next, not able to come straight out with it.

"Very easily."

"Can you picture us married and living at Jeanette's?"

Nate stared at her, surprised, but also feeling things fall into place. He would have been the first to admit that such a thing had never occurred to him, but that didn't mean he was against it. He looked at the woman facing him, a woman orphaned as an infant whose only family was Jeanette Fulbright and Becky Liburn. In light of that, such a thing made complete sense to him. And in truth, as long as Heather was his wife, he didn't care where they lived.

Without warning, Nate dropped Heather's hand so he could cup her face in his hands. He tipped her head back just enough and kissed her for the first time. Heather's eyes closed, and she felt herself melting in sensation. When she finally opened her eyes, Nate was smiling at her.

"Have you already discussed this with Jeanette?" Nate asked, still gently holding her face.

"It was her idea."

"Well, then, I think we'd better head back and see what she has in mind."

"Really?" Heather asked, almost afraid to hope.

"For the woman I love, anything."

Heather threw her arms around him and kissed him for all she was worth. When she could breathe, she said, "I love you, Nate Kaderly."

Nate wasn't sure what they talked about on the way back to the house; he wasn't sure how they arrived. At the moment all he could do was hear Heather's words and remember her kiss. He hoped Jeanette had a great plan for their future living arrangements. The sooner, the better.

Chapter Twenty-One

Seth went on his own to finalize the deal for the land. Jessie was excited, but it was a Saturday. She couldn't leave the store, but neither could she stand to wait another moment. The girls naturally asked where Seth was going, but their mother wouldn't tell them. Not until they were eating supper did Seth tell the girls.

"A house?" Hannah repeated several times.

"That's right, and," Seth started and then looked at the clock on the wall, "we're headed to the Vicks' tonight to discuss it."

"You didn't tell me that," Jessie got in, but Seth only smiled at her, more than a little pleased with surprising her. Jessie was pleased too but did her best to hide it. Her daughters were already bouncing in their seats, and she figured someone should remain calm. However, there was no masking the lightness of her step as they walked toward the Vick home. This was a dream come true for Jessie, a dream that had lived in her heart for as long as she could remember. She was going to enjoy every minute.

"This is the room I shared with my husband," Jeanette told Nate on Sunday afternoon; Heather had opted to stay downstairs. A lot of talking had gone on since Heather asked Nate about living with Jeanette, but Jeanette had not shown him what she had in mind. "I moved out after Owen died. It was just too large and lonely for me."

Nate looked around the gigantic *L*-shaped bedroom. The bottom of the *L* was a sitting area, warm and comfortable with its own fireplace. Another fireplace sat across from the wide bed, and Nate thought most of his house would fit in this room.

"It's beautiful," Nate said, taking in the windows and curtains, the rich dark carpet and wallpaper.

"We count it a privilege that you and Heather would live with us," Jeanette went on, "but we understand that you would still be a married couple. If you leave the supper table each evening to be alone in your own sitting room, we will understand completely."

"Thank you, Jeanette," Nate said. "I haven't talked to Heather about this, but it's not unusual for me to be needed on the job after dark and even in the middle of the night. Our living at my house was going to make that hard for me. I don't like the thought of leaving Heather on her own after dark."

"She's not afraid," Jeanette said. "We've talked about it, and she's already realized all of that. She knows that her bent would be fear, but she's decided to fight that and trust."

Nate had to smile. That sounded just like the Heather he knew. So many things were new for her, but she was embracing each and every one.

"You must be thinking about Heather," Jeanette said as the two moved toward the hallway.

"How did you know that?"

"You have a certain smile that you get when she's in your thoughts."

Nate smiled that smile again, not able to help himself. He was still smiling when the two found Heather and Becky in the parlor and spent the evening together.

Indian summer hit Token Creek with a vengeance. September was rushing into October, and the days were boiling. Men were back in shirtsleeves, and women who wore their hair down piled it high to offer some relief at the backs of their necks.

It was during this time that Chas Vick began work on the house. Now Seth and Jessie never had to coax the girls to finish breakfast. They wanted to be downstairs at the storeroom door as soon as they could gain permission. Getting them to leave for school had become much harder, however. Both girls would have gladly given up their education if they could have sat and watched Chas work all day.

They were never allowed on the work site while Chas was on the job and were forbidden to bother Chas and his assistant with questions. Nevertheless, their small eyes took in every detail, and they nearly ran from the schoolhouse each day to see what progress had been made.

Jessie was not much better. Seth often found her at the back door or storeroom windows. She wouldn't stay too long, but the urge to peek out and check to see how things were taking shape was simply too tempting.

Chas had been working only about eight days when Seth found Jessie at the door. The storeroom felt like an oven at the moment, and Seth was about to comment on that when Jessie turned from the door. She wore an odd expression, and he watched her hand grope in midair before her knees went out and she crumpled to the floor.

Seth didn't quite make it, but he was lifting her in his arms a second after she hit the floor.

"Jessie!" Seth called her name. Her eyes fluttered and then opened.

"Seth?" she whispered.

"I'm right here. What's going on?"

"What do you mean?" Jessie asked, looking very confused.

Seth took the chair that always sat at the storeroom table and held Jessie across his lap. Her face was moist with perspiration and swiftly going from ashen to flushed. Seth stared down at her, willing his own heart to beat normally. Thankfully Chas had chanced to look up and saw Jessie go down. He was at the door without warning, and Seth was able to ask him to run for the doctor. None of this took very long, but in Seth's mind it was the longest ten minutes of his life.

"When was your last menses, Jessie?" Doctor Ertz was asking less than 30 minutes later. After hearing the way she'd fainted, the doctor had wasted little time asking that question. They were in the living room of the apartment without Seth. Jessie had told him she felt better and talked him into going back to the store.

"Let me think," Jessie said, knowing immediately why he had asked. At the moment her mind was more on the fact that she and Seth had been living as man and wife for only about three weeks.

"Jessie?" the doctor tried again.

That woman worked to gather her thoughts, the past weeks all blurring together, but she eventually answered.

With Jessie's answer the doctor did some thinking of his own and said, "With that date it's a little hard to say, but do you think you could be pregnant?"

Jessie nearly started to have the word said aloud but knew in an instant he was correct. She had never actually fainted with Hannah, but at times she'd been lightheaded while carrying Clancy.

"I think you're right," she said quietly and worked not to panic.

"I figured as much. It's too hot right now for someone *not* in your condition, so you're going to have to watch what you do until this heat passes."

Jessie nodded, but was only half listening. The doctor had another question, and she did her best to answer and then take in what he was saying. He left her on her own not ten minutes later, and Jessie sat still on the sofa, panic starting to fill her.

Seth had not seen the doctor leave and was starting to think he'd been crazy for listening to Jessie. He should have put a sign on the door and gone upstairs with her and the doctor. He absentmindedly finished with a customer and then took the stairs two at a time. He found Jessie sitting on the sofa, staring into space.

"Are you all right?"

"I'm pregnant," she said, her voice expressionless.

Seth stared at her, afraid to look pleased. She was clearly not happy.

"I take it you don't want another child," Seth said, keeping all censure from his voice.

"Not that I have to raise by myself."

Seth began to relax. This made sense to him. He didn't rush but moved toward the sofa. He sat down next to his wife and put his arms around her. He didn't speak until she looked into his eyes.

"Then it's a good thing I'm going to be here."

To her credit she did not look skeptical. Seth waited only a few seconds and then began to kiss her. He took his time about it, and things were growing passionate when Jessie's reason returned.

"The store," she mumbled.

"Hush, Jessica."

They continued to kiss and hold each other until a thump sounded downstairs that could not be ignored. Seth made himself stand, but he bent long enough to take Jessie's face in his hands.

"We'll continue this when the girls are in bed tonight."

Jessie nodded, her eyes closing when he pressed a kiss to her forehead. She watched him head toward the door and heard his feet on the stairs, working with all of her heart to believe him and not panic.

Nate didn't know when he'd been so nervous. He told himself that this was Heather, his Heather, and there was nothing to fear, but his heart still pounded. This was the night. It seemed silly to worry when they'd already made plans as to where they would live, but he hadn't officially asked Heather to marry him and tonight was the night.

He had gone to supper at the house and now they were on a walk. Sometimes they walked toward town, and sometimes they walked away from the main businesses of Token Creek. Tonight Nate had taken her hand and walked away from downtown. Heather was talking about something that Becky had told her concerning Danny, and he was doing his best to listen, but he wasn't quite able to pull it off.

"Nate?" Heather suddenly said, but that man didn't answer. She turned her head to watch him, but he looked distracted. Heather grew quiet then, and it took a minute for Nate to notice.

"Did you ask me something?"

"I did, but I think you're far away tonight."

"I'm sorry, what did you need?"

Heather smiled. Her question had been tied in to the story with Becky and Danny.

"What did I miss?" Nate asked, catching her look.

"It wasn't important," Heather said kindly, not at all offended.

Nate stopped and looked at her. He stepped until he was directly in front of her and took her other hand in his.

"Are you sure? I'm listening now."

"I'm very sure. What did you have on your mind?"

"Mostly you."

"Oh," Heather was surprised. "Is anything wrong?"

"No, I'm just out of practice."

"With what?"

"Asking someone to marry me."

Heather's mouth opened, but Nate wasn't ready. He took just one of her hands and walked them on to a place they'd sat a few times. Large rocks provided natural seating, and Nate sat Heather down before sitting next to her. He kept her hand and looked into her eyes.

"The greatest gift I've ever known is eternal life. I think I've told you that."

Heather nodded.

"I would never wish to insult God's work on the cross by comparing you to eternal life, Heather, but you are a gift to me."

Heather watched his eyes grow moist, and she worked desperately not to cry.

"I didn't understand what a marriage in Christ could look like until I watched Rylan and Bri in their home. Then I spotted you. I certainly had known that you lived in town and thought you were beautiful, but that was about as far as it went.

"Then I kept seeing you at church and during fellowships. I couldn't stop thinking about how sweet and kind you were. At times I would see your face during the sermon and know that you were taking in every word. Your honesty and humility have been a huge example to me and are all part of the gift."

Nate stopped, thinking he was saying this all wrong. There was so much in his heart, and he didn't know how to begin or end. He knew it was time to give up and ask.

"Will you marry me, Heather?"

"Yes."

Nate's sigh was so huge that Heather had to laugh.

"What did you think I was going to say?"

"I don't know why I had myself so worked up over this, but I did."

Heather reached up and touched his face and told him she loved him. Nate put his arms around her and kissed her. Heather kissed him right back. The sky was growing dark earlier these days, but they stayed out as long as they could, talking about the firsts. The first time they kissed, the first time Nate noticed her, and the first time Heather had a clue.

As they walked back to the house hand in hand, Heather realized Nate was as much a gift to her as she was to him. There was only one Person to thank for that, and Heather did with all her heart.

Jessie woke while it was still very dark out. She could hear Seth sleeping hard beside her and quietly slipped from the bed and bedroom. She had found her robe and slipped into it as she went to the living room and shut the door behind her. Moonlight flooded into both front windows, and Jessie stared at it. For a long time she felt nothing. Seth had said many reassuring things the night before, but everything had changed.

Two days earlier she would have said it was all going to last forever. She would have believed that nothing could alter the wonderful place she'd come back to, one where Seth loved and cared for her again. And even in those moments when she doubted he would stay, she was able to push the thought aside. Not now. If he left now, there would be a third child looking for his or her father. She had become weak, letting Seth get close, and this is what it got her.

Without warning the girls' faces came to mind. Jessie moved for the sofa and sat down wearily. Had she been on her own, she would have sent him away before he could hurt her. She remembered that he had changed and so had she, but in her mind this new baby altered everything.

Jessie wanted to cry but forced the tears away. The girls were more important now. She had to be strong for them. She would not let them know that she hadn't wanted this. She would not let them know that their father was not a man to be trusted. He had left before when she was carrying Clancy. He would leave again.

Eventually Jessie lay down on the sofa, fatigue covering her. Nevertheless, sleep did not come. She had no idea what time it was, and then realized she didn't care. At the moment she didn't care about anything but her daughters, forcing herself not to even think about the small life growing inside of her.

The girls were off to school, the store was open, and Jessie had not said ten words to Seth. They had talked for a long time the night before, and Seth had fallen asleep with his wife in his arms, but when he'd awakened, Jessie was not in bed. Seth found her on the sofa, lying down but wide awake.

She had not wanted to talk. He'd watched her be normal with the girls, sending them off with hugs, kisses, and laughter, but the moment they were gone, the sober look covered her face once again, and she moved to busy herself in the back room. Seth watched her for a time, noting that she didn't even peek at Chas' progress.

Several times Seth tried to speak with her, but her answers were nonexistent or so brief that he knew he was not getting through. Working not to panic, Seth ran the store, taking every spare moment to ask God for wisdom and help. He knew it was the baby and the fact that no matter what he said, she was sure he would leave again. There was simply no way to convince her that that wasn't going to happen.

The day felt like a week. When the girls came home, it brought some of the life back into Jessie, but Seth could see it was going to be a rough time. He felt almost desperate to talk to Rylan and gain his advice but thought leaving the apartment for even a short time was the worst thing he could do. Instead he stuck it out, was as normal for the girls as he could manage, and stayed right by his silent wife's side all through the evening. When she turned in, going in to sleep with the girls, Seth dropped to his knees right by the sofa. Only God could save his marriage now, and Seth began to ask for a miracle.

The doctor had given Bri permission to be up and around, but he had warned her to take it easy. He didn't want her doing much, but being downstairs, back in every room of the house, and even doing some work on meals was wonderful. Danny was at her side almost constantly, which suited Bri very well. She could not get enough of her small son, who seemed to smile and laugh all the time.

Rylan had left nearly all medical advice to Doctor Ertz, but when it came to Danny, he had set down one rule. He did not want Bri lifting their son. She had grown accustomed to lifting him as he grew, but that didn't change the fact that he was a heavy bundle. And because Bri was tall, bending that low over her extended stomach seemed not a good idea to him.

At the moment, however, none of that was an issue. Becky had come and cleaned the entire house, and Danny was taking a nap. Bri was on the front porch with her feet up. The day wasn't quite as warm as it had been, and there was a breeze that made sitting outside irresistible.

A fly came past her ear just then, and Bri watched it struggle in the wind. She thought about creatures that were born with wings and the different times Scripture mentioned flight. If memory served, it usually involved angels.

For a few minutes she wondered if she would fly in heaven. Would there be a purpose? Was there a verse that could tell her? And if she could, would her ability to fly glorify God?

Lately the topic of glorifying God was often on her mind. How did being bedridden and unable to take care of her husband and son glorify God? She had had many hours to think about this question, and her conclusion was the reason Rylan noticed. She never complained. Not at any point did she allow her troubled pregnancy to give her permission to sin. She could have so easily, but fretting and anxious thoughts were taken captive and dealt with. She called them what they were, hated them, and stopped, putting into practice one of the most practical exercises Rylan had ever shared with her.

Bri's thoughts were interrupted when she heard the pounding of hammers in the distance. When the air or wind was just right, she could hear Chas building Seth and Jessie's house. Until she heard Danny stirring from his place on the living room floor, she prayed for Jessie. She knew exactly what her friend needed. She only hoped the blindness concerning God would leave her friend very, very soon.

Jessie spent most of her time in the storeroom now. It was peaceful there, and she didn't have to see much of Seth or her customers. It gave her time to think. Jessie knew it was only a matter of time. She could hear the interest and belief in the girls' voices. They loved going to church with their father and listened intently to every Bible story and prayer he prayed. The baby would be the same way. It was only a matter of time before their young, impressionable hearts would believe just as their father did. After all, didn't she believe just as her father had?

Seth said he wasn't leaving, and Jessie knew he meant well. But she could see the future. He wouldn't plan to leave, but how long can a man of faith live with an atheist? And with the baby coming, there would soon be four of them. She would be the only one who did not embrace belief in God.

Oh, they would be like Rylan and Bri, wonderful and caring, but Jessie knew she was different. Jessie knew there was something she didn't have. Ry and Bri didn't say those things, not so much as a hint, but she knew what they believed. They believed that all people needed a relationship with God. She knew they prayed for her, but she couldn't believe.

At one time she had actually tried. After Seth had left for Texas, she had tried to pray. She had told God that if He was truly there and He would bring her husband back, she would believe in Him. But He didn't do it. And she'd been alone for eight years.

And now you're no longer alone, Jessie, and look at where it's gotten you.

Jessie eventually sat down with the account books, deciding that there was such a thing as too much time to think.

"Did you pick one?" Nate asked Heather. They were discussing a date for their wedding; the couple was in Jeanette's small parlor.

"I thought we would do that together," Heather said.

"That sounds fine. Have you got a calendar handy?"

Heather did have a calendar in her room, and the two began to study the dates.

"What day of the week do we want to be married on?" Heather asked.

"I don't think I have a preference. Do you?"

"I've never been particularly fond of Thursdays, so not that day."

Nate began to smile.

"Don't you laugh at me," Heather said, knowing she was about to be teased.

"Me? I would never."

Heather only shook her head and tried not to even smile at his sparkling eyes, knowing it would only bring more teasing. "All right," she said, getting down to business. "Today is the ninth of October. We could get married four weeks from Friday, which would be the seventh of November."

"A Friday?"

"Yes, I think an evening wedding would be fun. What do you think?"

"Does four weeks give you time to make a dress?" Nate asked.

"It's made," Heather said, staring at the man she loved. Sure enough, his brows rose and his mouth opened.

"How did that work?" he asked when he could find words.

"Jeanette started it the day after I agreed to our first walk."

Just as Heather knew he would, Nate laughed. This was the last thing he expected. It was Heather's turn to sit and be amused by his response. She had been waiting for this to come up, and his laughter had been worth not mentioning it before.

"I think living with the three of you is going to make my premarried life look completely dull."

"You might also think it looks more sane," Heather suggested dryly.

"I'm willing to take the risk."

The two smiled before they shared a kiss and then continued to talk. Before Nate left, they checked the date with Jeanette and Becky. Both women thought the date sounded perfect; it meant Nate would be with them for Christmas. Meg's baby was due soon after that, but Meg was usually late. Only Rylan and Bri were left, and checking with them was Nate's job.

Becky made the assumption that the Jarviks would be most agreeable about the date and served dessert to celebrate. The four of them talked nonstop until it grew too late, getting a taste of life in the near future. The prospect made each of them smile.

Chapter Twenty-Two

"BE CAREFUL NOW," SETH said to the girls after supper as they stepped carefully into their "house." Seth had sensed a need to give Jessie the apartment on her own. "Mr. Vick might have tools or nails lying around."

The girls moved carefully and with almost reverential silence. The house was partially framed and Seth was able to show the girls where things in the downstairs would be and where the stairway would go upstairs. The new boards smelled wonderful, and for Seth things were shaping up just as he'd pictured.

For the moment, it was nice to get his mind off of his marriage. Things were still strained, and he'd still had no chance to see Rylan.

"Is Mama coming down?" Clancy asked.

"No, she's resting," Seth said. They had not told the girls about the baby. Jessie was not happy about the prospect, and it would be yet one more thing she would have to pretend about.

"Has she seen the house?" Hannah asked.

"Sure," Seth said honestly. He didn't know if she'd come outside, but she'd certainly seen plenty from the storeroom.

"I want to see my bedroom," Clancy said.

"It won't be long now," her father said. "Come here to the bottom of the stairs and I'll show you how it will look."

Seth kept them busy as long as the light would allow, but the days were growing shorter, and it wasn't long before they headed back inside. Jessie was buried in the newspaper, and the girls left her alone. Seth did the same, wondering how long the situation could last.

"I feel I need to do something desperate," Seth finally had a chance to tell Rylan. "I'm planning something, and I might need your help."

"Anything we can do."

"Thank you," Seth said, and then slowly shook his head. "She thinks I'm leaving. Outside of staying for the next 30 years, I can't prove to her that I'm not, so I guess that's just what I'll do."

"I wish she would come and see Sabrina," Rylan said, knowing that his wife could not get out much right now. "Maybe if they talked, it would help."

"I don't know. She's not even the same with the girls anymore."

Seth stayed as long as he dared, and Rylan encouraged him with God's unfailing goodness. Seth explained to Rylan what he wanted to do, but only if Jessie did not soften toward him. Seth left with great hope that God might choose to change his wife, but he also knew he was not afraid to act if need be.

Seth slipped into the store in time to start the day, but as soon as Jessie saw he was back, she headed for the storeroom.

Nate and Heather's wedding night was crisp and beautiful. The ceremony was simple and just what the bride had imagined. Nate's face as he vowed his life to Heather was sober, but his eyes were filled with love.

The reception was at Jeanette's. With Nate being so well known in town, it was a full house, but there was still plenty of room. Everyone welcomed an opportunity to visit and enjoy the cakes Becky had spent all week making.

All the Holdens were in attendance, babies and all, as were Nate's deputies. The church family was there and many of the townsfolk. Jeanette moved around from group to group, as did Nate and Heather. Some folks had cleared out at a reasonable time, but some were clearly going to stay half the night. Heather had gone to the kitchen to check on Becky and was headed back to the guests when Nate caught her at the stairway.

"Why don't you head upstairs?"

"Can we do that?"

Nate only smiled and told her to go.

Heather did not argue. She slipped up the stairs to their bedroom, shut the door, and waited. She didn't have long. Nate told Jeanette they were slipping away and joined his bride.

"How are you?" Nate asked when he gained the room. Heather was in front of the fire, and if her clasped hands were any indication, she was tense.

"Fine," she said, but her voice was small.

Nate was not feeling overly confident himself, but he still went and took her in his arms. For a long time they just held each other. Some noise drifted up from the crowd downstairs, but for the most part they felt they were in a world all their own.

"Better?" Nate asked when he felt Heather relax against him.

"Much."

"Are you sorry we left the party?" Nate asked.

"No," Heather said, a smile in her voice. She tipped her head back to see him, and he kissed her.

"Nate," Heather suddenly asked. "Do you mind if I take my hair down?"

"Mind?" he asked with a smile in his voice. "I've been looking forward to seeing you with your hair down."

Heather sighed with contentment and put her hands up, but Nate beat her to it.

"Allow me, Mrs. Kaderly," he offered, and Heather, with a soft laugh did just that.

"Well this is nice timing," Rylan teased Bri between contractions. She had waited until the next morning to have her first pains.

"You'll even be able to preach," Bri teased right back, hoping that Danny, who had been taken to Jeanette's, would not think he was going to be separated for weeks this time.

"When do I go for the doctor?" Rylan asked, remembering how long labor with Danny had taken.

"Not yet, I don't think."

Rylan hoped she would know and continued to sit with her as the time passed. He thought she was doing well, but things seemed to grow intense without warning. Bri's water broke, and she felt a desperate need to push almost at the same time.

"I've got to find him, Bri," Rylan said at one point, both of them dripping with sweat.

"But I feel like I have to push," Bri just managed, contractions coming one on top of the other.

Rylan knew he couldn't leave. He would ask himself for a long time if he should have done something differently, but for right now, the die was cast. Working for all they were worth, Rylan and Bri delivered their next baby together. James Rylan Jarvik came into the world, howling almost from the first moment. He was big like his brother and looked none the worse for wear once he'd calmed down. Staring at him, Rylan and Bri felt amazed. They counted fingers and toes and then laughed when he ate with great appetite.

"Oh, Rylan," was all Bri could say when the two took a moment to look at each other.

"He's here," Rylan said, kissing her forehead. "And I still have you."

Seth had brought the horse and carriage close to the storeroom door. The girls had just left for school, bundled against the cold, and he was sure Jessie would be missing him soon. He was going to have to move fast. Jeb and Patience would be along any minute.

Nothing had worked. With the cold weather coming, Chas had hired extra help, and the house was finished in excellent time. It was beautiful—warm and snug and everything Seth had dreamed of. They were all moved in, but the girls slept in one bedroom, Jessie in another, and Seth had his own. Jessie's waist was starting to expand, and time was moving on, but she was as unbelieving and as upset with him as she had been when she got the news.

For a long time he had thought it was only about his leaving, but there was something more going on and he was going to find out what it was. He knew what he was doing could be disastrous, but part of him didn't feel he had anything to lose. His wife was already becoming a stranger, and the girls were noticing more every day. For a time she was normal for them, but she could no longer keep it up. The uncertain glances that came her way from them were breaking his heart. For the first time he feared that Jessie would be the one to leave them.

"Hey, Jessie," Seth called from the storeroom door.

"Just a minute," she called back. "Jeb and Patience just got here."

"Can you come anyway?" Seth asked.

Jessie did not look pleased with him when she got there, but he ignored this.

"Come here," he said and took her arm.

Jessie looked surprised by this but did not protest. Not until they were outside at the back of the store and Seth was lifting her into the carriage did she find her voice.

"Seth, what in the world!"

"Your coat is right there," Seth cut her off, climbing in over the top of her. He put the rig into motion before she could climb out. "I'll cover you with the blanket as soon as you get it on."

Seth had the horse moving at a good pace, cutting along the back of the Main Street businesses until he got to the side street. The freezing wind gave Jessie no choice. She was struggling into her coat when she began to speak.

"Where are we going?"

"Away" was all Seth said.

"Out of town?" Jessie asked, her voice incredulous.

"Yes."

"You can't be serious. The girls?" Jessie said with sudden panic.

"Will be with Rylan and Bri."

"The store?"

"That's why Jeb and Patience were there."

Jessie's mouth swung open in shock that swiftly gave way to anger. She didn't speak, but Seth could feel her frustration. They rode in silence until Jessie saw that Seth was indeed taking them out of town. She pulled the blanket a little closer around her and asked where they were going.

"To the Carlisle ranch, the original cabin to be exact."

"What are we doing there?"

"Getting away for a few days."

"To do what?"

"Mostly to give us time."

"To do what?" Jessie would not let it drop.

"For me to find out what's wrong."

It did not bode well in Seth's mind when Jessie said not a word to him the rest of the drive, which was more than ten miles. He drove onto the Carlisle ranch and saw right away that there was smoke coming from the chimney at the cabin. Lying some distance beyond the main house, the cabin was the house Bart and Marty had started in when they began to ranch.

Seth pulled alongside the old front porch and jumped down. He reached for Jessie and kept her in his arms until he was on the porch, and then he set her down. Jessie was not happy about any of this, but it was cold enough to propel her inside.

Seth followed her inside with one satchel of clothing and a few baskets holding food. He didn't have plans to stay for more than one night, but he wanted to make sure they had plenty to eat. Something told him food would not be the predominant thought in anyone's mind, but those were the plans he'd made.

Seth told Jessie he was going to see to the horse, but she didn't answer him. When he got back to the cabin, he found her sitting before the fire, staring into the flames. He didn't think he would be very welcome at the moment but still took the seat across from her.

And he was right. For the next three hours, Seth tried to start conversation, only to be met with cold silence. Had there not been a fire burning hot in the fireplace, Seth thought he might freeze.

"I had to bring you here, Jessie. I had to find a way to reach you."

Jessie could not believe this was happening. She had decided to ignore Seth until he gave up and took her home.

"I've actually feared that you would leave me," Seth admitted finally, bringing Jessie's face to his for the first time.

"*I* would leave?" Jessie asked, sure she was hearing wrong.

Seth only nodded.

"Why would you think such a thing?"

"Because of how much you've changed with this pregnancy. You're clearly sorry you ever set eyes on me, but I didn't think you would ever reject the girls."

"What are you talking about?"

"You can't even see it, Jessie," Seth said, realizing just how true it was. "You act like you don't care anymore about anyone or anything. You go through the motions, but your heart is not in it—not in the store and not at the house."

Jessie had never been so angry. She knew she didn't lose her temper like she used to, but this was too much. She came to her feet, the fire lighting only half of her face in the dim cabin, ready to have her say.

"Do you think I don't know? Do you think I can't see? Hannah told me about her decision for Jesus. My own little daughter believes in God, but I don't! Clancy will be next, and then this baby. What am I to do then?"

The silence that fell between them was painful. This was not what Seth imagined. He had known that the root of Jessie's problem was spiritual, but not that she had worked this out for herself. However, he was not going to ignore her questions.

"You're to stay and be part of our family, that's what you're to do. We love you and need you."

"That's not true. You won't need me for much longer," Jessie said with more calm, sitting down, her eyes going back to the fire. "You'll all have God."

"We'll always need you, but I'm not going to try to persuade you of that. I have some questions for you," Seth said, starting in even though she wouldn't look at him. "Why don't you believe there is a God?"

"I just don't. I don't know how anyone can."

Seth stared at her and then stood and went for his Bible. It was in one of the food baskets, and he brought it back and turned to the New Testament.

"I need to read something to you. This is from the book of Romans, chapter one and verses 19 and 20. It says, 'Because that which may be known of God is manifest in them; for God hath shown it unto them. For the invisible things of him from the creation of the world are clearly seen, being understood by the things that are made, even his eternal power and Godhead; so that they are without excuse.'"

Seth didn't think she'd looked at him at all, but he kept talking.

"These verses say that all that's been made shows that God exists. You're staring at the flames right now, Jessie. Can you imagine trying to make that? Can you imagine anyone you know, the most brilliant or talented person you've ever known, creating fire?"

Jessie didn't look at him or answer, but she did as he said. She tried to think of how fire was made, realizing for the first time that there had to have been a start.

"Everything around us speaks of a creator. Nothing just happens. Every flower, every fire, every person has a designer. Nothing so miraculous as the human body can just happen."

Seth waited, but Jessie still watched the fire. She didn't look upset, and Seth only hoped she was listening.

"If Hannah can understand that there's a God, why can't you?" Seth asked next.

Jessie looked at him, sure it was some sort of trick. The question seemed unfair to her, and she felt attacked. Her gaze went back to the flames.

"I'll tell you why," Seth continued, knowing the risk was huge. "Your pride won't allow you to need anyone or anything. If you admit there's a God, then you'll have to admit that you were wrong about something. But worse than that, it would mean you can't handle everything alone."

He knew she'd heard him this time because her jaw clenched in anger. Seth did not want to do battle with her, so he came to his feet. He began to work on a meal, putting together some of the food he'd brought. He told Jessie what was there and sat down at the small table to eat, leaving it up to her if she wanted something.

"How much food did you bring?" Jessie asked about noon the next day. They had talked off and on for hours, sleeping very little in the night.

"There's enough here for a week," Seth said, having brought plenty and also seeing that Marty Carlisle had things well stocked. "Why do you ask?"

"Leave me," Jessie said. "Head back to town and leave me here. Come back for me on Friday night."

"Why, Jessie? Why would I do that?"

"I need some time. I need to think about what to do."

"I can't leave you here alone," Seth said, but Jessie was shaking her head at him.

"Bart and Marty are home. Tell them as you leave that I'll be here for the week and that if I have a need I'll come."

Seth wrestled with his heart. It was a reasonable request, but he hated leaving her this far from town, even with the Carlisles nearby.

"Please, Seth."

Seth managed a tortured nod and then reached for her. He held onto Jessie tightly and she hugged him in return. His heart felt broken for what had become of them, but he knew there was nothing more he could do. This was between Jessie and God, and she needed to work it out.

"If you change your mind," Seth said, "have Bart take you to Brad and Meg's. They'll bring you home."

Jessie nodded and then Seth kissed her carefully and with great tenderness. He looked into her eyes and begged her with every fiber of his being.

"Find Him, Jessie," he whispered. "Search in humility with your whole heart and find God.

"Or don't find Him," Seth added, surprising Jessie's mouth open. "Come Friday, I'll be coming for my wife. I *need* my wife. I need her beside me all my days. I want you to know God and have a relationship with His Son, but the girls and I love and need you. No conditions. We want you back no matter what."

Seth looked at her for a long time before slipping out the door. Jessie stood very still, his words still sounding in her ear. She looked into the fire and thought about every word Seth had said to her, knowing it was best that she be on her own.

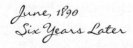

June, 1890
Six Years Later

"Was that the train?" Seth asked for the fifth time.

"Oh, Papa," Hannah laughed at him. "That was Milly's dog next door."

"Oh," Seth said, sitting back in his chair in the living room, working not to be disappointed.

Eliot was headed their way. Eliot, Cassy, Nate, and Lindy were coming from Texas to Token Creek for a visit. Seth knew what day they should arrive, but not which train. The morning train had come and gone—actually on time for once—but the afternoon train had yet to make an appearance.

"Clancy," Seth suddenly said, "did you dust your room?"

"Yes," she said, smiling a little because he'd already asked.

"And the beds are all ready?" Seth asked next.

Both girls assured him all was well, and a moment later, five-year-old Susan made a sound from her bed.

"Go and get her, will you, Hannah?" her father asked.

Hannah did as she was asked, carrying her youngest sister, flushed and sleepy from her nap, down the stairs and into the living room.

"Did you sleep well?" Seth asked her when Hannah placed Susan in his lap.

The little girl lay against him, smiling when their eyes met. Seth began to talk into her precious face and missed the sound of the back door opening. Hannah went that way and met her mother.

"How is he?" Jessie asked.

"He keeps asking us the same questions, and he thought Milly's dog was the train."

Mother and daughter shared a warm, fond smile before Jessie fell to putting things away. Clancy arrived to help, and it wasn't long before Jessie made it into the living room.

"How are you?" she asked, bending down to kiss Susan's flushed cheek.

Seth said nothing, watching Susan and Jessie absently.

"Seth," Jessie tried again. "How are you?"

"Oh, you were talking to me? I thought you were asking Sue."

Jessie bit her lip, but Seth still saw the hidden laughter.

"All right, you can tease me, but your brother isn't visiting for the first time."

Jessie kept smiling and took the sofa. Susan wanted into her lap, and that's when they heard it. The unmistakable sound of the train whistle. The girls ran from the kitchen, and Seth nearly leaped from his seat. His brother had arrived.

As usually happens when cousins haven't met or seen each other, it was awkward at first between Nate, who was 17, and Lindy, who had just turned 14, and Hannah and Clancy who were 15 and 13 respectively. Susan was only too delighted to be playing with all of these big kids, and her cousin Lindy could not get enough of her. Indeed the youngest of the group served as the icebreaker, and before long all were talking and finding things to do in the yard as if they'd known each other for years.

Unlike the children, there was no awkwardness in the living room. Seth and Eliot took up as though they had never been apart, and Jessie and Cassy grew comfortable with each other almost from the first moment.

They talked about the long train trip and different things they'd seen, and then Jessie asked about Texas. She'd never been out of Montana, which had become a state, and was fascinated by the things Cassy shared about Texas.

It didn't take long, however, for the talk to turn to personal and spiritual matters. They had corresponded over the years, but there was nothing like sharing news face-to-face.

"Cassy," Seth said, "tell Jessie about Lindy's voice."

"Oh, my," the mother remembered. "That was a miracle."

"How long had she gone without talking?" Jessie asked.

"Well, she'd watched her father die when she was just shy of three, and I came to Christ when she was seven, so almost five years."

"And it happened overnight?"

"The moment I told them. I had prayed and asked Christ to save me, but I hadn't told anyone. I knew it was time to sit the kids down and explain it to them, and the moment I did, Lindy spoke."

"What did Nate do?" Seth asked.

"He cried at first and then grew scared. He said he'd done a lot of wrong things, but I told him he could be forgiven."

"Did he believe then?"

"No, but it was soon after. Lindy actually believed first."

"Your turn," Eliot said to Jessie. "I want to know your side of what happened at the cabin."

"Oh, my," Jessie said, repeating her sister-in-law's words and then turning to exchange a look with Seth. He only smiled and sat back, looking forward to hearing this again. "That was a hard time. I was so upset that he'd taken me out there, and then I could have kicked myself when I asked him to leave me on my own.

"I remember sitting in front of that fire and thinking it was no use. I couldn't believe in God. I looked at the fire for a long time, and it didn't help."

"I had asked her who had made the fire," Seth put in. "I had challenged her to think about that."

"Yes, and I tried," Jessie continued. "I don't know what I would have done if Seth hadn't forgotten his Bible."

"Did you really forget it?" Cassy asked him.

"Really," Seth said, shaking his head at the memory. "Jess was in a bad enough way. I thought she might burn it to get back at me."

"But you read it," Eliot said.

"Yes. I started in Genesis. I had never read any of it before, and I was captured. I could not stop reading. It got dark out, it got light again, I ate a little, I slept a little, and I read."

"How far did you get?" Cassy asked.

"Through Genesis, and then I remembered that Seth said he'd been reading in John. So I found the book of John and read that. I did not understand everything. In some ways it only brought more questions, but I knew I'd been selling God short. I didn't know if I could have the personal relationship that Seth had, but I knew God was there."

"Tell about the mouse," Seth prompted.

"Oh, that mouse!" Jessie exclaimed and then laughed with the memory. "I'd almost forgotten. I had been very afraid of mice my whole life. It was the last day, I knew Seth was coming that night, and I was looking forward to seeing him and telling him I wanted to know more. I had just made myself something to eat when I spotted a mouse by the fireplace.

"At first I froze, but then something came over me. I remember thinking that God must have created mice and all other animals. It was the first time I found myself assuming that God had a part in creation. I somehow found the courage to use a broom and chase it away, and as soon as it was gone I started reading in Genesis again, this time choosing to believe that God is the Creator."

"What happened when Seth got there?"

"I just told him I needed more. I told him I was ready to hear more."

"How long before you believed?" Cassy asked.

"It was the next summer. We met every week with our pastor and his wife, and one night I knelt in their living room and made God my Savior."

"How about the girls?" Eliot asked, and Seth took that one.

"Hannah believed before Jessie, not long after we moved into the house. Clancy was after Jessie and Sue was last year."

"How are you doing with yourself?" Cassy asked, and Jessie knew just what she was talking about.

"I don't think God has any more children for us," Jessie said. "I don't know if Seth wrote you after the last one, but I've had three miscarriages in a row. Some days are hard, but I'm so thankful for the girls, and I know God has a plan. I'm willing for that plan."

The adults talked about their church families until the kids came in looking for supper. Jessie had prepared a feast, and they all talked their way through the meal. Seth caught up with Nate and Lindy, and Eliot got to know his nieces. Eventually someone remembered that they were all going to be together for four days and not everything had to be talked about the first night.

"Tired?" Seth asked Jessie as they turned in. The four of them had talked until the kids went to bed, and then talked again until their own bedtime.

"I am," Jessie admitted, "but wound up too."

Seth put his arms around her. "I'm so excited to have them here. It's a dream come true."

"They're so special. I loved hearing about their church and the ranch."

"Shall we visit them next time?"

Jessie smiled. "Talk about a dream come true."

Seth's hands framed her face as he looked into her eyes.

"It was great to hear your salvation story again."

Jessie had to smile. "In some ways it seems like yesterday."

"I'm glad it wasn't," Seth said dryly. "We've learned too many things to lose them now."

Jessie wrapped her arms around him and held him close. God had done the most amazing thing in her heart. He had done the impossible. He had taken a lifeless heart, one that was cold and dead to Him, and brought it back to life. Since those days alone in the cabin, Jessie had never been the same.

"You've never been the same," Seth suddenly said.

Jessie laughed and said, "I was just thinking the same thing."

Jessie stared into Seth's eyes, still amazed at how far they'd come. Seth looked right back, more in love with this woman today than he'd ever been. He knew only God could do what had been done in their lives, and the woman in his arms that he was just about to kiss was sweet proof of that each and every day.

Dear Reader,

Please allow me a few words of greeting. I hope you enjoyed *Jessie* and the other two Big Sky books. In this book I incorporated a character from another series, something I've never attempted before. It was a challenge, but I think it was worth the time and energy.

For my readers who have been with me for a while and suspected that Seth was from another book, you were right! For my first-time readers, you'll find Seth Redding in the Yellow Rose Trilogy, in the middle book titled *A Texas Sky.*

Whether you are a first-timer or a long-time Lori Wick reader, I thank you for choosing this book. I pray for all my readers and thank God for you.

Warmly in Christ,
Lori Wick

P.S. Meg presented Brad with a third daughter. They named her Elizabeth.

About the Author

LORI WICK is a multifaceted author of Christian fiction. As comfortable writing period stories as she is penning contemporary works, Lori's books (6 million in print) vary widely in location and time period. Lori's faithful fans consistently put her series and stand-alone works on the bestseller lists. Lori and her husband, Bob, live with their swiftly growing family in the Midwest.

To read about other Lori Wick novels, visit
www.harvesthousepublishers.com

Books by Lori Wick

A Place Called Home Series
A Place Called Home
A Song for Silas
The Long Road Home
A Gathering of Memories

The Californians
Whatever Tomorrow Brings
As Time Goes By
Sean Donovan
Donovan's Daughter

Kensington Chronicles
The Hawk and the Jewel
Wings of the Morning
Who Brings Forth the Wind
The Knight and the Dove

Rocky Mountain Memories
Where the Wild Rose Blooms
Whispers of Moonlight
To Know Her by Name
Promise Me Tomorrow

The Yellow Rose Trilogy
Every Little Thing About You
A Texas Sky
City Girl

English Garden Series
The Proposal
The Rescue
The Visitor
The Pursuit

The Tucker Mills Trilogy
Moonlight on the Millpond
Just Above a Whisper
Leave a Candle Burning

Big Sky Dreams
Cassidy
Sabrina
Jessie

Contemporary Fiction
Sophie's Heart
Pretense
The Princess
Bamboo & Lace
Every Storm
White Chocolate Moments